MECHANICS' INSTITUTE
MECHANICS'
MERCANTILE LIBRARY

Games

of the Blind

Evelin Sullivan

Games

of the Blind

Fromm International Publishing Corporation
New York

Published in 1994 by Fromm International Publishing Corporation,
560 Lexington Avenue, New York, NY 10022.

Manufactured in the United States of America

Designed by Gene Crofts

Printed on acid-free, recycled paper

First U.S. Edition 1994

Library of Congress Cataloging-in-Publication Data

Sullivan, Evelin E., 1947–
    Games of the blind / Evelin Sullivan.
        p.   cm.
    ISBN 0-88064-158-4 (acid-free) : $19.95
    1. Prisoners—Fiction. 2. Psychiatrists—Fiction. I. Title.
PS3569.U3467G3   1994
813'.54—dc20   93-46670
                                                              CIP

to Thomas Thornton

Finstermeister: Remember, nothing is what it seems.
Bosco: Nothing?
Finstermeister: Is what it seems!

— *C.G. Nicklausse*

Part
One

My impossible parents. Amazing mother, absurd father—or reshuffle the adjectives with no loss in accuracy.

I begin this "investigation" with my parents because our progenitors are according to the more popular theories of psychology the root of our ills and because I emphatically claim an exception in my case. In the outline I'll trace of them here, they'll be seen ministering guilelessly to their separate obsessions and inflicting no harm whatsoever on their moody son during that impossible (and amazing and absurd) week in the summer of 1961.

I was fourteen that summer. The three of us were staying at the Albergo Attila near the town of Aquileia in the Gulf of Venice. The hotel was a converted palazzo whose last ducal owner had died ten years earlier in objectionable lunacy (he had, my father learned from the locals, made it a habit to stride through the town naked, conducting agitated dialogues on Papal Infallibility with an invisible man). In addition to its mad duke, Aquileia had the usual colorful history of ancient Italian towns: spells as a stronghold against the barbarians, several sackings, the one the town most prided itself on by Attila. Its island port Grado, a popular resort, had the most level beach I had seen in my life: people walking into the bay shrank to figurines by the time the water lapped their buttocks.

We settled into a routine that summer. After breakfast on the hotel's flagstone terrace, my mother would leave for the town, carrying an easel, a box of paints and brushes, and her canvas. She'd take a taxi to the piazza where the town's famed eleventh-century Romanesque basilica brooded in a manner that has surely been described in some tourist brochure with literary pretensions as "self-ab-

3

sorbed." She'd set up easel and canvas facing the gray bulk of masonry, would study it and her painting, and would begin deftly to add color.

But there was more to the scene than met the casual eye. The sightseeing tourists, mostly Germans, who strolled across the piazza to admire the work in progress must have been shocked when the more or less faithful rendition of the basilica they expected not merely wrenched itself before their eyes into a post-modern mockery of the object, replete perhaps with a gratuitous tearful eye and erect phallus (something the less timid must have considered possible—art, after all!), but turned, presto, into a silver and blue fish arched in a steely leap above a reflecting pond and spewing from its round mouth a bouquet of summer flowers.

Those who weren't cowed into retreat by this display of treacherous imagination and spoke to the artist discovered that she was French, and, after culling enough vocabulary entries from their remembered *Sprechen wir Französisch!* schoolbook to tack together: "Votre peinture est très jolie," were informed with a dramatic gesture toward the basilica that the painting had private religious significance. They departed for other sights, probably suspecting that their legs had been pulled in one of the myriad ways in which the legs of stolid German tourists have been pulled by the subtle inhabitants of exotic climes since Saxons and Visigoths first cast their blue saucer eyes at the cunning perversions of Rome.

But baffling tourists was only incidental to my mother's art. Her problem—if I can give so utilitarian a name to an artist's psychic quirk—was that although she had an eidetic memory and could paint anything she had once seen, she needed some other visual reference during the act of painting. In my readings in art history I've found no other painter quite as peculiar. The Pre-Raphaelites may have departed from the anatomy of their mistresses/models by furnishing them with two or three extra vertebrae in the neck to achieve the effect of a woman keeping the observer transfixed by her snakelike gaze—or were disdainful swans the intended subliminal image?

But if they veered from reality by a few eerie inches, my mother leaped into a different dimension altogether in finding models that were totally unrelated to her subject. Another example, and I don't know why this one stuck to my mind: a pair of galoshes for a tower bent like a reed by a giant's fishing net.

I have no idea what secret associative processes were at work in the artist's mind. Nor do I know what symbolic meaning that summer's bouquet-spewing fish held for my mother. The possible Freudian interpretation is too obvious to bear mentioning; what Jung would make of the image, beyond its mandala-like appearance, I have no idea. I myself am perfectly willing to call my mother's choice of subjects arbitrary and incomprehensible without any anguished wringing of hands. Those who, based on her eccentricity and the scantiest of evidence provided by an overpriced lawyer at my trial, have concluded that insanity not so much ran as galloped in my family, I charge with an uncharitable interpretation of art, if not of murder.

I don't know that I ever asked my mother a single question about her paintings. As a child, I found her odd juxtapositions of objects funny but was also aware that I was nervously substituting that response for another, truer, one I didn't understand. Now I think I was simply afraid of the chaos invoked by surrealism. Her paintings threatened the rational, comprehensible edifice I was struggling to make of the world. Where I, with the fervent conservatism of the artist's child, cherished the thought of all things in their proper places and serving their proper functions, where I prided myself on knowledge that was indisputable fact (at six I knew that the moon was a satellite orbiting the earth, the sun a mediocre star, and that everything, including me, was made up of atoms), where I nailed proclamations of Absolute Certainty on all my walls and had LIARS KEEP OUT posted on my door, my mother was forever confronting me with impossible images, oblivious to how much I objected to absurdities like a net bending a tower—which would certainly break rather than curve in a ridiculous arc.

Which is not to say that I have after all doubled back to the dreary notion that mothers and/or fathers are to blame for all our woes: A mother paints a fish vomiting a jet of flowers and thirty years later her son stands in a living room, a smoking gun in his hand, and stares in bewilderment at the red bloom spreading on the chest of a dying man—not that I remember the reputed tendril of smoke curling upward at the nozzle of the murder weapon, only a jolt in my hand, and in my ears a noise like wind whistling through a desert canyon. But my point is that the mind is the strangest thing in the universe and the forces that shape it unknowable. (This, yes, from a man with a doctorate in psychology and an erstwhile thriving practice.) Still, it is unlikely that I hurled a slug of lead through a man's beating heart because my mother painted that particular painting that particular summer.

By the time of my mother's fishy painting I was, at any rate, shed of my childish insistence on pigeonholes; I allowed imagination and its strange excrescences a role in my world even to the point of being in love with one of my mother's canvases: A young man, barefoot and shirtless, in sky-blue pants; next to him, sitting at his feet, a dragon the size of a cat. The beast was half real, with gleaming scales and folds of delicately wrinkled skin where legs and body joined, half an artist's figurine, embellished with jeweled eyes and a serrated ridge of hammered gold running down its back. From its gaping mouth a torrent of fire poured, and a wreath of flames was wrapped around the young man's calves. And he, bent down, was stroking the dragon's head as he would that of a cat. Why I was so inordinately fond of that creation of hers I don't know. There was grace in its lines and composition, but my response was more than aesthetic pleasure awakened by form. Whenever I saw the painting, it was as if someone I absolutely trusted were telling me that improbably, against all odds, what I most desired would be mine.

I should add that again the painting departed from its model, which was, unless my memory fools me, a Spanish fan with the image of a matador or flamenco dancer or some other figure of stylized male flamboyance.

My mother sold the painting to a French collector a few months before her death; I found out by accident that it was recently destroyed in a fire, possibly an appropriate fate for a fire-breathing dragon and its friend. Still, I'm sorry to think of it as lost. The postcard-sized reproduction I taped over my bed (I'm not allowed thumbtacks—are the authorities afraid I'd put out my eyes or find some other dramatic and futile use for them?) doesn't do it justice.

Incidentally, I assure whatever curious soul may stumble across these pages (in addition to my primary audience of one) that they will not be the pathetic fabrications of a murderer trying to be "understood." I judge the likelihood of being understood by another member of the human race on a par with the likelihood of gaining entry into the Kingdom of Heaven—a place of such unmitigated boredom that I don't remember believing in it even in my kiddy years. But a desire, probably futile, of giving the poor, bedraggled truth its day out of court seized me when I was approached some weeks ago by a reporter for no less venerated an organ than *Vanity Fair*. The woman, assertive, bright and, judging by her comments on the appalling affair, endowed with a surprising amount of empathic imagination, was bent on securing a series of interviews from which to distill a more thoughtful version of the events than the scandal sheets had spat up during the trial. I squirmed at the thought of the five thousand distortions contained in the average article because of things misunderstood by even the most conscientious reporter, and made her a counterproposal: I would undertake my own inquiry into the remembered past and would put the results on paper, and she would draw on my self-reflexive exposé.

Although the idea of renewed public interest nauseates me, I'm attracted to this prospect of creating a record of the facts, not merely those that speak against me (of which there are many!) but also those that exist only as what an earlier age called "secrets of the heart": the actual turmoil, the actual hurt and loathing and heartache (but also—surprise!—delight and bliss)—the true remorse at the deed never to be undone.

I am acutely aware that in writing behind bars about my "romantic" life, I join a distinguished group of literary lunatics. I hope to be more amusing than de Sade and less notorious than Humbert Humbert or Felix Krull, but I promise my *hypocrite lectrice* that whatever charms or horrors I'll present in these pages will be as close to the truth as memory and psychological probing will allow me to get in the matter of my own life, personality, weaknesses, depravities, etc.

My mother was dark-haired and small-boned, with deep brown eyes, wide cheekbones and a narrow chin, and with the quick and graceful movements of an aerial acrobat. I resembled her uncannily in childhood although by the time I was fourteen I was half a head taller than she. That I was my mother's son was obvious to anyone who saw us together, and I grew at an early age tired of people rhapsodizing about the resemblance between us: *her* beautiful long eyelashes, *her* nose, *her* eyes, *her* porcelain complexion—and look at how he has the same shrug, so disdainful, so Gallic! I strove not to shrug disdainfully, not to look Gallic. When I was nine or ten, I studied her gestures for some weeks and checked myself whenever I found myself using one of them, the flick of the wrist to indicate the unimportance of something, the head tossed back expressively to indicate amusement. I succeeded at eliminating the most obvious similarities, but when I saw her smile at something that pleased her, or knit her brow at something distasteful, a tug and a shiver told me that hers were my smile, my frown, and that I could no more rid myself of them without doing harm to myself than I could rid myself of my thighbones.

She had met my father, the American writer, at Marseilles, where he was doing research for a novel and she was attending the *Académie des Beaux Arts*. A few weeks later they got married at Lyons, home of her parents (father, upper-echelon civil servant; mother, owner of a photography studio specializing in silk-purses-from-sows'-ears portraiture). When she promised to love, etc. him and vice versa, they knew as much about one another as any two people can know who are temporarily deprived of their wits by mutual enthrallment (or, for the less jaded, "who are deeply in love"). But they were luckier than most: when in the course of a few years he, no longer "deeply in love," found out that she loathed the idea of a large family, he settled without rancor for the one son; when she, equally cured of romance, discovered the weak core of the red-bearded colossus she had married, she accepted the truth without resentment and found his indifference to failure quite as attractive as the nonchalant way in which he had treated his laurels when first she met him.

In those early weeks of courtship, his unaffected lack of interest in his monstrous success (a Pulitzer Prize for his novel *Sea Dreams on Dry Land*, and a freakish—for a literary book—place on *The New York Times* best-seller list for nine weeks) would have impressed her even if her heart had not been set atrilling by...what? the mellow baritone of his voice? the way he bared his small, white teeth when he laughed? the brute strength of his bulk? or even less obvious clues that propel the human brain into a state virtually indistinguishable from severe neurosis.

That this physical and literary giant, so full of energy and purpose at the prospect of the next book he'd write, had done his one great deed and would spend the rest of his life planning and researching, collecting material, outlining sections—and would never again produce a single finished chapter, she couldn't have anticipated. Maybe her serene resignation to his epic writer's block was sign of an innate unwillingness to fret over the unalterable. But maybe it also had to do with her awareness as a fellow artist that the muse is a fickle bitch and can turn her snowy back on any lover and take her leave in a steel-blue rustle of taffeta and disdain. At any rate, unlike his publisher and unlike his son, his wife was not dismayed when she recognized the unfailing dynamics of her husband's "creativity."

I don't know when I first became aware of the pattern. One day I simply knew how it was and would always be: My father would have an idea for a new novel, a book so spectacular and stunning that it would make *Sea Dreams* look like practice. First, though, he'd have to do research, visit his story's locales, see the sights, talk to the people, observe, record. That part of the enterprise determined, and our erratic finances permitting, we'd journey to Málaga or Cologne or elsewhere and spend a few weeks or months there—typically in the summer, although on two occasions we played exiles for longer spans: I spent my first year in school in Paris, learning to read and write to the cadence of "Où est Jean? Jean est avec Paulette. Ils sont amis"; and when I was eleven we lived for a year in a run-down flat in grimy Newcastle-upon-Tyne (the Newcastle of coals-to-Newcastle fame)—in each case for the sole reason of a book fermenting in my father's imagination. Unlike my mother, who preferred anything American to anything in "embalmed Europe," the writer found the Old World endlessly fascinating. So Europe it was most summers, and we'd set up quarters at a lowly Pension or opulent Albergo, our finances, again, determining our standard of vacation living.

On the scene, my mother would paint, my father would wander through the town, visit parks, stop at pubs, and talk to the locals, either in English or workmanlike French to those who had a smattering of those languages or else by means of imaginative renditions of Spanish, German, Italian. He also, I should add, visited churches, cemeteries and brothels—always as an observer, not participant in the entertainments offered, and he studied buildings, the layout of streets, rivers and their bridges, parks, theater districts, the houses of birth or death of artists, writers, philosophers. He'd take notes and come back after a hard day's investigating well-satisfied and eager to relate to us his discoveries.

I, left to do as I pleased, would swim at the *Schwimmbad* or *piaggia,* go to movie theaters, visit amusement parks. I was a great museum-goer, and I loved exhibits with life-sized figures in period costumes and historic settings. I remember to this day gazing in mute rapture at an apothecary in burgundy velvet and wearing a Vandyke bent over his assistant in a cavernous hall filled with dusty jars on shelves. Before the two men was a scale, mortar and pestle, and the powdery answer, I was convinced, to a man's life or death. (I was, if nothing, a romantic.) Another time, when I was twelve or thirteen, I stumbled upon a dress rehearsal of *The Tales of Hoffmann* and sat in an empty theater mesmerized by the tricks played on gullible Hoffmann by his evil rivals in love.

Our vacation at an end, we'd return to whatever place we currently called home—usually in New York, but the part of town and amenities varied depending on my mother's unpredictable income from the sale of her paintings, on her parents' just-as-unpredictable transfer of sometimes extravagant sums of money into our bank account (grandmère every so often knew with clairvoyant certainty that my mother would be saved from starvation only by an emergency transfusion of funds), and my father's even more unpredictable income as a visiting writer at obscure but usually enthusiastic colleges.

Then the process of non-writing would begin with vigor and determination. Busily and energetically, my father would consolidate his notes, reorganize them, catalogue them, cross-reference them. He would bring home armloads of books from the library for supplementary reading. He would outline his story and present it to us at dinner, change his mind, present a revised version, elaborate on details. He'd refine his theme, give us short descriptions of how this or that fragment of history or architectural peculiarity would fit in: the claustrophobic *Gassen* through which the plague carts had rumbled setting the mood for an encounter between the protagonist and her demented lover; the bells of the cathedral counting off the deadly sins one by one.

This went on for months and months. But inevitably days came when nothing was said about the new novel. There was a vagueness about the writer, an absentmindedness and puzzledness, as if he were forever standing in the middle of a room, scratching his head, wondering what had brought him here. I had no difficulty recognizing the state as one of pain, and I worried about him. Now, I suspect I was wrong and my imaginative putting myself in his shoes simply meant I assigned to him what *I* would have felt under these circumstances. *I* would have been in pain if a thing I had loved with passion and devotion had suddenly stopped being interesting. For that was what happened to my father, he lost interest. The book that had excited him and moved him and had made the rich blood of the creator course through his veins had suddenly, overnight, become dull. It was as if he had wooed with passionate intensity and heroic effort a woman who enticed him, made his pulse race, his breath catch in his throat. He had dreamt day and night of the hour when she would yield to him, be coupled to him at his throbbing loins. Then the moment arrived. She was in his bed, naked, moist-breasted, her legs wantonly parted, awaiting his caresses. And he walked in, looked at her and scratched his head, unable to understand for the life of him what had possessed her to take off her clothes.

I would have been heartbroken at finding that riot of desire, that feeling of being alive with every quivering particle of self, gone without a trace. But some happy God of Forgetfulness had kissed my father's brow at his birth. A week or two of puzzled vagueness was all he was capable of, then, one morning or evening there'd be the announcement of an idea about a novel, which would be spectacular, stunning, marvelous—only, there'd have to be a good deal of research. My mother and I would listen, ask questions, enter into the spirit of the new glittering bauble—and neither of us would ask what had become of the novel about the woman who lived in Strasbourg and made mechanical dolls and fell in love with a man who used her automatons to rob banks.

For me, my father's relationship with his books solved the puzzle of my physical appearance when I first learned about sperm and ovum. His combining of energy, determination and unquenchable enthusiasm with easy resignation made obvious what had happened in the process of my generation: My father's sperms had launched themselves on the journey toward their destination with fervor and vim. But before the pregnable goal was reached, the effort had proven too much and they had drifted to a halt in the milky tide, vaguely unhappy with the failure of their mission but too disinterested to exert themselves further. Whereupon the ovum, impatient with the flagging suitors, had decided to go it alone, and I, fatherless tadpole, had begun to grow without having been given any of my sire's (or non-sire's) characteristics, neither his red hair, nor his large bones; neither his lack of staying power nor the deathless optimism that kept him from ever seeing the hopeless pattern and forever bucked him up with the happy conviction that he was about to write a masterwork.

An aside is in order here. There was in fact a break in the pattern in the last two months of my father's life. Two months before he died in a much-publicized freak accident (two Staten Island ferries; collision in heavy fog; seven people drowned), he began to write a novel. This time there was no announcement, no research, no synopsis presented at dinner. He simply began to fill page after page in his amazingly small hand—at the kitchen table when my mother and I were out of the apartment, at a minuscule desk squeezed into a corner of my parents' bedroom otherwise. When he returned to "reality" at the end of the day he looked disoriented, and he was absentminded in conversation; the few times I asked him about the new project, he told me with a mixture of pride and abashedness that I'd have to wait.

Whether his book would have turned into the stunning work he had always thought himself capable of writing there is no way of knowing. Some ten years ago, when I went through boxes full of things left over from my adolescence (notebooks, letters, books, a box of condoms—of the latter more in due course) I found a folder, labeled "Mister Faustus," with my father's manuscript. I read page after page of surpassing strangeness: A man puts a bullet through his head and dies but returns to life telepathic and obsessed with the idea of learning everything about the human mind. He finds lust and anarchy in the mind of the first person he encounters, his teenage son. The plot, however, seemed almost a subtext to an *omnium gatherum* of odd digressions proceeding, in the first chapter, from the reproductive habits of the aardvark to the death of Zwingli.

If my father had after years of failure discovered the Philosopher's Stone that would have allowed him to synthesize the elements of a lifetime of research and observation and to transmute them into what would make him immortal (in the dubious sense in which immortality is granted the author of an immortal work), he was betrayed by a fate that was as indifferent to his heart's desire as to the advancement of literature in the second half of the twentieth century.

I suppose a fair question is whether we were a happy family. Happier than a great many, I would guess from my clinical experience. My mother lived with the artist's blissful knowledge that she was creating the world anew, endowing it with meaning through the magic hand of illusion. My father lived and breathed illusion and was forever trembling on the threshold of endowing the stuff of his imagination with the life of words.

Which leaves only me. Although there would come a time when comparison tried to tell me otherwise, I don't remember being happy. Not that I was unhappy. (For those interested in semantic fine points, I see the difference between not being happy and being unhappy as the difference between the absence of something positive and the presence of something negative in one's life. Since things absent usually carry less weight than things present, I conclude that lacking happiness is preferable to possessing unhappiness.) I know that for many years I thought my sensibility ample compensation for not being blessed with my parents' frivolity. My mother called me Monsieur Laplace whenever she marveled that two free spirits had produced as methodical and deterministic a soul as me. When at age twelve I became moody, oppressed by a sense of futility and often irritable and sardonic (Monsieur Mélancolique?), she probably saw this development as a mixed bag of tricks. I became more difficult to live with, but she also may have felt that I had finally joined the human race as a creature of doubt and imagination. If my father was disappointed at the change, he gave no indication of it.

And I? I was waiting, although I didn't know that I was, or why, or for what or whom.

And so it came about that, in the fifteenth summer of my life, in the ancient town of Aquileia, I was born and died, and learned nothing from the experience (except how to be happy and how not).

On the fateful day, I came back from the beach sun-dazzled, water-logged, abrasive, with sand in my hair, teeth, toes. My eyes slits against the white sun, I entered the shuttered marble cool of the hotel's foyer. I opened my eyes to the dark grotto, and there was summer brightness again, only soft and pleasing to the eye: a

woman skipping down the stairs in a lilting stepstep, stepstep ca- ⌐
dence. Leather sandals, bare legs, an off-white, shortsleeved linen
dress, a hat of pale straw on blond hair that curved in on either side
of her face to brush against her throat. This was how she looked,
and my memory of her will always be a vision of brightness and
infinite delight to the eye.

Yet I immediately have to contradict myself. I cannot resurrect in
my mind the image of her face. Like a photo too often handled, too
often cried over, left ruthlessly in the sun, angrily crammed out of
sight in a drawer full of junk, it has lost all but a blurry suspicion of
the former likeness. I know it was a delicate face, with lips surprisingly full. (The latter I remember only because I remember her
telling me that she had her mother's fat lips, "hooker lips," she said.)
I know the eyes were a startling bright blue, and cheek and jaw had a
velvety sheen at certain angles of the light. But I can form no composite picture out of these fragments. I'm not sure it was a beautiful
face, though it probably suggested to me vulnerability and a capacity for passion—or how else can I explain what happened to me?

She stepstepped down the stairs, I looked at her from across the
foyer, and I was flooded—every chamber, every hollow, every infinitesimal space of my being—by longing. My mouth went dry, my
knees were ready to buckle, my heart beat weakly, as longing lifted
me up and pulled me toward her, so that I felt I had to lean back to
keep from either falling forward or rushing to her.

This was what all my years of living had held in store for me.
This was why I had been born, had grown, was here and nowhere
else. The reason for all things, the solution to all puzzles, the answer
to all secret murmurs of a desirous heart. To be here now and to
know what it meant to want another human being with every atom
of my being. I felt faint and I might have collapsed if there hadn't
been at the same time, or separated from it by a tick of my pulse, a
wild surge of energy at being in the presence of the one I loved. And
separated from that moment by the space it took for her to skip
down the stairs, her eyes on something in the foyer—that some-

thing at her approach turning into a balding, pink, fattish man, who rose and folded his newspaper—was the shock of violent pain.

For he rose and said something to her in English with a German accent, and she laughed a clear high laugh and hooked her arm through his. They left the hotel, her gaze skipping over me as lightly as she had skipped down the stairs.

If I had died then, struck down by divine fiat and a burst aorta, I would have been buried under stately cypresses having known all I was ever to know about desire. Nothing that happened to me in my life after that moment, no experience great or small, added in any substantial way to what I knew then of the workings of my heart. Even the thrill and terror of killing a man, or the disagreeable repercussions of his death, did not have the feel of the new, never-before-experienced but struck me as simply the natural result of feelings brought to life all those years ago when I saw the woman I loved trip lightly down those marble stairs and move past me on her husband's arm after an uncurious glance at me.

What do I remember of her? What clings to me still when so much else has been effaced beyond recognition, sloughed off, jettisoned as worthless because not sufficiently odd, amusing or tormenting to keep around? (No restored castle without its torture chamber to revitalize the sightseer after the polite tedium of ballroom, bedroom and chapel.) Most vividly, a splash of color: a fire-engine-red bikini and the aesthetic delight of seeing the clean way the smooth cotton fabric was folded around small breasts and a narrow pelvis. But also so many other, subtler things that set my heart afloat. In that sterile courtroom, I could never make a jury of my peers understand for even the span of a sigh the delight mixed with mortal anguish I felt when I looked at her blue, green-flecked eyes, how my breath caught in my throat when I saw the veins in her lower arms—an aquamarine web in alabaster—her bony upper chest. And yet, if that delight, that terror, weren't understood, how was anything else to make sense?

What do I remember? Her on a beach chair, one of those colorful striped canvas and wood contraptions; her upper half in the shade of an umbrella; her legs, slim legs, full in the calf (at home she took long walks), glistening with lotion in the sun. I sit next to her on a blanket, and she, with closed eyes and in a low voice, tells me about herself. Around us are bathers and sun worshipers, but they seem to be moving in a silent dream of splashing, and bouncing beach balls, and running children. They make no sound as I listen to the voice of my beloved, afraid to move, afraid to break the enchantment—although I already feel so close to her, so intimate, so much a part of her, that there seems nothing strange about a woman of twenty-seven telling a fourteen-year-old boy the story of her abominable childhood.

She told me much on that first day, and effortlessly—for I loved her!—I found the right responses: Were you afraid? Were you angry? That must have hurt. Mostly, though, I listened to her with a passionate intentness, knowing that I would love the blood pulsing in her veins, and her narrow wrists and long fingers, and the blue hollows between her throat and collarbones till the day I died.

But that was day two of our six-day romance. On day one, the day of our first encounter, she and her husband returned to the hotel for dinner. They sat a few tables from us. From my place I had a clear view of her. She had changed for dinner into a pale pink dress and it was clear that my impression of her had not been a trick of the moment, one of those cheap laughs nature has at our expense when she composes the perfect tableau for our delectation—a marble stairway, light muted by shutters, the clean lines of a summer dress, a filigreed straw hat, all artistically arranged to give loveliness to something that, seen against a more prosaic backdrop, by a harsher light, in a less fetching costume, turns out to have no power over our spirit. No trick, she, but the true answer to my heart's desire (a desire, for the record, that is infinitely more treacherous than any lie presented by outward forms).

Of her husband I saw only a pink neck and a head equally pink where scant blond strands of hair didn't cover it—a young pig's pink, but he was older, much older, than she. An hour earlier, propelled by the sudden wild hope that he might be her father, I had asked one of the owner's sons, who worked at reception, about the new arrivals, and he had told me that the couple was il signore Reinhart Seeler and la signora (not signorina) Jennifer Seeler from Frankfurt.

So it was Jennifer, lovely Jennifer, married Jennifer, I glanced at when reaching for my glass of diluted chianti, when reaching for the salt, when looking around the dining room to observe to my parents that it seemed more crowded than usual.

Then the hotel's owner stopped at our table and invited us to a party, a weekend extravaganza, for his special guests—to be held upstairs in the duke's "Hall of Lights." I loathed the man for his phony charm and joviality, which hid, as I had discovered, genuine nastiness. A few days earlier, I had turned a corner and had surprised him striking one of his sons, a boy of nine, in the face. The boy cried out, covered his cheek and ran away. His father turned, murder in his eyes, saw me, and effortlessly transformed his face into one of comical dismay: "Mamma mia, questi bambini! They will drive you crazy!"

I knew from my father, ever a font of local lore, that Signor Carlucci had been a small-time operator, the owner and captain of a barge that ferried people and goods along the coast, until he had inherited his great-uncle's palazzo. Then he had gone into business with a brother-in-law in construction, had refurbished the place and turned it into a hotel, becoming the hotelier with a vengeance—dressed in blinding white shirt and trousers, his dyed black hair and mustache slicked. The hotel was a financial success, but some hidden discontent kept driving its owner. He was unwilling to settle for lucre alone and lusted for a prestigious clientele, not the run-of-the-mill tourist with enough cash to spend a week in a ritzy place but people with real money or with some other legitimate pretension. My parents were on his "approved" list because they were artists. Others qualified because of conspicuous wealth and/or social standing.

I mention Carlucci at some length because when, thirty years later, my lawyer looked for an improbable defense in the events of that week, he found that the man had been stabbed to death in the hotel's kitchen in the small hours of the night a year after our stay at the Albergo Attila. The police had suspected a rival in love but had been unable to prove anything. I've always been fascinated by coincidences of this sort and I'm convinced that hidden within them lie all the secrets of the universe.

Having secured the artists for his extravaganza, Carlucci ingratiated himself with a Roman professor of archaeology, a world authority on Etruscan funeral art, and his lawyer wife. Next came the table of a Liverpudlian industrialist and his loud wife, and their carp-faced sixteen-year-old daughter, who was rumored by her loud mother to have a crush on me—we'd exchanged maybe a dozen words—and who as far as I could tell thought me a perfect baby and was desperately in love with Giorgio at reception. Then a table was skipped—a young German couple with no credentials other than a winning number in a soccer pool and a BMW motorcycle. Another table was given an even wider berth, the mocking eyes of the old American woman sitting at it exerting a repelling influence. The woman was a retired M.D. who had begun practicing medicine during World War I. She was big boned and had shockingly bad taste in clothing. In the sequined dresses she wore for dinner she looked like Charlie's Aunt played by a tackle. I was fond of her because she relished intimidating Carlucci with her black, observant eyes, acerbic humor and harsh laugh. Our host gingerly skirted the reef of the formidable doctor, and then, oozing charm like iridescent slime, performed for Herr Seeler, the owner of half a dozen home electronics stores in as many German cities, and his lovely young wife.

Who, in the middle of his spiel, allowed her eyes to stray from him and to catch mine. And who smiled at me a sly, conspiratorial smile that blinded me to all but its memory for the rest of the meal. I don't remember returning it, but I must have because when after dinner I "accidentally on purpose" ran into her on the terrace, she asked me, in unaccented American, "Is he as awful as he sounds?"

I had, doomed mariner, failed to tie myself to a mast or at least ask someone to belay me with a sturdy rope by which I could be dragged to safety at the first sign of enthrallment. (Incidentally, I used to think of Odysseus in the presence of the Sirens as the wisest man in all mythology—aware of the frailty of his own mind, nevertheless unwilling to forego experience, but smart enough to protect himself against its worst consequences. Now it seems to me that Homer shortchanged the human psyche's propensity for self-destruction: realistically, formerly "crafty" Odysseus ought to have spent the rest of his life sitting on Ithaca's strand, staring out to sea, unable to free his mind of the voices that had spoken to his soul. Meanwhile, back at the palace, Penelope impales herself on the phallus of one suitor after another in reckless grief and Telemachos offers the use of his anus to all comers—yes, a pun—for a small fee.)

I had no rope mooring me to wax-deafened companions. That elementary precaution omitted, what could I have done when Jennifer spoke to me? Turn and run away? Hastily plead a chronic toothache or consumption and spend the rest of our stay locked in my room? Tell her that I was very sorry, but the mere sight of her induced derangement in me and the only way I could hope to save my sanity—possibly my life—was to have no contact with her? (True, oh so true, that last apology would have been!)

I did none of the above, and I can't honestly blame myself. We don't encounter what our soul has thirsted for all our days and turn away from it—not even if an expert tells us that what we've found is poison. I speak from experience, having been such an expert and having saved few if any of the poor wretches clutching glittering flasks of deadly concoctions. But on that terrace, that evening, there was no one to draw me away, no one to whisper a warning into my ear or slip into my hand a scrap of paper with a hastily drawn skull and crossbones.

So I talked to Jennifer. Actually spoke words that made sense about our loathsome host, found out that she had been looking forward to this vacation for months. Reinhart couldn't take the sun and had brought a suitcase of work. But she'd be sunbathing and enjoying herself.

I told her I knew a beach that wasn't too crowded, where I went swimming every day. I'd show her where it was.

"I don't know how to swim," she said. "I almost drowned when I was little."

If I hadn't been achingly in love with her before, I would have been so after she made that confession. There was a wistful note in her voice, a rueful reluctance to admit to something that embarrassed her, coupled with the resolve to be honest even if she felt silly. My answer? "I'll teach you. It isn't hard."

Hence the scene on the sand: red bikini, beach chair, talk about her childhood. What did she tell me? Nothing that was the apex of hideousness; nothing approaching in horror the case studies of child abuse I read in graduate school. She grew up in Las Vegas; her father abandoned her and her mother when she was five; her mother turned to prostitution. She began to drink when she was thirteen, was seduced/raped by one of her mother's johns at fourteen, tried to kill herself with whiskey and sleeping pills at fifteen. When she was sixteen, Reinhart Seeler, German businessman sightseeing in the U.S., asked her directions at an intersection, bought her dinner, took her to his motel and did not sleep with her but cleaned her up and put her to bed. Three months later they were married and living in Frankfurt, where Reinhart owned a home electronics store. He now owned half a dozen such stores; they lived in a large villa with an English maid and a dog and a cat.

I listened attentively, but my mind was drawn to a desert scene of red sand, high, white clouds, tumbleweeds wheeling in the wind (the production of some otherwise forgotten Technicolor western). At a desolate intersection, dwarfed by a giant sky, stood a thin, untidy girl in a flimsy cotton dress. I felt a dreadful yearning to leap back in time and become the traveler who stopped his car for her. Me to take her to a place of safety; me to put her in a warm shower and gently soap her down, thinking no evil thoughts; me to put her to bed and tuck her in, kiss her drowsy eyes, wish her a good night with no bad dreams. Me to marry her and love her all my days.

The following day we waded out into the bay, half a mile it seemed, until the water reached our rib cages, and we tossed back and forth a blue rubber ball Jennifer had bought from a vendor. Whenever she failed to catch it, she waded after it, awkwardly paddling water aside with her arms to speed up her progress. When the ball sailed past me, I pursued it with the smooth freestyle I had taught myself on a previous vacation.

We also played tag in the water. (The innocence and charm of it all!) Jennifer protested when I eluded her by diving and swimming circles around her underwater. I was careful not to frighten her by splashing or pushing her over, and she squatted down as far as she could while still keeping her head above water and blindly swept her arms around in search of me. I surfaced, blowing water like a Triton in a fountain, and we laughed at my cheating, and she gave chase and caught me because I needed to be caught.

On that same day, I buried her in hot sand and she giggled when rills from the first handfuls trickled down her midriff. When the mound was complete, I was reminded of a primitive burial lacking only the heaped rocks meant to protect the loved form from ravenous beasts. (Have I mentioned that my mind is as morbid as it is melancholical?) The sarcophagus—the scene was, of course, more Egyptian than Anglo-Saxon—baked in the sun, and pharaoh's fair child, unswaddled, her head sheltered by an umbrella, talked of her husband. Either jealousy rendered me deaf or what she told me didn't interest me—the only bits of information I brought away were that he had studied medicine before the war but had changed his mind about his surgical vocation before taking his exams, and that in the war he had served in Northern Africa. Infinitely more important than Reinhart's bloodthirsty past was the bittersweet impression I got that she didn't love him.

In the evening, at Carlucci's party, I availed myself of the lights in the Sala delle Luci, an array of chandeliers reflected in dozens of mirrors, to take a cold-eyed look at Herr Reinhart Seeler. I found that I disliked him intensely. The man exuded a smooth and polished arrogance, a cultivated sophistication that I found hard to swallow in someone who spoke in heavily accented English (as in, "Sis town vas vonce fortified") and who would have fit better in a butcher's apron than in the silk dinner jacket he sported. He was probably in his mid-forties but to me was simply old. His porcine pinkness was emphasized by the black jacket. He had a distinct spread around his middle and was generally beefy, with a fatty neck and short sausage fingers. It was grotesque to think that Jennifer occasionally (I couldn't imagine it being frequently) submitted to his embrace. She had to be physically bruised by his sheer heft, my slim love, and there was no telling what emotional bruises his piggishness inflicted on her in these encounters.

It should be noted here how effortlessly I had already cast her as the victim, used, misunderstood, unloved—how could a pretentious vulgarian like he understand or love her?—hopelessly trapped in a situation over which she had no control. Already I bled for her, already I was in a rage about the unfairness of a life that had chained her to an unworthy object. A quarter of a century later, when I had virtually the same response to what I facetiously dubbed "Model Two," one of the sensations accompanying the experience was a nauseating familiarity. Another was incredulity at not being able to avoid having a certain response to a certain type of creature despite a marked increase in my sophistication.

The next day, it was back to the beach for the poor wife and her hopeless swain. Now that I resurrect these days and reassemble them fragment by fragment (and what feelings cling to some of the fragments!), I realize that most of what the poor wife and her hopeless swain did, they did in sun, sand and sea—even though the two impressions that remain most vividly in my mind are cloaked in semi-darkness and darkness (the former her descent down the stairs, the latter her minnowlike nakedness glimmering in the moon shadow cast by a beached fishing boat—but two more days were to elapse before she glimmered naked for my loving eyes).

She was leery, but I coaxed and cajoled, and in the end she was game: I would teach her to swim. The breaststroke was easiest, I told her, managing to sound matter-of-fact and adult, as if neither the word "breast" nor the word "stroke" nor their juxtaposition had any meaning other than that related to swimming.

She sat on her beach chair, and, alternately giggly and serious, imitated the motion of my arms: stab stiffened hands forward, turn them to make the palms face outward, sweep them back in a semi-circle, repeat. The legs were more of a problem. I lay on my back and demonstrated the kick, but she broke into laughter and laughing said she'd look too damn silly if she did that. Surmising that she thought I looked silly, I was momentarily peeved. But I quickly checked myself: she couldn't possibly find me silly. Had she not, smiling a sweet smile, told me that I looked like a fairy-tale prince? (Reinhart had bought her collections of fairy tales when she had started to learn German—which, I imagine, had a larger than ordinary influence on the little girl he had saved from the wicked den of Las Vegas.)

And while we're on the subject of make-believe—I haven't mentioned the multitude of pleasantries Jennifer uttered in those giddy days concerning my appearance and personality. For the record: In addition to being as handsome as a fairy-tale prince, I was "charming" and "sweet" and exactly like the boy she'd always dreamt of meeting in the desert when she was growing up—the one with whom she'd fall in love and run away. Maybe I've failed to mention my virtues and attractions according to the woman I was in love with for fear of appearing vain. More probably the reason is that to this day the remembered lies flood my mouth with gall.

But back to the swimming lesson. That she was having a laugh at my expense as I was lying on my back, for her benefit moving my legs like a stricken beetle, bothered me for an instant and then was forgotten as I cast about for other ways to teach her the frog kick. I finally hit upon the idea of a life preserver. From a man renting umbrellas and other beach gear, we borrowed a contraption of cork blocks on a rope, which was tied around the lower chest and waist to give the non-swimmer buoyancy. And there we were in the gentle rise and fall of the Adriatic, me holding on to Jennifer's cork-encased middle, she churning up the water with energetic limbs and startling ineptness. I took one of her wrists and guided her arm through the motion. I tried to do the same with one of her ankles and caught a kick in the stomach when, alarmed by her face taking a dip in the water, she struggled to get her legs under her.

After some time, she had a rudimentary idea of what she was supposed to do, and we returned to shore. She told me about her near-drowning when she was four in an algae-covered pool. She had slipped and had suddenly been under green water, everything around her green, everything slimy, no air, then darkness.

Poor Jennifer, and to think that if some misguided do-gooder hadn't jumped in and pulled her from her slimy grave she would have been dead close to a quarter of a century at the time when it was my particular misfortune to lay eyes on her—not an ankle bone left intact, no face to gladden my heart, no mouth to please me, no brain to deceive and mock and wound me to the core. (Am I making too much of this? I don't think so, even though my false love has been dead these ten years, as was also determined by my ever-anxious lawyer—killed in an accident on the autobahn. Poor Jennifer, I murdered a man because of you, when you had been a heap of ashes sealed in a stone-cold urn for ten long years.)

In the afternoon, my new method was a variation of one I had used to teach myself to swim at age six. We stood in waist-high water. She squatted down, launched herself in my direction, executed one rapid stroke of arms and legs and held on to me while getting her legs under her and standing up. We repeated the maneuver over and over, then I moved two yards further away and she had to reach me with two strokes. And so on. All of this entailed a good deal of touching. She, often on the verge of panic, would grab any convenient part of me. I, to help her steady herself, did the same. So that by the time she was taking three strokes to reach me, I had touched her arms, shoulders, waist, breasts, and once had gotten my wrist trapped between her legs and had touched in a confusion of fingers and thumb the smooth crotch of her bikini.

All this was entirely innocent. Even contact with "that" part of her anatomy was merely an embarrassment I hid with prattle about her improvement. That no erotic thrill accompanied this episode, either right then or later, when I was alone in my room, may seem odd but is not unusual, as any number of experts on the subject of romantic attachment corroborate: A sizable percentage of adolescents report a marked difference between the experience of romantic love and that of sexual interest, romantic love typically focusing on one person and involving an aesthetic response to a face, a feathered brow shading a lustrous eye, a delicate hand, or the way a voice resonates or a laugh rings melodiously, whereas sexual interest tends to focus generically on primary sexual characteristics and to result in a sexual response to, for instance, any girl's or woman's large breasts or buttocks, or, in extreme cases, any female's pudendum.

I knew then, and I know now, that my feelings toward Jennifer were chaste. My ardor burned clean, a pure flame of ethereal delight and yearning uncompromised by the rankness of sex. Which is not to say that I was chaste. I had found on a park bench in Lyon, where at twelve I spent two months with grandmère et grandpère, a French paperback, which, even with my limited French, revealed itself to be pornography. One male and a difficult-to-keep-track-of number of female "characters" went through the standard unimaginative repertoire of lust in action—this position, that motion, imbecilic dialogue à la: "Oo, chéri, tu es très dur"—and many an hour did I spend leafing with sweaty fingers through a dictionary, deciphering such tidbits as *écarquiller les jambes* and *mouiller le ventre*. Other expressions were palpably filthy but not to be found in my reference work; I had to imaginatively surmise from the surrounding text what untranslatable acts they might be referring to. I acquired from this volume an idea of the rudiments of the act of copulation as well as of a sizable number of its permutations, and even though the fact that the text was in French gave the action an elusive quality that I was never able to translate into hardcore American reality, there was enough material to enliven my masturbatory fantasies when I applied it to women I saw on the covers of magazines or in the proverbial flesh in peekaboo bathing suits.

But I insist that none of this had anything to do with Jennifer. Although I had no difficulty thinking of her as victimized by her husband, piggy Reinhart, the victimization being in a vague sense connected to the fact that he was by virtue of holy matrimony entitled to sex with her, that thought, inchoate and unreified by words or pictures in my imagination, did not turn her into a sexual being in my mind. For me she was, in the simplest terms, in another world, one in which sex had no meaning. In that world, she appeared to my chaste gaze a figure of heartstopping loveliness, invested with all that was good and to be cherished. She dwelled in a blue and golden land, and meeting her there meant meeting my own best self. There, with her before me, I was noble and wise and thoughtful and unselfish, ready to be hers forever, ready to give up my life to protect her from harm. At the same time, she imbued this land with such delight that I could not help but be witty and charming, ready to amuse and be amused at the slightest provocation because my heart was so light, ready to see all things as reflections of a cosmos combining the highest seriousness of purpose with the greatest gaiety. I desired Jennifer, but it was my best self that desired her. My longing, that breathless urgency that kept me awake most of the night with thoughts of her, and occupied all of my day with thoughts of her, took the form of the wish to be close to her, her eyes meeting mine with an inward smile that told me she loved me, her narrow hand in mine, her shoulder touching mine. Smiling, she'd turn to me and say, I love you; I've loved you from the moment I first saw you.

My yearning stopped there, with that moment of ecstasy. It held nothing base, nothing carnal, only infinite tenderness, infinite happiness, infinite delight, and the knowledge that in some unfathomable way every instance of sight and touch was connected with being understood by her, not through Saint Paul's glass darkly but face to face: with calm, penetrating eyes my love looked through the mottled surface of mundane concerns and petty aims and saw the lucid, harmonious whole that was my soul. Symbolically speaking.

One more day of frolic in sand and sea followed, then we took a day off from the beach to go sightseeing. It was a magical day (according to the platitude of young love); all things made exciting and gay and full of whimsy by Jennifer at my side. Every moment infused with charm, the young donkey nuzzling her bare arm at the vegetable stand, the old man saluting the "bella ragazza" with an elegant sweep of hand to forehead. Every moment significant, every instant important, a treasure lavished upon me by a world that had an inexhaustible supply of such treasures and a boundless munificence.

Jennifer posed for a snapshot before an excavated wall. The two of us, arms clasped about each other's waists, posed before a fountain while a young Belgian took our picture, after which I returned the favor for him and his young bride, wondering whether he thought Jennifer and I were in love. We strolled down the streets, arms interlinked, bantering, laughing, our closeness seeming the most natural thing in the world. And in the background, just at the edge of consciousness, my heart chanted to me over and over, She's fond of me.

She thinks I'm remarkable; she thinks I'm beautiful. I'm funny, I'm charming, I make her laugh, she loves to be with me, she prefers being with me to being with anybody else.—Und, as they say in zee old country, so weiter.

My parents were spending two days in Venice, and Jennifer invited the temporary orphan to have dinner with her and Reinhart. I accepted because it meant being in her company, and I grimly resolved to be pleasant to Ruddy Reinhart (who was growing ruddier by the day despite spending most of his time in their suite). I suppose we talked about sightseeing, Italy and other innocuous topics, and I suppose I didn't fold my hands around Reinhart's neck and strangle him notwithstanding my antipathy for him as a superficially clever, patronizing fool, who seemed unable to address a single remark to me that was not in some mocking way connected with my youth and inexperience in all worldly areas.

Dinner ended, Reinhart retired, and Jennifer invited me to have ice cream with her in town. We lingered at the *gelateria* for a while, then walked around the town, enjoying the night. To my great delight, Jennifer showed no interest in returning to the hotel but wanted to take a stroll on the beach. We got there close to one and walked at the lapping edge of the water by starlight. Jennifer talked about how much she had hated the desert, especially at night, because it had made her feel small and unimportant. I (Monsieur Laplace even in love) told her that some of the stars we saw had been dead for thousands of years and their light was still reaching us from far away.

"That can happen to people too," she said. "They can be dead and not even know it. They go through the motions but there's no longer any feeling."

She sounded sad and my heart quavered. "But you're alive," I said. "You're more alive than anybody I know."

"Am I?" she said. "Maybe I'm now. Maybe because of this week."

I don't know what I replied. That I too felt alive? More alive than I'd felt in my entire life—and all because of her?

We walked and talked, about the vastness of space, the shortness of life, the possible meaning or lack thereof of life, the possibility of alien civilizations on other planets—the deep, trite things people talk about when awed into thought by a starry night. Jennifer, poor child, "sort of" believed in the transmigration of souls and in God, no particular God but some all-knowing, all-loving, all-forgiving entity floating amorphously in space. I forgave her her innocent superstition, and I thought that if I were granted one wish in my life it would be for this night never to end.

A quarter moon rose and sea and sand crept palely into view. Jennifer walked next to me, no longer a disembodied voice but a delicate face grayed by the moon and bruised by shadows.

She stopped and looked around. "It's beautiful, isn't it?" she said. "It gives me the feeling that something magical can happen any moment." She turned to me. "Are you tired?"

I told her no, not at all, I'd never been so awake.

"Me too," she said. "Isn't it strange after all the walking we've done?"

A little further down the beach we came upon a beached fishing boat. Jennifer suddenly nudged me. "Quick, before we get moon-burned," she said, and she took my hand and pulling me ran to the boat, tossing her legs backward in the awkward, foal-like gait I loved. She threw herself to the ground and pulled me down next to her in the wide shadow cast by the boat. Out of breath, she abruptly asked, "Have you ever made love?"

Assaulted by a jumble of emotions—for I knew what would happen and was confused, afraid, excited—I said no, never.

"Would you like to?" she asked.

I said, "Yes, but I don't know how."

She put her arms around me and kissed me on the mouth. "It's easy, I'll teach you," she said in a low voice that thrilled me. "Remember? That's what you said about swimming. When you said it that evening I thought, Maybe I'll teach him something too."

I can say with perfect honesty (the truth, the whole truth…) that I remember with the vividness of total recall every infinitesimal part of everything that ensued, every move made by her—the unhurried way she unbuttoned her dress and spread it on the sand for a blanket, the awkward way (but what lovely awkwardness!) she stepped out of her panties, the small laugh she gave when she unhooked her bra in the back and shrugged off that last barrier between me and her nakedness. I fumbled with my shirt and pants awkwardly and felt shy when taking off my shorts. Then her hands were on my chest and belly and buttocks and her body rubbed against mine, and there was the startling surprise of her tongue in my mouth, hot and flexing like an eel. I held her, feeling with every pore the sensation of her nakedness, my nipples pressed against her small breasts, my belly and thighs against hers. My heart was a fluttering wren in my rib cage; my breathing was labored; my blood roared in my ears. She touched the most intimate parts of me, stroked them, kneaded them. I trembled and all my feelings merged into a single sensation of wanting. I kissed her, ran my hands over her body, felt in my palms her nipples. She pulled me down, on top of her, guided me, and suddenly I was inside her, thrusting spasmodically. Then it was over in a shuddering moment, and I eased myself off her and lay next to her out of breath and almost faint. I said to her in a voice choked with feeling, "I love you. I've loved you from when I first saw you coming down the stairs. I can't tell you how much."

She turned on her side, put her forehead against mine and said, "Me too. I dreamt about you in the desert but I didn't think you were real. But you're real, aren't you?" She kissed me, again filling my mouth with her sinewy tongue, and she took my hand and put it between her legs, closing them firmly around it. I tried to please her clumsily and apparently I succeeded. She shuddered and sighed and said, "Ah, you're sweet."

I kept my hand there, still caressing her wet curls, so like the horse-hair stuffing of a pillow I had torn in childhood, and thinking that I would never in all my life be closer to anyone than I was to her.

"You can't leave," I said to her. "You have to tell him that you want to stay." (I couldn't bear pronouncing the name of the loathsome toad, her husband.)

"Don't I wish," she said. "I'd like to stay here forever and ever."

I heard her words. At first I didn't understand the awful meaning they held, and then, suddenly, I did. With the consummate gift at ignoring reality that is granted lovers and fanatics I had, until this precise moment, managed to keep out of my head all thoughts of the inevitability of our separation. The future had been a thing cloaked in densest fog, unknown and unknowable, about which it made as little sense to think as it made sense to think about a gruesome death that was unlikely to occur. Now it attacked me like a fiend unmasked, in the garb of countable days, vanishing minutes, inescapable endings. Dismay put a stranglehold around my throat and clapped iron bands around my chest. "You can't go back to him after this," I protested ("this" meaning of course the monumental thing we had done together). Reprimand quickly followed. "How can you leave me if you love me?"

She laughed a sad little laugh. "I have to. How would I live if I didn't?" she said (managing without effort to sound as if leaving her husband would mean starvation or worse in the cruel streets of Frankfurt).

With the cunning born of desperation, my brain came up with an answer. My answer showed the depth of my feelings, the sincerity of my commitment, and an impressive—for an adolescent—perspective of time. I told her, yes, she had to leave me now, but that would not be the end. We would write to each other, and in four years I'd come to Germany and study at Frankfurt. I'd find work and we'd be able to get married.

Jennifer said, "You *are* sweet," and kissed me on the forehead. She sat up, found her panties and put them on, meanwhile explaining to me why my plan wouldn't work: three years earlier she had fallen in love with a student and Reinhart had found out. "He's very possessive. He hired a man to put him in the hospital," she said, looking around for her bra.

I was appalled but, to my credit, less at the thought that my Jennifer had been in love with someone else than at another thought. "Did he hurt you?" I asked.

"Oh no, he'd never do that. He loves me." She fastened her bra, got up, picked up her dress and shook out the sand.

Fighting incomprehension and despair, I began to put on my clothes. "Didn't it hurt you that he hurt the student?" was the only question that came to my shell-shocked mind.

"Not really. He wasn't very nice." She slipped into her dress and buttoned it down its length with a deft rapidity that terrified me. Suddenly time was the great enemy, sand running out, a clock ticking away inexorably toward the moment of doom. I fought dread and despair. So little time for eloquence, so little time for reasoning, for persuading, for making her see that without each other we'd never again know a moment's happiness, that without her I'd die, that she had to wait for me to become an adult with the ability to go anywhere I chose and do anything I chose, and then she had to live with me.

We headed back to the hotel. One landmark after another appeared to sight and was passed—each one closer than the previous to the place where my fate would be sealed if I hadn't persuaded her. I stopped, to get her to stop. She kept moving. I pleaded with her, I argued, I implored. Her answers were all hopeless: She couldn't leave Reinhart; staying in contact with me would be too dangerous with Reinhart on the scene; there was nothing she could do.

"Don't you love me?" I pleaded, in tears.

"Of course I love you." There was a tremor in her voice when she said it.

"As much as your student?" I asked bitterly.

She finally did stop and turn to me. She kissed me and I tasted tears on her lips.

"Don't cry," I said. "I can't stand it if you're hurt." But in my heart of hearts I rejoiced because she was crying because of me.

All this, as the lover of literature will pages ago have noted, took place by the light of the inconstant moon ("O! swear not by the moon"), whose sickle was high overhead when we made our way through the quiet town to find at its edge, like a place of evil enchantment, the hotel where the evil wizard waited for the return of the spellbound queen. The door was locked, and we had to ring the bell and wait for a sleepy Giorgio to let us in. He vanished and we stood in the lobby at the selfsame spot where I had first seen her a lifetime ago. We embraced and kissed. I wanted to hold her and never let go of her. But she pulled away from me, saying, "I really have to go." And then she was gone with a clatter of leather sandals up the stairs.

I dragged my weary self up those same stairs, found my room and lay down on the bed in my clothes. I recalled Jennifer's nakedness and mine, the intimacy of touch, love in her arms—all of which I relived as things sacred, a blending of the purest passion with a feeling of great awe—both juxtaposed with a sense of utter peace, as if I had returned to a place of ecstasy and reverence I had missed for so long that barely a wisp of its memory had survived. And yet such wretched dismay encircled my safe and holy place. She would leave; she would be gone. I would die of grief, for how could I go on living without her now that I had found her. How would I be able to breathe and eat and do the thousand things one needed to do to live, when longing for her was tearing me apart? I wouldn't. I couldn't. I heard myself say: I can't; I can't; I can't—over and over, until the words turned into sobs and I pulled my pillow to me and cried into it inconsolably. My chest heaved, my shoulders jerked and the sounds that issued from me were inhuman. Never before had I given myself over to grief so completely.

In the midst of this turmoil I had the curiously dispassionate thought that maybe if I went to her room and she saw how dreadful I felt, she'd relent—and if Reinhart beat me up, what of it? that would show her what a monster he was. But I didn't follow my impulse, not because I was afraid to spill blood for my beloved—I would have bled away my life for her and suffered the torments of hell in addition—but out of the fear that I might rashly destroy what tiny hope there was. This hope gradually gained in strength fed by need and desire and worked its way through my misery, taking the form of the thought that I would see Jennifer in a few hours and would be able to talk to her. There had to be a way to move her. She would have to see that there could be no life for either of us without the other. Once that notion took hold of me, I began rehearsing what I would say to her and I found comfort in that. I constructed one appeal after another, each more urgent, each more persuasive, each more certain to sway her and make her understand the unthinkable horror of my separation from her.

Finally I fell asleep from sheer weariness, and in my sleep I had a dream. I was rowing a boat on a lake and Jennifer was sitting opposite me at the tiller. She said: "I've told Reinhart about us and he'll have us both killed." Her words frightened me and at the same time made me happy because I knew that if we died together, we would be reincarnated as a couple. The dream ended with me feeling that my life was ebbing away because of a poisoned barb Reinhart had shot into my calf with a blowpipe.

I won't apologize for this prosaic burp of my subconscious, which, with the exception of the sexual metaphors of boat, rowing and tiller, sadly lacks latent content. Until about five years ago I suffered all my life from embarrassingly literal dreams. In my practice I used to envy patients who came to me with dreams that were orgies of obvious symbolism. I'd decipher their manifest content and would at times use in therapy insights I'd gain from it, but I could never completely shake off the feeling that some people's subconscious was having a field day at their expense by presenting them with symbols of things it could very easily have handed to them straightforwardly. (Yes, I take the sainted Jung with a salt cellar.) Still, I didn't deny the Gothic impressiveness of certain dreams. A witch thrusting a flaming torch at the dreamer, and he wresting it from her hand and turning it into a magic sword with which he cuts her in half are far more powerful images than the probable literal meaning of a son's wish to break away from his possessive mother.

A few years ago, I suddenly began to have dreams in which a veritable gallery of archetypal images popped up. I thought at first that my subconscious had simply found a new game for its amusement in imitating my patients' dreams, in other words that whereas their dreams autobiographically referred to them, mine were invented stories with no true connection to my life. Then I realized that they did—arcanely, symbolically—refer to my life and I was as pleased at this broadening of my experience as I could be at a time when my life was coming apart at the seams.

I awoke with a start when there was a knock on the door and the *cameriere* entered. It was late, and I jumped out of bed alarmed, thinking of Jennifer and precious hours lost. I staggered downstairs and stood dazed in the lobby not knowing what to do since I had no idea where Jennifer was; still asleep? on the terrace, having breakfast? (In the past days of innocent friendship either I or she had waited for the other to finish breakfast and then we had taken our leave from my parents and Reinhart.)

An architectural note is in order at this point. The terrace could be approached in two ways: through the dining room on the second floor or from outside via a flagstone stairway running along a rock wall. On top, blooming azaleas, red, purple, lavender, rimmed the terrace, and having climbed high enough on the stairs, one could glimpse the terrace through blossoming branches. I give this detailed description not in order to belatedly provide local color but because this arrangement was responsible for the major event of that morning and possibly for the course of the rest of my life.

I went around the hotel and gingerly made my way up the stairs. If Jennifer was having breakfast with Ridiculous Reinhart I had no intention of joining them. I peeked through the bushes and saw that the terrace was deserted except for precisely my heart's detestation, who was nursing a cup of espresso while reading a book. I was about to withdraw when Jennifer came through the French doors. Even then my instinct was to leave, because it would hurt too much to see her in the company of the man who owned her. But there was another instinct, even stronger, the desire to see her for just a moment because every moment of seeing her was pleasure even if it was now pleasure accompanied by the most awful pain. Of course I should have left, and if there had been any supernatural force in the cosmos who was my friend, I would have been picked up by a firm hand and set down gently in a bower of whispering leaves and murmuring brook, out of earshot of the couple. But I had no friend in high places. I stayed, I looked, I listened; I saw Reinhart close his book and put it down, and I heard him say, "So, tell me, how was the little seraph? Did he reach ethereal heights?"

Jennifer gave a little bell-like trill of a laugh, sat down and said, "He was sweet. It was like being ravished by a bunny rabbit."

Whereupon Reinhart leaned back in his chair, cocked back his head and laughed, transported by mirth.

I'm not interested in transcribing the entire conversation, especially not the part pertaining to my substandard (but sweet!) performance on the sexual front. I'm afraid the ink would flow pure acid and the letters dissolve in a sulfuric hiss. Two things are perhaps worth mentioning since they are "informative." The first is that Jennifer told her husband that she had given me "the story of the student." To which he replied, "If you have me thrash that poor bastard one more time because of my insane jealousy, he'll never leave the hospital alive." The second is that throughout their conversation, which focused mainly on the premature ejaculation and lack of sexual savoir-faire and repertoire of adolescents versus the sustained erection and variety of techniques available to the mature male, Jennifer's diction was that of an educated, articulate woman. There were no moronic: "Me too"s or "When I was little"s. My innocent, vulnerable, childlike dear was not innocent, not vulnerable, not childlike, but was a jaded man's sophisticated wife. In the end, the lie, the monumental, monstrous lie of who she was hurt me far more than her casual betrayal of our intimacy.

Interestingly (from the point of view of mental states), after an initial surge of pain so intense that I felt like crying out, I had no feelings at all while listening to this diabolical discourse. I was neither in agony, nor angry, nor grief-stricken, nor (a conceivable reaction when all is said) in stitches. The only thing that approached any kind of feeling was a dull ache in my stomach—the same ache, curiouser and curiouser, that I feel these days and that I claim with as yet unsubstantiated conviction is the symptom of a terminal illness.

Rescue finally—too, too late—arrived in the form of one of the waiters, who took the signora's order. His appearance made me realize that there was no point in my standing there garlanded by flowering branches, eavesdropping on the tedious babble of a tedious couple.

🔲🔲🔲. In my memory, the rest of the day is snatches of sights and impressions, very like the snapshots of the previous day. There are scenes of the town, streets, shops, people. Then a country road lined with trees, fields on either side. All of this is perceived with a lightheadedness that translates punningly to an impression of brightness everywhere, the houses white, the road chalk, the trees their own poor representations in an overexposed photograph. I stand in the doorway of a house, drinking water offered to me by a peasant woman. Inside is darkness. Outside, a little girl with huge brown eyes and four fingers in her mouth stares at me as if I were a thing of surpassing strangeness. I think, How peculiar; she sees me exactly as I see myself. Then, walking along another chalk road with overexposed trees, I think, I ought to feel something, and I might if I could become interested in what that something ought to be. Or maybe I was asleep on my feet and dreamt that those were my thoughts.

My aimless wandering might have taken me in any direction—to Yugoslavia, where I might have joined the national chapter of the Komsomol, or to Venice, where I might have collapsed fevered and delirious in the arms of my mother, or to the Alps, where I might have fallen into a crevasse to be found encased in a block of ice in the twenty-fifth century and unthawed and returned to wretched life. But where it took me in the end was the sea. Maybe despair always seeks the lowest level and nudged me, once my initial flight had lost its momentum, in the direction of lower ground at every crossroads—which could only mean toward the sea. Or maybe I knew all along subconsciously what I was going to do, and the sun was my guiding star.

I arrived at the shore late afternoon and sat down in the shadow of a wall. I fell asleep. When I awoke, I was in darkness under an immense, starry sky. I sat up and thought that I really had been hurt very badly and that because I had been hurt so badly I ought to cry. But although I agreed with the logic of my argument, the thought made no sense because, although I abstractly understood the concept of hurt, I had no idea what it would feel like to be hurt.

I did, however, know what to do. I went close to the edge of the water and took off all my clothes and arranged them in a neat bundle. (I didn't know I was following a standard protocol of suicide in returning myself to the state in which I had entered the world and tidying up before taking my final leave. Years later I was pleased to discover that I had unwittingly provided evidence for the theory that symbolic acts are not learned behavior.) I waded out into the bay. When the water had risen to my belly, I began to swim away from shore.

It goes without saying that when embarking on my journey to my final end, I didn't think of the physiological process of drowning. From what I recall of that night, the future presented itself to me gently, as if it respected my need not to be hurt further. I would simply swim until I got tired. Then, leaden-limbed and drowsy, I would sink through darkness and oblivion, to lie on a bed of kelp, stirred by gentle currents, nevermore subject to betrayal and hurt. The idea of struggling for air and coughing and retching, or the blind panic of sucking water into my lungs, were not part of the scenario. Nor did I consider the bloated corpse that would be washed up a few days hence, its eyes not pearls and of its bones not coral made.

I swam in darkness, away from shore, out to sea—thinking of what? Not betrayal and hurt. Not of Jennifer laughing at my performance. Not of how much I loved her, more than I'd loved anyone or anything in my life. I thought of swimming. I concentrated on my freestyle form: breathe, stroke, stroke, breathe, stroke, stroke, the hypnotic cadence of my progress. At first I didn't know I had a goal, but as I swam and there was only darkness and the rhythm of my strokes, the goal appeared to me. It was massive yet dimensionless, perfectly black, perfectly quiet. Like a giant mouth or hole. It would swallow me, arms, legs, heartbeat, motion, everything in any way connected with me. I would cease to be. There'd be nothing of me; no thought, no feeling, no memory. In all my dreams (for some reason, I thought I'd still have dreams), I would be in total darkness and whatever brushed against me there would hold no power to harm me.

I don't know for how many hours I swam. I became aware that the moon had risen. The water changed to black and silver molasses. I was tired. My arms were leaden, my legs numb. I kept swimming, never changing my strokes or resting, sensing that my goal was near because I was so very tired and wanted to sleep more than I wanted anything else.

Then my hand struck sand, I breathed in a mouthful of water and frantically thrashed about in water too shallow for swimming but deep enough for drowning. I finally got my legs under me, and spitting and coughing I staggered toward shore. When I reached dry sand, I collapsed and slipped instantly from exhaustion into sleep.

Someone shook me and talked to me. I was lying on my belly. Around me was darkness but the beam of a flashlight was on my half-face and illuminated the sand and my hand stirring in it like a torpid crab. At first all I heard was gibberish, then it became intelligible as a foreign language, German. The voice, a young man's, was joined by two other voices, both female. They tried questions in Italian and French and finally the boy said, "Are you all right? Should we get an ambulance?"

I rolled over and sat up. I said, "No, I'm fine. I'm just tired."

They asked me where I was staying and I told them. They said they'd drive me there. The boy and one of the girls helped me to my feet and led me up the beach to their beat-up Opel Kadett. There, the boy opened the trunk and rummaged about in a duffel bag and handed me a pair of shorts. "You'll need these; it'll be light soon," he said and steadied me while I put them on.

On the way to the hotel, the three of them chatted about themselves: one of the girls was the boy's fiancée, the other was his twin sister; all three were students vacationing on a shoestring budget. They didn't ask me how I had ended up on a beach in the early morning hours, naked and almost too weak to walk, and it didn't strike me as odd that they didn't ask, nor did it surprise me when upon our arrival at the hotel at the first graying of day, they all got out of the car and shook my hand. One of the girls said: "Peace," the other, "Happiness." And the boy, with a seriousness that gave his young face framed by blond curls a classical severity, said, "Rejoice in life."

I watched them drive off in a cloud of exhaust smoke. I suppose I should have felt that the world was not such a dreadful place after all if a poor sinner could be found and clothed by angels and wished well by them, but I was too tired to care even about divine intervention.

I didn't want to wake up Giorgio or wait until the kitchen started stirring. There was a way into my room via a wide ledge leading from the terrace to its window and I gingerly made my way along it, past several other dark windows, behind none of which slept my faithless love. My window was open but the mosquito netting was a barrier. I knocked it out and climbed into my room. I was thirsty and gulped handfuls of water in the bathroom. Then, for the first time since infancy, I was asleep before my head hit the pillow.

I woke up parched and with a vicious headache, my arms and legs so sore I could hardly move, and itchy swellings all over my body. I had left the light on in the bathroom and it had attracted droves of mosquitoes. Fat with my blood, they sat on the ceiling. I stared at them, scratching the swellings on my forehead and chest until I drew blood, and thought that surely I had died and gone to hell.

⌐⌐⌐⌐ This was how my father found me when around noon he and my mother returned from their trip to Venice. With little help from me in the diagnosis, he surmised that something was seriously wrong with me and having just seen the old doctor in the lobby, he went to fetch her. She took my pulse, felt my forehead and then sent my father for a tray of lemonade and sweet rolls from the kitchen and headache pills from reception. She sent Carlucci's nine-year-old to a pharmacy to get lotion for the mosquito bites and had my father dab it on. When she left, it was with strict orders for me to stay in bed.

But I didn't. Alone, I stared at the high ceiling dotted with mosquitoes and an idea slowly worked its way into my brain. Although every move was torture, I found the blue rubber ball Jennifer and I had played with on the beach. I placed myself directly under one of the blood-engorged insects and two-handedly I tossed the ball up. It struck and bounced back, leaving a splotch of red on the ceiling.

The next half hour saw me with deadly surehandedness destroy mosquito after mosquito. The ball sailed up, made contact and returned into my hands leaving the splattered remains. I moved into position for the next kill. Toss, catch, move, repeat. Occasionally one of my intended victims would take to flight, to land at another place every bit as unsafe as the one it had left. A few minutes at most were all it gained. I killed as if in a dream. Up the ball went, down it came, a red smear marked the spot. Again and again. When not one enemy was left alive, I crawled back into bed and fell into a deep sleep.

When she visited me in the afternoon, the doctor looked at the dark splotches of dried blood on the ceiling but made no comment. She examined me again and her prescription was bed rest until further notice. For the next three days, the good doctor accompanied the *cameriere* when he brought me breakfast and dinner, and she stayed while I ate and told me anecdotes about her life, all having to do with the men she had been in love with when she was young. I listened attentively but without engagement because the things she spoke of seemed infinitely remote from my life. To keep me amused the rest of the day, she procured from somewhere an armful of science fiction paperbacks in English. I read them with the most avid attention when I wasn't sleeping—maybe because they shrank the world in size and importance by positioning it among stars and galaxies. Maybe I needed clichés like "the cold vastness of space" to help me fight the suffocating closing down of possibilities and options that obsession is—blinkers and shutters blocking out all but one individual, nothing but her mattering, nothing but her having meaning. I wanted swirling clusters of gases forming primordial stars, and planets in another dimension in which hyperspace distortions allowed instantaneous access to any point on the surface, and 10,000-year-old travelers meeting their 20-year-old selves in parallel universes. The miraculous, the amazing, the far, far away.

On the third day of my retreat, the old doctor said to me, "That little fraud and her fat husband have left."

I said, "Why do you call her that?" prepared for an unthinking instant to come to the defense of my wronged love.

"Because that's what she is." She looked at me with piercing eyes. "I hope she didn't break your heart into too many pieces." I protested that she didn't break it at all; I didn't even like her very much. She said, "Good," and left it at that. If she suspected that I had tried to take my own life for the love of a fraud, I never confirmed her suspicion.

This would be the logical place to end Part One of these reminiscences since a few days later I too was on my way back home, leaving behind the settings and props of my summer romance (props in the form of the insecticidal ball, which I gave to Carlucci's nine-year-old, and Jennifer's suntan lotion, which I found with my beach things and tossed into a wastepaper basket).

But the episode did not come to a clean, well-defined end since there were lingering effects of the harm that had been done to me. First I experienced the stereotypical symptoms of depression: sadness, an aching awareness of loss, the unshakable conviction that I would never again be fine. When those feelings departed after a few months, for no reason other than the passage of time as far as I could tell, what remained was a deep sense of loneliness. I had always thought of myself as alone, but in the past my aloneness had been connected with a sense of self-containedness and independence. Now that I had been happy, truly happy, with someone else, it was as if an essential part of me that I had valued had suddenly turned leprous. The obvious metaphor is that I had caught a glimpse of paradise and that after such a glimpse the life one was content with becomes unbearable. I had been in paradise with Jennifer; without her I could never again be happy. I had no faith in the ability of anyone else to take her place. So that I didn't even play the lonely man's lonely game of walking the streets looking for her in every face I saw, but lived wrapped up in my loneliness, without hope.

Then, eight months after my seaside adventure, I got a letter with a German stamp and postmark but no return address. Yellowed and creased, it has survived thirty years and is co-incarcerated with me and a stack of notebooks and files that my *Vanity Fair* "contact"—who is quite as resourceful as Becky Sharp—unearthed and delivered into my hands to help me in these reminiscences. (I may be an inept murderer but never let it be said I'm not a scrupulous curator of the past.) The letter read:

Dear Paul,

I got your address by writing to the Albergo Attila and telling them that I found a ring belonging to you when I emptied my purse. I hope you won't mind getting a letter from me after all this time. I was so sorry that we couldn't talk before I left. I sneaked into your room once but you were asleep and I didn't want to wake you up because your father told me how sick you were. I was afraid you'd get upset if I said goodbye. I wanted to tell you how much that week with you meant to me. I told you I love you and I meant it. In all my life I've never had this feeling about anyone. Making love to you on the beach that night was the most wonderful thing that ever happened to me. There are times when I feel I can't live without you and today is one of them. Please don't write to me. I couldn't bear it.

Yours,
Jennifer

I studied this anguished document for several days of near-manic mental activity. I retraced my memories and sifted and compared evidence, and struggled to create a version of reality into which all the facts would fit. I wrestled with serpents and tried to get fleas to stay put in a hat: she loved me but she had ridiculed me before her husband; she had never felt this way about anyone but she had told me she couldn't have anything further to do with me almost the instant she had told me she loved me; she couldn't live without me but she didn't want me to contact her since she hadn't given me her return address; she had lied to me; was she lying to me now? had she lied to Reinhart then? was Reinhart in on the joke now—the little fraud and her fat husband? Or had I misheard or misunderstood the scene on the terrace and did she really love me? Or had I heard and understood correctly, but she nevertheless loved me?

I don't know how close my mental gyrations brought me to the "brain fever" postulated by nineteenth-century students of the mind, but I know that I was as close to psychotic as I've ever been—wanting desperately to believe Jennifer and brutally forcing myself not to. A few days later, my attention was savagely yanked into another direction when my parents were killed in the ferry collision I mentioned. Neither could swim and both drowned, which convinces me, as do so many other things, that we live in an ironic universe that projects its coincidental humor in both directions of the temporal axis.

At any rate, the event and its aftermath pushed all thoughts of love out of my mind. When the issue next appeared in my life some six months later, I was no longer who I had been but had turned into a minor monster.

Theoretical Interlude One

⌐⌐⌐ Few autobiographers are in a position to enlighten their public with authoritative speculations on what "really" happened to them in psychological terms at certain times in their lives. The reader of what academics forever coyly refer to as "the present work" is fortunate to have as guide through the knotty subject of my emotional life a man capable of examining the events of a certain week of a certain summer by the light of psychological theory. Even my well-read "journalist acquaintance" (whom I'd like to call a friend, but who can blame her if she won't go out of her way to procure an eleven-foot pole with which to touch me?) may find the digression useful.

The facts themselves are simple: I was the victim of a violent emotional disturbance induced by my exposure to Jennifer; the combination of romantic fixation, fierce hurt at the destruction of my happiness, and extreme mental as well as physical fatigue brought on by prolonged excitement and lack of sleep almost cost me my life. As far as the cause of my affliction goes, I provide below a lightning-quick overview of educated guesses on that inexhaustible subject, the nature of love, and I invite the reader to decide which best fits the case of Paul Avery in love with Jennifer Seeler.

Freud, unsurprisingly, sees romantic, falling-in-love type love as sublimation—the conversion of sexual desire into adoration, tenderness, admiration of charming qualities. Romantic love, he argues, would not exist if social barriers did not block the physical impulse to copulate on the spot (any spot). Why this "aim-inhibited sexual impulse" would be directed at a particular individual rather than at anyone encountered who possesses the characteristics requisite for copulation, Freud is silent about in this instance. At any rate, by this light, I would never have experienced the euphoric bliss, the ecstasy

I felt when I saw my love descend those stairs, if social mores hadn't kept me from launching myself at her, hoisting up her pale linen dress and possessing her in the lobby under the presumably amused eyes of her husband and anyone else in the vicinity.

Elsewhere in the Freudian corpus, love originates in one of the instincts and is subject to vicissitudes—the most interesting of which is succession by hate. (Ha!)

Yet elsewhere—in his essay *Introduction to Narcissism*—Freud speaks of "object-directed desire," which prefers to attach itself to a certain type of woman and impoverishes the libido. To the object of desire, he attributes the blissful self-absorption of a Narcissus. By this reading, I was drawn to Jennifer precisely because I coveted her self-absorption and her refusal to allow her own libido to be impoverished by an attachment to me (in other words, her cold shoulder was what drew me to her). Since, as far as I know, I never aspired to narcissistic qualities, this coveting—a door giving onto a greasy slide and a swift descent to torment and self-degradation—does not seem to apply in my case.

Theodore Reik, less famous than Freud but more voluble on sex psychology, proposes a very different etiology of romantic love. Not only is romantic love unrelated to sexual desire, or desire of the object's narcissistic qualities according to Reik, but it belongs to a different mental realm altogether. Reik sees the ego, ego needs and ego frustrations responsible for love: Before we can fall in love, we must have low self-esteem because we must desire to attain admirable qualities we recognize in the love object. The beloved represents on some level the ideal self, and the possessive aspects of romantic love are expressions of the desire to own the attractive qualities that the lover himself lacks. Hence, when I loved Jennifer, I really admired and envied my own idealized personality. In other words, I was in love with her actual self only to the extent to which what I thought I recognized in her (and recognized as lacking in me) was truly hers. I fail to remember how, if at all, Reik addresses the question of why I and myriad other lovers find the idealized self in an oppositely sexed member of the species.

Jung, more brutal and more honest, turns the gap between the perceived and the real that Reik hints at into a yawning abyss between lover and loved, unbridgeable by any means. He sees love as a projection of the anima in the male lover's doomed attempt to fuse with his own feminine soul (and vice versa for the female's animus). What we fall in love with is not the person we think we fall in love with but our own adored souls superimposed on the features and personality of another. When the power and charm of the projection wear off—as they must eventually—what appears is lusterless, unmoving, dull, since it is now simply another imperfect human being. (To which process may be attributed the high rate of divorce in countries in which people marry for love, as well as the slew of love-is-blind/smoke-gets-in-your-eyes adages.) By this theory, I was not given the chance to see the projection of my soul fade from Jennifer, which may explain why it has forever remained with her.

I've already mentioned the theory of romantic love as an aesthetic response: the lover's rapture, ecstasy, delight, etc. elicited by the face, frame, voice, etc. of his beloved is no different from an aesthetic response to a painting, Alpine sunset, or piece of music. The root of the aesthetic sense—the question of whether it is innate or acquired—is a matter that is (in the quaint mumblings of learned discourse) beyond the scope of the current investigation. In my own case, I have never experienced an authentic aesthetic response to anything but women (a grand total of two of the fair creatures). So the comparison would seem to be moot.

Behaviorism, as usual matching tedium with grimness, holds imprinting responsible for the curious phenomenon of the heart opening its doors while the rational faculty flies out the window: One day, while rocking in the cradle, I noticed a feature of a face, and at that moment, a pursed lip, a drooping eye, a furled brow, merged with my infantile sense of bliss at being the coddled and nurtured center of the universe. Any future encounter with a facsimile of that feature will propel me back to the visceral contentment of that moment, and from that feeling springs love. Unfortunately I have no way of verifying the claim. Even if at the door to my cell were to appear a woman who remembered visiting my parents when she was twenty-seven and peeping into my crib—"you were such a beautiful baby"—she would now be in her early seventies and it is unlikely that I would recognize beneath the destructive work of time that fatal feature. Model Two, at any rate, bears little resemblance to Model One according to my memory; if there were shared features (other than monumental selfishness and a ruthless disregard for my feelings), the match was so subtle it never registered in my consciousness.

Leaving the realm of pseudo-scientific speculation, a more daring and off-beat interpretation is found in the theory of the transmigration of souls. According to it, the sense of recognition and import that accompanies the experience of love for someone is simply the recognition of having known and loved that someone in a previous life. I don't have at my fingertips a work on this topic, and I wonder how its gurus answer the obvious objection that this explanation begs the question of the origin of love, since it merely transposes it backwards in time ad infinitum. If I fell in love with Jennifer because I fell in love with her in a previous life, then why did I fall in love with her in that life? Because I fell in love with her in a yet more previous life? And so forth, and so on, while we regress in time to reach the milestone of her and me as troglodyte and troglodette in love, and, leaving homo sapiens altogether, move backwards to pre-human, pre-mammalian, pre-etc. times—until we behold the love of Paul and Jennifer as amoebae in primordial slime (probably their earliest stab at it since we run out of organic molecules if we back up much further). Or is the answer that Jennifer and I were lovers in the ethereal realm before we ever assumed mortal shape? Which would seem to leave unaddressed the question of love unrequited—my soul recognizing hers and hers perversely refusing to recognize mine? Or recognizing mine and instead of joyously reuniting with me choosing to play a nasty trick on me?

What all of the above models glaringly have in common is that

none of their purported mechanisms of infatuation is in any meaningful way connected with the object of infatuation proper. If I project my anima or ego ideal on someone in order to love myself, God
save the poor flesh-and-blood creature whom I choose as the vehi-
cle for this sick traffic with myself. If the response is purely aesthetic
or purely the result of a feathered brow or bisque-colored cheek
connected with my earliest pleasurable memories—God help her
and me. In all these cases, the question of who she is in terms of an
autonomous, unique, separate entity is lost in my mad quest to
make her what I need her to be for my own gratification.

So much for theory. Then there is practice, which beats theory
to a pulp any day of the week in making experience a thing of the
viscera and demonstrating, by holding up hearts torn to bloody tat-
ters, how deficient models are at capturing the true feel of dry, leeched,
fevered desire wanting with every pore to touch, with every fiber to
embrace, eyes blinded by inner images, thoughts sealed off by love,
lips cracked with longing, yearning, pleading for that other to be
here, to stay, never, never to leave.

Part
Two

After my parents' death came the years I'd most like to expunge from my life. I'd gladly settle for a gap in my past—three years erased, a frown clouding my placid features at someone's question of my "experiences" between the ages of fifteen and eighteen, a puzzled shake of the head the answer. In the absence of a convenient lapse in memory, I wish I could skim—too busy for tiresome details—over that span of time in this chronicle. ("From 1962 to 1965, I lived with my uncle, aunt and cousin Diana in Chicago. The years were largely uneventful. Then, in the fall of 1965...") But I can't escape the past so easily, if only for the greater glory of science. Studies have shown (ha!) that monsters engender monsters, and my own, private findings indicate that studies are right.

There had been nothing monstrous about me when I met Jennifer, but what happened to me during that week of exposure to her was like the misadventure of a science-fiction hero: While exploring a jungle planet at the far edge of the galaxy, he encounters a beguiling, elusive creature. He is in pursuit of it when a barb shot from the fleshy-leaved vegetation pierces his thigh. He staggers, clutches the wound, limps back to the base. The doctor removes the hook-shaped thorn, examines it, mumbles something about an odd nucleic acid. The wound heals and all is well.—Except all is of course desperately unwell. There are changes in our hero's behavior toward his fellow spacemen. He grows moody, is attacked by strange fits, finds patches of scales on his chest. Then, one night, his transmogrification is complete. And now his companions hear the freakish laugh and in the erratic beams of their torches see the pincer claws, the faceted eyes, the monstrous, blood-dripping snout. Half a dozen gruesome deaths later, a laser blast brings him down, and only now as he lies dying in the arms of his best friend does he revert to human form. The End.

My mouth never dripped with blood, but I nevertheless became monstrous, with no outward signs to warn my victim. My victim was my cousin Diana—a clumsy creature matching neither Keats's "Diana, Queen of Earth, and Heaven, and Hell," nor her Greek antecedent, chaste and cruel Artemis, and more will shortly be said about poor Diana.

While we're on the subject of mythology in that household, and not to digress from our monstrous topic: Diana's mother, my aunt, was melodiously hailed Phaedra—a name suggestive of maximum pretentiousness and minimum learning. I have no doubt that her parents chose it for its aristocratic sound and did not bother consulting a classical dictionary. Else they would have learned to their possible consternation that Phaedra, daughter of Minos and wife of Theseus, after falling in love with and making unsuccessful advances to her stepson Hippolytus, claimed the boy had attempted to seduce her—whereupon hapless Hippolytus, riding in a chariot along the shore, was killed when Poseidon, urged by Theseus, sent a bull from the water. The bull frightened the horses, who overturned the chariot and dragged the charioteer until he was dead. (So much for my conviction that Jennifer, my love, was the greatest bitch that ever lived.) According to Roman mythology, interestingly, none other than Diana restored Hippolytus to life, in other words, mitigated Phaedra's evil deed. I told my cousin Diana about this bit of nomenclatorial irony and she derived some small satisfaction from her own namesake getting the better of her mother's.

As for Diana's father, he was simply Rex—no resemblance to Oedipus or any other king of old, except possibly in terms of stature and appearance, the latter the result of weekend tennis. He was more than six feet tall and had the physique of a not-too-greatly-gone-to-seed college athlete. (Or were the ancients even shorter than knights in armor, those pint-sized butchers in coats of plate and mail fitting the average modern-day thirteen-year-old? Were the battles on the ringing plains of windy Troy fought by midget warriors? And can our tame imagination accommodate the idea of a five-foot-tall Hector towering over the flower of Trojan manhood?) I will not, by the way, prolong my digressions ad infinitum; I'll return to the topic of my monstrosity as soon as I've set the stage, wiped my beaded brow and waited for the effects of a small yellow pill to set in. (I'm allowed tranquilizers, but I medicate myself only when my nerves vibrate like incandescent filaments in a bulb shaken by a madman's fist.)

I lived in this mythical household—Paul among the pagans—for three years after my parents' death. Rex was my late father's brother, older by two years and, according to one of the few statements I heard my father make about him, "a royal jackass." I had last seen my uncle, aunt and cousin some five years earlier when my parents and I had spent a few days in Chicago for forgotten reasons. I had noted Rex's cultivated joviality and Phaedra's irritability when she realized that she was still unable to faze my mother's old-world aplomb with ostentation. My cousin, a year older than I, simply did not penetrate into my consciousness and left me only with the dim impression that there was something hamsterish about her (an impression I understood when five years later I took a closer look at her and noticed her bulging cheeks, result of an overabundance of fatty tissue in those facial regions).

Rex and Phaedra came to New York to arrange the funeral service. Grandmère also came, sans Grandpère, who was in a clinic recovering from a heart attack he had suffered when named a co-defendant in a civil-service bribery scandal *Le*

Monde had unearthed a few months earlier. (My paternal grandparents did not attend for the compelling reason that they had departed for a better world years ago, she dead of a brain tumor at forty-two, he of a heart attack at fifty-six; a curiously short-lived clan: athletic Rex was to follow in his father's footsteps, cut down by a coronary a few days before his fifty-seventh birthday.)

My parents were cremated, and friends strewed their ashes from a boat in Long Island Sound, the location having no particular significance as far as I know. I remember wondering at the time whether they really would have wanted to be "buried" in the same element that took their lives but not saying anything because I would have hated to see their poor dust imprisoned in urns—cold ugly things like perverted eggs.

After the funeral came the question of me, underage and in need of adult support. I was in a cocoon of grief but knew that I would have preferred to go live in France. But my grandmother would have her hands full when my grandfather was released from the clinic. So the decision was for me to live with my uncle and aunt. (I assume the courts also had some say in all this and in the trust fund established for me from my parents' meager assets, but the condition I was in insulated me from most things, and the details of the decision were one of them.) I helped pack my and some of my parents' belongings and a week or so later was on a plane to Chicago.

Little need be said about my aunt and uncle provided it is said with a minimum of delicacy. Phaedra was the quintessential rich bitch, descended from real-estate and car-dealership money. At college (the University of Chicago) she had fashionably majored in psychology and minored in English and had (crazy kid!) emerged engaged to Rex—unmoneyed and his family to be found in no social register. He had gotten his degree in some useless field (sociology or hermeneutics), which, however, qualified him for an entry-level position in an ad agency. Phaedra, an astute judge of character even when crazily in love, had seen promise in this up-from-the-boondocks lad. Maybe there was an aggressive obnoxiousness in the way he asserted dominion over her flesh in the sack, or maybe she was struck by his man-with-a-vision quality when he talked of the future in terms of the size of the house he had to have, the kinds of vacation homes, the kinds of cars. She married him and was not disappointed when he rose rapidly at the agency, established his own firm before he was thirty, and, at forty, was president of one of the largest ad agencies in Chicago, a firm specializing in high-concept copy for high-profile accounts. The house they lived in was palatial (cathedral ceilings, skylights, solarium, two two-car garages, etc. etc.), the vacation homes (one on Lake Michigan, the other in Aspen, Colorado, for the skiing) comfortable. The family cars were his Porsche, her Mercedes SL, and a Mercedes sedan for family excursions. On Diana's seventeenth birthday, they broke the pricey-imports pattern by giving her a Chevy Nova.

The years I spent with them, the master of the house, dynamic and driven, put in twelve-hour days at work, the mistress led the strenuous life of the idle rich: luncheons in town, shopping, tennis, golf, beauty salons, massages, visits to art galleries. I don't think she was involved in any extramarital dalliances in the years I lived with the family. Her vices were the possession of material things and pride of status, neither of which is enhanced by a lover unless he is a figure of fabulous wealth or social standing. Her husband, on the other hand, was almost certainly having an affair, or, if not that (or in addition to that), was having early evening shtupping sessions with open-minded and -legged staff members on the wide leather sofa in his office—afterwards a quick cleanup in his private toilet, scooping water over his limp wienie, then home to wife and kid. I base my verdict on my professional experience: most of the dynamic, driven, middle-aged men I met in my practice boasted of such goings-on on the side.

I double back to Phaedra to add that in my unflattering description of her I am not indulging in a misogynistic reflex. If I think of her as an obnoxious parasite, I think of her husband as no less so. Her life was what the life of any talentless, brainless individual in her position would have been. The hostile reflex I indulge in is one against stupidity, a characteristic that is no respecter of gender.

So the commercial branch of the Avery clan clasped the sprig of the severed artistic branch to its innocent bosom and gave suck to a viper. Not that unconscious Phaedra and Rex ever knew it. They must have thought they had gotten not too bad a thing: a quiet, polite, self-contained boy, who spent much of his time in his room reading books and made barely a ripple in their household routine. In the fall, they enrolled me in Diana's high school, and that first semester my cousin and I took the bus together, I reading or doing homework, she dreamily or gloomily looking out the window. Then she got her car and I my driver's license, and on most days I drove us to and from school. An outside observer unaware of the infinite complexity of the mind might have concluded I was settling in nicely and was coming to terms with all my losses. A somewhat more knowledgeable diagnostician might have said, Wait and see. And Diana, poor Diana, an inside observer if ever there was one, waited and ended up seeing far more than she could ever have wanted to see.

Big, bulbous breasts, curved shoulders to make the former less conspicuous, a heavy rump, fat (facial) cheeks emphasized by a hairstyle straight and parted at the center, and a mild case of acne—thus Diana in her seventeenth year. Not outright fat but pudgy enough to make beautiful, greyhound-slim Phaedra heave sighs about poor (a term of endearment) Diana not having her mother's genes.

Poor Diana hated her looks. Although she had a closet full of expensive clothes purchased by her mother in the hope of turning the ugly duckling into at least a sartorial swan, Diana wore a uniform of drab, mid-calf-length pleated skirts and cardigans—her sole sustained attempt at rebellion, and even that one was a sham since she kept justifying her get-up, claiming petulantly that it was what everybody at school was wearing (which it wasn't—not the pretty girls, who pranced around in skirts as short and tight as they could get away with).

According to that family's lore of "known facts," poor Diana also did not have her father's genes (eyes rolled heavenwards, sigh heaved at the evidence of yet another dumb thing done or said by her). It was a known fact that her father had brains, and Diana, ah well, was Diana.

How much my own opinion of my cousin was influenced by the household doctrine I don't know. I certainly didn't swallow the poor-brainless-thing myth any more than I swallowed the Rex-as-mental-giant one. If asked, I would have said that she had probably been smarter than momsy and daddykins since age ten, but that that in itself wasn't saying a great deal. Nevertheless, her parents' matter-of-fact verdict that their daughter was "no genius" could not have raised my estimation of her. As far as I recall, my feelings were that, left to her own devices, she would have been all right. Not brilliant, not stupid. Average.

As it turned out, I was almost as wrong about my cousin's talents and intellectual acumen as her imbecilic parents were. But surely my blindness will be excused once the reader realizes that my designs on her (once I started having designs on her) were quite limited in scope. Limited and elementary.

Diana was a virgin. When I met her, her only non-autoerotic sexual experience had been three frantic minutes in a broom closet at school after hours. The senior who had wooed her for a few days with the intent to add a notch to his sex pistol had playfully pulled her into the closet and had not so playfully tried to rape her. Realizing from up close how much she loathed him, she had fought him off, and he had countered the rebuke with the successful jab (down for a count of ten and then some) that she was "too ugly for fucking."

This was the full extent of my cousin's grappling with heterosexuality until I appeared in her life and—to put it in terms both vague and pregnant—"changed all that."

But first the background.

By the time I had lived with the family for maybe six months, essentially ignored by the parents and avoided with tongue-tied awkwardness by the daughter, I had become conscious of the "interpersonal dynamics" between mother and daughter. I add quickly that, when I recognized the relentless war that was being waged against my cousin's sense of self-worth, I felt no sympathy or compassion for her. That she rebelled rarely and ineffectually against her mother the bitch made me as contemptuous of her as I could be of someone who existed only at the periphery of my awareness. But a coincidence as much as my mounting irritation with Phaedra finally made me take sides one day—and thereby made me begin the sequence of events that in short order led to my becoming intimately acquainted with my cousin's plump flesh.

I had run across an article about new findings that discredited the then-accepted notion of there being a link between the consumption of chocolate and acne. About a week later, Diana's bad complexion and refusal to renounce chocolate (the unhappy child's only vice) was, not for the first time, a topic that cropped up at the dinner table. Phaedra, noticing two new eruptions on her daughter's chin, and ever the soul of tact, opined that Diana's face might look less frightful if she stopped stuffing herself with chocolate. Diana blushed, which made her pimples an even more startling red, scowled at her plate and muttered that she didn't believe chocolate had anything to do with anything. Her mother said it was a scientific fact that acne "comes from chocolate" (did I mention that Madame was as illiterate as she was pretentious?). Rex chuckled and said that when he was Diana's age it came from something else, and he tried to include me in this bit of ribald humor with a wink. Whereupon I, polite and articulate, informed everyone at the table about the article I had read, citing chapter and verse—the authorities no less than a team of researchers at Johns Hopkins; the largest, most thorough study of its kind, several years in the making; the finding: no correlation whatsoever. Phaedra, miracle of miracles, was speechless. Rex thought I had supported his joke and grinned inanely. And Diana, poor Diana, looked at me from across the table so full of gratitude and admiration and tenderness that I decided then and there to make her my slave.

Not too many days after this epiphany, my cousin made to me the joyous confession that I was the only good thing that had ever happened to her. Her claim was open for discussion since what I had by then set out to do was debauch her, by which term I mean possibly more than was meant by it when it was popular: I not only committed defloration on her (with my slender index and middle fingers) but in the course of time introduced her to as many sexual practices as I had knowledge of then—not by any means as many as I have at my professional fingertips now, but a fair sampling of standard and not-so-standard practices, some of them (I did say monster) painful to her.

It was all ridiculously easy. Once I had decided what I wanted from her, I showed some interest in her, paid attention to what she said, told her she was remarkable and unlike the bubble-headed nitwits the school abounded in. She blushed with pleasure, said no one had ever said anything nice about her. The rest was child's play, me being the child. It took no persuasive skills at all to get to that afternoon—Dad, of course, at work; Mom as usual tripping the light fantastic in town—Diana and I in my room, on my bed, her jeans off, mine unzipped, my hands between her white thighs, my fingers parting her nether lips, probing, then deftly deflowering her. She gasped, bled a little, but a short while later masturbated me without grace but with a crude effectiveness.

Afterwards she confessed to me in tears ("please don't laugh at me if I tell you, but I have to tell you") that she had been in love with me from the moment of my arrival. She recounted touchingly how I had stood in the hallway looking so dark, so tragic, so mysterious, and how she had wanted—more than anything she had ever wanted in her life—for me to take her into my arms.

Anyone who has ever had fantasies of absolute sexual domination will agree that for the next two and a half years I had a delicious deal. Unlike the typical lecherous cad who has to coax his coy sweetheart gradually from the missionary position into more adventurous placements and doings, I had but to decide on the particular variation on the theme of copulation I wanted to subject my cousin to and the next time the opportunity presented itself (usually three to four times a week), there she was, naked, ass down or belly down or on her hands and knees, legs open or closed, while my penis was working the orifice of my choice.

I'd spend entire mornings in school mentally rehearsing the afternoon's diversions and playing imaginatively the scales of arousal, consummation and climax.

A random sample from my grab bag of lust: Although her fat rump was aesthetically repulsive, its bared sight gave me an instant erection and once I discovered anal sex, I sodomized her routinely (wearing a condom then as always—in this case because I was fastidious rather than fearful of impregnating her). I liked what—savoring the plosive and sibilant as much as the vulgarity—I called "fucking her ass"; alas, she didn't. But the one time she said meekly that it was uncomfortable "to do it that way," I was upset and told her that I was hurt because I sensed in her complaint the charge that I was only using her sexually and didn't really care about her. No, that wasn't it at all, she protested. It was just that that kind of sex was uncomfortable—but not that uncomfortable; she wouldn't mind if we did it again. It took some cajoling on her part, but eventually I relented and once again gave my penis the run of her rectum.

This, in general, was how I responded to any resistance I met: I became annoyed, accused her of not understanding me, of not believing that I cared about her, of mistaking my physically desiring her for the average horny teenager's lust. Sex for me wasn't just sex, I told her, it was a metaphor (I took time out to explain the meaning of the word). Sex stood for experience, mystery, life itself, hence my constant questing for the different experience. If she found repulsive what I did and asked her to do, then it was me she found repulsive. And if this was the case, then I wanted no further part of her.

Her reply was invariably that of course she didn't find me repulsive; how could I even think of a thing like that; she loved me; of course she wanted to do all the things I wanted to do; she was so sorry she had upset me.

I found these discussions tedious but tolerable since afterwards, once I had forgiven her, I invariably got to have the sex of my choice on her grateful, quivering form.

On rereading the above, I realize that I have not yet conveyed with sufficient vividness how monstrously adept I was at manipulating poor Diana into doing what she hated. An earlier (pre-anal-sex) episode should convince anyone who has struggled to maintain an ounce of sympathy for me that sympathy is ill invested in the case of Paul Avery from 1962 to 1965. (Later we'll see appalling Paul grow into a moderately enlightened and conscientious adult.) In that episode, oral sex, or to be clinically precise, fellatio, was the larger context, and the question was the fate of my jism. For a few months I allowed my partner to discreetly spit out the bodily fluid in question and was magnanimous in ignoring her pallor and the queasy quiver of her jaw. In fact, the mental game I was playing (after the initial excitement of the sex of my choice had worn off even my delicious deal needed some additional mental work) was to imagine that she hated me and I was forcing her to suck me off; the make-believe fear of her vengeful incisors cutting into my throbbing member added frisson to the experience, and her spitting out my semen ("a viscid whitish fluid of the male reproductive tract consisting of spermatozoa suspended in secretions of accessory glands," as Webster's Ninth New Collegiate unappetizingly puts it) matched that fantasy.

But the afternoon came when the thrill of even that cherry-on-the-top invention faded and I was irritated by her dainty expectoration. My punishment was delayed and thoughtful: The next day, I ignored her on the way to school and on the way home, acting distracted and aloof. When, as soon as we had closed the front door, she asked me to please tell her what was wrong, I shrugged and said it was nothing she would understand; there was no point in even talking about it. She cried, said she knew she had screwed up, she always did, pleaded with me to tell her what she'd done wrong. I finally relented and told her that I was hurt by her spitting out my cum; to me it meant that she didn't truly care about me; but this was something personal and she wouldn't understand. Oh no, she said, she did understand—of course I was hurt by her rejecting something of mine, of course that was like an insult and painful; it had been so thoughtless of her not to think of that. But it wouldn't happen again; she promised!

I was cold at first, saying, No, it was perfectly all right; I'd never force her to do anything she didn't want to do. But more tearful pleading got me to relent and I allowed her to follow me into my room. "All right, if you really want to," I said and took off my jeans and shorts. I sat down on the chair, my legs comfortably apart, and let her moist mouth work my member into an erection. She was quite good by then at licking and applying pressure with her lips and tongue. I came profusely, she pulled back, and I saw the revulsion in her eyes and the struggle against the instinct to spit out my hot goop. She swallowed once, nervously, dryly, then the fear of losing my love won: she closed her eyes and swallowed and almost instantly retched. But the spit of my loins stayed down and she smiled at me through tears, a brave smile that almost made me feel guilty and made me tell her that I believed she truly loved me.

I don't remember whether she was forced to ingest more of me because shortly after this moving scene I discovered that I preferred being in her ass to being in her mouth and the problem of swallowing was obviated. (There was, as I mentioned, the new problem of her anal discomfort, solved by my lightning-quick "It hurts me to be told I'm hurting you" response.)

I'll say a few more things about sex with my cousin because my pathology in this area is the thing I remember most clearly—with appalling lucidity in fact—about these years and because even if a complete picture is impossible, a few of the peaks of horror must be climbed if any sort of panoramic view is attempted. Regarding my cousin's aesthetically unappealing but sexually stimulating buttocks: I not only "enjoyed" the use of her anus but also liked to position her on her hands and knees and to mount her in barnyard fashion from behind (the entry portal being the traditional one in this case). The slapslapslap of my lean belly against her fat rump teased my thinking into the direction of beating her, and for a while I toyed imaginatively with a variety of disciplinary scenarios.

I did not, I quickly add, beat her—one stroke across her pale, plump lower cheeks with Rex's rubber-soled house slipper (I told her it was an experiment testing de Sade's pleasure/pain principle) was enough to make me stop, not, I'm afraid, because she buried her face in the pillow but because the livid weal I raised alarmed me: what if Phaedra inadvertently entered her daughter's bathroom when Diana was about to take a bath and espied her daughter's maltreated derriere?

The question of possible discovery aside, my "experiment" probably made me realize that my interest in that area of sexuality had less to do with an urge to inflict pain than with curiosity about just how much Diana was willing to put up with from me. Which brings me to one more terse disclosure about my life as a sex fiend before I temporarily move on to a less overwrought topic. Of course my erotic predilections changed over the months. For a while I derived satisfaction from a rather sterile sexual activity: Diana would lie on her back, her legs pulled up and spread; I would almost but not quite sit on her face, looking in the direction of her privates. Squeezing her large breasts together with both hands I would create a tight tunnel for my penis and I'd stimulate myself by rocking back and forth and using the friction of her breasts and breastbone. A gratuitous thrill of this particular enterprise was that I could imagine the view that was staring her in the face while I was availing myself of her endowments.

Naturally (and unnaturally), I experimented with other sexual variations in the years I had my cousin by the proverbial short hairs, too many to enumerate them without inducing boredom. What I will do to put things in perspective is establish an upper limit of extreme behavior in terms of activities I did *not* indulge in with unfortunate Diana, lest the reader be left with the impression that I worked my way through *The Story of O* or some other manual of strenuous perversions. I did *not* in general, deliberately inflict pain. As I said, there was an intellectual curiosity in the question of how abjectly my cousin was attached to me and how much I might be able to get away with in that area, but my curiosity was kept in check by the fear of discovery. The one time she was earnestly in pain after anal sex (I must have ruptured a blood vessel for there was considerable bleeding) I, not she, declared a one-month moratorium on that particular activity.

Also in terms of upper limits, I never defecated on her, nor did I ever ask her to stick her tongue up my rectum. Coprophilia was not my bag, man. Nor did I lap up her menstrual blood or indulge in the more flamboyant fetishisms presented to the eyes of an incredulous (but not uninterested) world by von Krafft-Ebing. In short, I did nothing that nowadays would be considered vastly bizarre in the sexual intercourse of consenting adults. But, of course, we were not adults and, of course, one of us can hardly be judged consenting unless acts she was being driven to by her own psychological injuries can be considered voluntary. And thus I temporarily close the book on my pre-adult sex life.

One logical conclusion that might be drawn from the above is that I deeply hated my cousin. How else to explain the physical and psychological abuse to which I routinely subjected her? The truth is that I didn't hate, or even dislike, Diana because she didn't occupy enough of my mental life for me to develop feelings of any kind for her. I used her, but without any genuine interest in her. Which suggests another possible reason for my shying away from sadistic sexual practices: maybe it wasn't fear of discovery but fear of being forced to get closer to my victim and becoming interested in her (the theory being that it is difficult to remain entirely aloof while tormenting someone). This may sound odd, and I'm sure Diana would have derived cold comfort from it, but strictly speaking what I did to her was "nothing personal."

Cursed with an attention span longer than two minutes, my reader may be shifting uneasily now, ready to lodge the complaint that since a few pages ago I was shown interested in the question of how far my lovesick cousin would allow me to go with respect to uncomfortable sexual doings, surely, a measure of personal interest must have entered.

I wish I could answer that, yes, I lied; I did hate Diana for some secret, complicated reason that I myself didn't understand, and that I did my utmost to have my revenge on her "personally." If this were the case, I would be somewhat more comprehensible, if not forgivable. But the truth is that what interested me with respect to the above issue was not Diana but Diana's attachment to me; my curiosity revolved around the question of how her infatuation with me turned her into an abject creature, as tied to me and responsive to my every breath and word as if I had absolute power over her mind, body and soul. What fascinated me was how certain feelings she had for me, feelings that meant absolutely nothing to me, made her incapable of dealing with me in terms other than those of submission and slavish devotion.

I found less fascinating, and in fact tedious and embarrassing, another type of evidence of her emotional fixation on me: Until I finally got it into her love-addled brain that I really couldn't stand it—it upset and depressed me—she insisted on speaking to me in the language of love. She would mention my delicate hands ("like a pianist's"), my smooth skin, my beautiful eyebrows, how sad my eyes always were and how moved she was by them, that I had a peculiar way of smiling that sent shivers through her.

I didn't then ask myself why her remarks drove me to fits of annoyance. It was enough that they did. More than three decades later I'm in a better position to take a stab at an answer. That answer in its most elementary form is that I did not love her and that to be loved by someone you do not love is an offense, an affronted voice saying: How dare you have these feelings for me if I'm not interested in you? How dare you violate my privacy by thinking of me in loving terms? How dare you force yourself into a region reserved for someone very different?

One example of the innumerable times in which my resentment at being loved by my cousin flared up was her wish to have a photo of me for her wallet. Since I avoided the holiday snapshots that Rex the family man took, or managed to have a comatose, eyes-closed expression when there was no avoiding them, no treasured portrait came from that direction, and the tiny picture she cut out of our yearbook and pasted on a piece of mauve paper trimmed to wallet size was so poor a likeness that I felt in no way responsible for it and didn't care what she did with it.

But in my junior year the story was different: the photo for the yearbook showed me "true to life," dark and handsome, with more than a hint of intellectual keenness and seriousness of purpose— although it failed to capture a certain amused detachment that I felt was emerging as an integral part of my adult personality. Catching a glimpse of the portrait, Diana asked me for one of the wallet-sized prints. I refused to give it to her, telling her that I hated the picture.

A few days later I noticed that one of the prints was missing from my drawer and that Diana flaunted a coy smugness. My reaction was fury. I was livid at the thought of me trapped in her bulging wallet, at the mercy of being touched and handled and adored by her cow eyes whenever she was in the mood to adore. For several days I plotted to steal the picture back, but in the end I settled for the minor revenge of being what she tearfully called "nasty" to her and then remaining unmoved when she, again tearfully, apologized for having lost her temper.

Ironically, my deep resentment of Diana's feelings for me was probably the closest I ever got to responding to her as an individual. In all other areas, I draw a blank when I ask myself what I thought of her or felt about her. I'm not sure that in the three years I lived in her house I once considered her as a person in her own right. This is difficult to explain, but when I manipulated her, I did not, in fact, manipulate *her* but a crude facsimile of her that I had fashioned in my mind. That rags-and-stuffing thing, though looking and sounding like Diana, lacked all complexity or autonomy. Strings were connected to it, and when it was not behaving the way I wanted it to, I pulled a few of them until I got the right motion. That that motion ultimately did come from a living, thinking, feeling creature who was reacting to my actions did not occur to me. Or maybe a better analogy would be an animal act: The trainer cares only about the result and is indifferent to how his commands and cracks of the whip are translated by the brain of, say, a bear into something that will make another part of that brain prompt Mr. Bruin to dance on his hind legs and beat the drum, rather than rip the innards out of The Great Sardo.

Which brings us to the interesting question of whether this means that if someone had asked me what in heaven's name I was doing with Diana I would have answered: I'm turning her into a dancing bear because I'm curious to see how difficult it is to turn someone who is in love with me into a circus act. The answer is, Not bloody likely. I was neither sophisticated nor honest enough, nor sufficiently plagued by existential angst, to be able to think of myself as a cold, calculating monster. I'm sure that, if asked, I would have swiftly found a less incriminating explanation, according to which I *was* attracted to Diana—in a way—and sex *was* a metaphor—of sorts—for life, and therefore not always tame, and according to which when she objected to some of my practices I *did* feel hurt or at least insulted and *did* believe my threat of withdrawing my affection from her. To put it simply: while there was a level on which I was aware that I was coldly manipulating her, there was another level on which I kept this awareness hidden from myself and believed in the things I told her. And on that level was probably to be found my adamant conviction that the world owed me—"the world" being represented at a snap of my fingers by anyone, no matter how blameless, who could, after this conceptual sleight of hand, be victimized at will. I carried a carte blanche for mayhem.

But what of my victim? When I think of her now in my monastic cell—four whitewashed walls spelling orderliness, hygiene and strictly enforced sanity—I quail at the thought of how she must have loathed me, and what mental contortions she must have practiced to keep her loathing hidden from herself. By her own words, I was the best thing that had ever happened to her. Obviously she was desperately in love with me and experienced me with that horrific combination of visceral and cerebral responses that assures monumental attachment. Obviously she thought of me every minute of the day, "knew" she couldn't live without me, gloried in the thought of our closeness—was I not hourly inside her in all manner of ways?—tried to believe with eyes pressed shut and fingers crossed that my sexual interest in her was sign and signal that her feelings were requited.

But under the tenacious fabric of illusion (rainbow colors and layer upon layer of self-deception) must have been a cold well from which a muffled voice shouted to her that I loved her not at all, that I used her, watched her suffering with indifference, that she had no hold on my emotional life. No matter how hard she worked on believing my rare professions or gestures of affection—like bones thrown to a starving mongrel—no matter how often she replayed them in her mind and treasured them as tokens of my true, if complicated (since I kept telling her that I was complicated), feelings for her—no matter how diligently she reminded herself that life had treated me terribly and that I was afraid of getting hurt again by feelings (I had told her about my summer romance with one revision: Jennifer wanted to leave her husband, but he found out and beat her so badly she ended up in the hospital; Diana had sighed for me and had understood my terrible hurt)—no matter how deperately she tried to believe in me, there must have been thousands of instances when overwhelming evidence glared her in the face—like the bright cleft moon of my buttocks—and the voice from the well of chill truths told her: "He doesn't give a damn about you; all you are for him is a piece of meat with swellings and holes for him to paw and plow." Or worse, infinitely worse: "He treats you like dirt and you're letting him, and that means it serves you right and you really are dirt."

What heroic battles she must have fought to outargue that voice: "No, you're wrong; he loves me! in his own way he does!" she must have shouted down that truth-telling well. "He loves me! He just can't show it!"

I imagine a mocking echo coming back: "Showit! showit! showit!" and her covering her ears with trembling hands and running away.

Still, all was not perennially awful for poor, used, unloved Diana and deplorable Paul. I've so far failed to mention the comical potential inherent in our clandestine "romance"—the multitudinous possibilities for humorous confusion and alarm. Consider only the eternal care I had to take to remove my used French letters from the premises and discard them in a public wastebin. I suspected they would clog pipes and did not want to risk a hairy-armed plumber dangling one of the yellow offenders under Rex's startled nose, telling him: "There's what did it: your nephew's rubber." I also did not want to be blackmailed by the cleaning woman after she dug a soiled Trojan out of the basket in my bathroom. Hence I had a standard routine of rinsing the evidence, and wrapping it in a tissue and hiding it in my briefcase. A few times, however, I forgot to do so and remembered my omission in the middle of dinner or on my way out the front door and madly dashed upstairs as soon as I could to take care of the oversight. Not that I really expected Phaedra or Rex to stick their heads into my bathroom, but the thought of the translucent balloon draped over the faucet like the epithelium of an unlucky slug unnerved me.

That in more than two years of leisurely sex we were never in typical bedroom-farce manner discovered in the act may seem bordering on the miraculous, but the dynamics of that household would have made it rather more of a surprise if Diana and I had been descried in the course of two years of afternoon fornication in the entrance hallway. The master of the house was busy adding to his boodle, the mistress was busy subtracting from it by patronizing the priciest stores in town, in addition to having a positive aversion to being "cooped up" in the house. Those rare afternoons on which she did unexpectedly come home earlier posed no problem because the master bedroom was on the other side of the mansion, so that even if Phaedra chose to go upstairs, she was half a mile from my den of iniquity (an exaggeration, but we are talking about a six-bedroom house). The cleaning woman came in every morning on weekdays and was done with her chores by one o'clock. Ergo, we could carry on with impunity.

Nevertheless, farce did rear its indelicate head on one occasion, sometime in the second year of sex with my cousin. On the afternoon in question I was for a change of pace joined to Diana in the traditional I-above/she-below, belly-to-belly way. I was energetically humping and was approaching climax, when there was a sudden outraged roar outside the door. I never lost an erection more quickly, was out of naked Diana and stood panting next to the bed, listening to the infernal noise of…the vacuum cleaner! The door was closed but not locked, a precaution I was no longer careful to take. But instead of lunging at it and depressing the button on the doorknob, I stood petrified. Diana recovered her wits more quickly. She scrambled out of bed, my abandoned rubber dangling from her, locked the door and rapidly gathered her clothes and clutching them to her nakedness fled into the bathroom.

I hurriedly got dressed while the vacuum cleaner was moving down the corridor. Then I changed my mind, took off my shirt, and bleary-eyed and irritable went outside to inquire whether Mariella *had* to make this racket while I was lying down with a monster headache. She turned off the dust sucker, apologized and explained that she was getting a late start because she'd had car trouble, but she didn't have to do the upstairs rugs or my and Diana's rooms today. She continued her work downstairs (probably grumbling to herself that with the exception of the girl there wasn't a single decent human being in the house—and how right she was!), and I returned to my room and safely got Diana out of my bathroom and into her own room.

For the next few weeks, being surprised in the act by a roaring vacuum cleaner became a coded joke between Diana and me. Being "hoovered" was our expression for it—which suggests that in the midst of the grimmest drama humor may lurk.

The saddest of sad things is that, all questions of my despicableness aside, a case may be made for my cousin having had a point in calling me the best thing that ever happened to her. Yes, an outrageous statement in need of justification. Our lives together did of course have more texture and variety than I've so far indicated. Unless one is a maniac who keeps his object of sexual abuse tied up in a cellar and visits her (or him) only to sate demented cravings, one cannot spend two and a half years of "intimacy" with someone without establishing ordinary, non-sexual connections as well.

I'm not trying to dilute the potency of my tale of horror, but the whole truth *is* more complicated. Although away from sex I was often distant and preoccupied with things that did not involve Diana, there was also plenty of casual contact occasioned by our living in the same house and going to the same school.

One composite image of a frequent routine I remember is my

sitting in the vast kitchen while Diana is fixing supper. (This was a responsibility Phaedra had passed on to her daughter as soon as Diana had been high enough to reach pots and pans, just as she had abrogated housecleaning the moment Rex's income had permitted the hiring of a cleaning woman. They could of course have afforded a full-time housekeeper cum cook, but Phaedra knew when to economize, to have spending money for the ludicrously overpriced and ugly *objets d'art* she, the *connaisseuse,* kept cluttering the premises with.) In that kitchen, often after sex upstairs, we'd talk about mundane things: books, movies, politics, religion. I was doing much reading and was contemplating becoming a writer or philosopher or film director; Diana was a rapt listener to my in-sights. Anyone overhearing us at those times could easily have been fooled into thinking that we were brother and sister—non-incestuous, reasonably intelligent adolescents with no major psychopathologies. In fact, I was the only person in that family to whom Diana could talk without being made to feel stupid or clumsy, and in this sense I was surely a good thing for her.

We also talked about her benighted mother, and this is probably the area in which I was of the greatest use to her since I made no attempt to hide my thoughts regarding the intellectual and moral caliber of that would-be filicidal bitch and thus buttressed Diana's grievances with a concurring second opinion. I was certainly the first person whom Diana could tell that her mother had never loved her—not even when she had been a little girl. She didn't remember ever being hugged by her mother, nor her mother ever playing with her. And there had been no love later either. Quivering and almost unable to control her voice, she told me of an argument between her and Mommy Dearest on her twelfth birthday, in the course of which Phaedra had informed her that she hadn't wanted her in the first place and that she was sorry she hadn't gotten rid of "the accident." I marveled that poor unaborted Diana was as normal as she was, given exposure to the miasma exuded by her mother. I don't know what I said to Diana on that occasion—with any luck something pungent and utilitarian like: "Ignore the shit she tries to feed you to make you feel bad." I know that on another occasion I told her: "Your mother doesn't have the brains of skunk cabbage; whenever she opens her mouth substitute in your mind 'garbage' for every word she says." Diana, a sucker for directional therapy if ever there was one, tried it and reported triumphantly that it worked.

With respect to her mother, I was an ally Diana sorely needed. But I helped her in other ways as well. It was I who, drawing on a sense of aesthetics I didn't even know I had, suggested a different hairstyle and went with her to that female sanctum, the beauty salon, and, un-fazed by curious femininity, leafed through several magazines until I found a style I thought would suit her better (wispy bangs; the rest of the hair swept back and consolidated in a short pony tail at the back of the head to balance her bottom-heavy face). I also studied up on makeup and made her buy lipstick, blusher, eye shadow and eye liner, and advised her on how to use them, stopping just short of dabbing on and blending in the pastel hues and contouring her eyebrows. In other excursions I accompanied her to Marshall Field's and Carson Pirie and selected muted-colored sweaters with open necklines, a stylish, deceptively understated coat, and dresses. I waited patiently while she tried on the latter, and I studied the various possibilities as she stood before the dressing room smoothing out non-existent creases and waiting for my thumbs-up or -down sign. Other women customers must have envied Diana for having a solicitous male in attendance when it would have taken two harnessed oxen to drag their husbands to Ladies' Apparel. If they had known my true feel-ings while pondering Diana in this frock or that, they would have changed their minds in a hurry. My true feelings? That I was trying to make a purse out of a sow's ear.

I should point out that my instigation of and participation in the beautification of Diana was no sign of increasing fondness or sym-pathy. The root motives of all things are hidden in obscurity, but one can feel around and take guesses at some of the hard or spongy shapes one encounters—razor blades or clammy putrescence? Diana posed a challenge to my sense of aesthetics and I was curious to see how much I could improve on miserly nature's handiwork with artifice. Call Motive One the challenge of art. Then, I loathed her mother, and nothing would more upset Phaedra than a radiant Diana; call spite Motive Two. Then again, I was seen often enough with my cousin to want her to look at least minimally presentable; which makes Motive Three vanity. Finally, I was interested in the beauty-salon, department-store world of women; possible reason: a latent homosexuality that has remained latent.

Interestingly, I did not put Diana on a diet; why, I don't know. Maybe I thought trying to get her to shed excess tonnage would be hopeless, or maybe the idea of sex with my cousin sporting emaciated haunches and thighs held no appeal. Or is the answer more subtle? Did I unthinkingly cast myself as the photographer rather than the painter in the matter of my artistic "project," and was my self-appointed challenge that of working in a medium that allowed only for minor touchups and not for the surgical improvements the painter can effect by falsifying a line here and there to slim a neck and tuck in a waist? Whatever the answer may be, the fact is that I never suggested to Diana to lose weight and devoted all my energy to improving what was at hand. (My cousin did eventually, grimly, go on a diet, but that episode in her life had nothing to do with any prompting on my part.)

Diana, of course, misinterpreted my interest in her appearance and was pathetically pleased at my willingness to expend my energy and talents in her direction. I wish I could report that somewhere in a hidden corner of my heart there was indeed a tiny impulse to please her or to make her feel better about herself. I've hunted high and low in my memory for that impulse, but although I know that I'm perfectly capable of doctoring memory in order to make remembered events less painful, and believe in virtually everything Freud said about repression, the revising mechanism (erase and overwrite) doesn't seem to work for me. It refuses to produce any version of my feelings toward my cousin containing a single charitable impulse.

Regarding the improvement of Diana, Mum, predictably, could not refrain from the not-so-occasional "flattering" remark about Diana's changed appearance and the not-so-subtle-hint that a crush on me was at the heart of the metamorphosis. (Ha, ha! laughed Rex at the thought of his awkward daughter gussying up because her silly heart was atremble over her elegant and remote cousin.) Since I had warned Diana to expect thinly veiled facetiousness from the penny seats, she was prepared and snubbed her idiot parents with a show of indifference. (Not that she wasn't hurt anyway, but hurrah for the bold front!)

But no good deed goes unpunished. There was a sinister side to the issue of Diana's revamped looks that surfaced with a vengeance during my last six or so months in Chicago. The indirect agent of this development zoomed into view bright-eyed and breathless at the bottom of a ski slope in Aspen, Colorado in December of 1964 and will shortly be introduced.

In fact the skiing vacation I allude to and the months preceding it were under a cloud because of what had happened in August of that year. In August, Diana had refused to pack her bags, wave Mom and Dad goodbye, blow me a kiss, and drive off to Normal, Illinois (not a joke; you can look it up on any detailed map of the heartland), the home of what was then called Illinois State Normal University, to begin college life.

She had applied at a few other places as well and had been accepted by several. Why she chose ISNU I neither knew nor cared, although two seconds' thought should have told me that since the University of Chicago had turned her down, Normal was the closest place to home, read: to me. Two hours by car from the one who mattered to her more than anyone else in the world.

But she sent her letter of intent in the spring, when the fall seemed a long way off. Then came summer; vacation in a plush Mexican resort since Rex was renting the house on Lake Michigan to one of his clients. In Mexico, Rex el Macho fished for marlin from high-powered boats; Phaedra, the modern conquistador, pillaged mercado after mercado, returning with a loot of handwoven cloth, silver trinkets, gold jewelry. I, bookish lad, read *Finnegans Wake* under an umbrella on our private patio. And Diana, poor Diana, was fifty feet away on the beach getting her ample thighs burned and staring morosely at water and horizon.

She asked me to walk with her on the beach. I declined, stating that I hated walks on beaches. When she asked me again, I accused her of insensitivity in not understanding why I hated walks on beaches, not remembering what had happened to me on a beach, etc. She apologized. Then she wanted me to go swimming with her. I did, but immediately put a sizable distance between her and me when she couldn't keep up. End of beach-related frolicking.

Diana was unhappy the entire week; I did my best to ignore her and her tiresome emotional state. On our last evening she whispered to me angry and in tears that she couldn't stand it anymore; she had to talk to me. Can't it wait till we're back home, I asked. No, she said. To avoid a hysterical scene, I consented, and we did walk on the beach under a tent of stars as obscenely luminous as the one over Aquileia had been a hundred years earlier. She cried and said she couldn't stand the thought of leaving and being without me just a month from now. It would kill her. I had no idea how much I meant to her, she said; how much it would hurt her to be away from me. I had no idea how much she loved me. I didn't understand!

I tried to hide my exasperation, told her patiently that all things in life came to an end. There was no guarantee of permanence in anything, least of all in human relationships. Surely she had known when we first began to be intimate that this was a phase she and I were going through and that sooner or later that phase would end.

She cried harder, always a disagreeable activity to be a witness to if the crier is someone who bores you, but especially distasteful if the intention is to make you feel guilty. No, she hadn't known that, and I had never told her, she said between sobs. All she had known then, and all she knew now, was that she loved me even if I'd forgotten everything I'd ever promised her; even if I didn't give a damn about her.

Don't be an idiot; of course I give a damn about you, said I—although I'll change my mind if you keep carrying on like a lunatic. I tried to reason with her: We have to be adult about this. We've had a fine time together but there's no point in tearing out our hair now that things are going to change.

Etc. Etc. Etc.

I thought I had taken care of the matter with my rational discourse, but ordinarily submissive Diana had other ideas. A week before she was to leave for college, she told her mother that she had changed her mind: she'd take off a year and then go to college. She wasn't sure what she wanted to do with her life and a year would give her a chance to make up her mind.

Phaedra was furious for reasons that weren't clear. Maybe she felt that a "problem child" reflected poorly on her maternal performance and wanted out of the house a constant reminder that it was unlikely the Order of the Nurturing Mother would be bestowed upon her in the near future.

Rex didn't care one way or another but sided with his wife since that was the most convenient thing to do.

I, little Beelzebub with cloven hoof and leer, had looked forward to my cousin's departure because in the last weeks of spring a new girl had appeared in my class. She combined shyness with voluptuousness, and in my ambitious forecast of future delights I had already seduced her and was spending afternoons in her apartment (her recently divorced mother conveniently worked downtown), initiating her into esoteric sexual practices. Diana staying in Chicago, waiting every day for me to return after school, like a dutiful wifey waiting for hubby to come home after work, was not my idea of bliss.

Nevertheless, I did not overtly object to Diana's plans, even when she told me half-triumphant, half-apprehensive that she meant to attend the same college I would attend. I said, Sure, why not? and made up my mind on the spot to apply only at Harvard and Yale, places my grades and SAT scores would get me into and hers wouldn't. I did feel like telling her that I had no intention to have her in tow the rest of my life simply because we'd screwed a few times a week, but I held my tongue and acted moderately pleased at her staying in Chicago. Privately I resolved to wean her of me even if it took a boot in her broad behind to do it.

In the fall it was back to school for me while Diana stayed at home, reading mountains of books, mostly on geology—I couldn't imagine a more boring subject. She welcomed me home with eagerness every afternoon. Or every afternoon in the first few weeks and then less and less often since I allowed myself to become immersed in the school's extracurricular activities. I joined the debating society and the Drama Club and became treasurer of the Latin Club. The reason I chose these avenues of entertainment rather than the more interesting one of sex with Theresa, the new-arrival sophomore at school, was that my shy, voluptuous quarry had been appropriated by a senior lettering in basketball, a quick operator miles ahead of me in speed even if light-years behind me in subtlety and ultimate effectiveness (as I discovered later, he never even got to second base with her).

Given the circumstances, it shouldn't be surprising that those months were not rich in domestic harmony. More than ever, Phaedra treated Diana as if she were mentally and physically defective. More than ever, Diana withdrew. In her contact with me, a note of desperate urgency appeared. After sex, she clung to me and "playfully" asked me to say that I cared for her just a little. I repeatedly protested that I felt odd about having to keep telling her what should be perfectly obvious to her from my actions, and she said she was just kidding. (Even "just kidding," she didn't dare ask me to tell her I loved her, probably because she knew that that lie would have been too hard to spit out even for the consummate liar I was.) Then there were tiresome arguments: she accusing me of lying to her about being busy after school (which I didn't) or of breaking promises of "being there" when she needed me (which I had never made in all my life)—I protesting that she distorted everything I said and didn't understand me at all.

The result of her behavior was of course the opposite of the intended: I more and more felt she was tying me down, fettering me, suffocating me, and I grew ever more eager to be rid of her. If it hadn't been for the fact that there were still many days on which my penis overruled all other priorities in absolutely insisting on being in one hot wet hole or another, conveniently furnished by my cousin, I probably would never have gone home except to eat and sleep.

As for Diana, I think I can say without the least exaggeration that she was in an antechamber of hell throughout that fall. She herself probably thought she had long ago arrived in the ninth circle and stood cut to the bone by cold, lenses of ice freezing over her eyeballs. It took my opening a door to make her realize that what she thought couldn't get any worse could. I cracked that door during the last ski vacation I went on with the family.

Skiing at Aspen meant staying at the modest cabin (three bedrooms downstairs, living room and kitchen under the A-frame) that Rex rented out the rest of the year. We had been there on the two previous winters and I had become a good, if not expert, skier. Rex, of course, was an expert and attacked the black diamond runs with an aggressive, take-charge style. On the intermediate runs he was that infernal bore who schusses down the pistes hollering: "On your left!" at souls less audacious while careering past them. Phaedra, immaculately dressed in whatever was "in" that season (sable pelts trimmed with ermine? gold lamé insulated with spun platinum?) carefully glided down groomed slopes. Diana, lacking all grace, toiled knock-kneed and bottom-heavy on the easier of the intermediate runs—turn, turn, turn, turn—making her descent look like an ordeal. My own form was a study in control as I executed crisp parallel turns with little effort. Despite my ability, I went out of my way to avoid Rex since I had no desire to be challenged to a race by Mr. Killer Instinct.

The vacation was not a success. Phaedra was still nursing her grudge against recalcitrant, non-collegiate Diana—my cousin had applied at Harvard and Yale, just as I had, but no one believed she stood a chance. Diana was morose and ill-tempered. Rex was wearing his bullet-proof veneer of good nature. I ignored the lot of them, skied alone and in the evening read *The Decline and Fall of the Roman Empire*.

Since I skied alone, I had to play the "Single!" game at the ski lift (for the non-initiate: you ski to the bottom of the lift but, on crowded days, instead of taking a chair alone, you yell, "Single!" and wait for another lone skier to join you before getting in line). For two days I drew few partners worth mentioning: no snake dancers, erotomaniacs, miners, or thaumaturgists as far as I remember. Mainly I was paired with an assortment of teenage males with whom conversation was limited to an economical, "Hi," or "How's it going?"

Then, deftly digging in her edges to stop her skis precisely parallel to mine, there was Caroline, my height and age, slim, with bright gray eyes and brown hair tucked under a red wool hat. "Single?" she asked out of breath. "Yes," I said, and we got in line.

In this way came into my life what might have been my salvation had I not by this time been beyond salvation by any agency human or divine.

We sailed up the mountain, panoramic white below and blue above, and we talked. She (still nameless) lived in Dayton, Ohio, I in Chicago. She had an older brother, Brad, who was a senior at the University of Washington; I had a cousin, Diana, one year older than me; we both had applied at Harvard and Yale. That was funny, she said, she had applied at her brother's college. She wondered whether it was common for kids in the same family to go to the same colleges. I said I doubted it, and refrained from adding that I fervently hoped not.

We arrived at the top of the lift, organized our poles, said, "Goodbye," "Have fun," and took off. But we skied down the same run, arrived at the bottom at the same time, and logically teamed up for the ride back up the mountain. Suspended in midair, we exchanged further notes: Her name was Caroline, mine was Paul. Her father managed a department store; her mother had stayed in Dayton to take care of the children and household of a sister who was in the hospital. My uncle was the head of an ad agency; I lived with him and my aunt and cousin—my parents had died two years earlier in an accident.

Caroline took a quick glance at me and said, "I'm sorry." She said it plainly, straightforwardly and for some totally obscure reason that simple act of kindness almost made me break out in tears. Fortunately a hot-dog skier on the slope below chose this moment for a spectacular crash (plume of snow; both skis flying off and being dragged along by the nylon bands with which skies used to be suicidally secured to ankles) and we got absorbed in watching him dig himself out.

At the top, it was goodbye again and off we were. But once again we skied the same run, and when she fell on an icy section close to the bottom, I waited for her to gather her skies under her and use her poles to push herself upright.

Half an hour later it was understood that we were skiing together; we decided which lifts to take and which runs. We tried one mogul-studded chute and found that we were matched in incompetence. It was in the midst of the strenuous effort of sliding down one steep bump after another that I became aware of how thoroughly I was

88

enjoying myself. "Moguls from hell!" I called to Caroline. "Is this fun?" she yelled back and attacked the next bump. I realized that my enjoyment came from liking her in an uncomplicated way that had more to do with who she was—fresh, lively, quick-witted—than with anything else. Not that I didn't find her attractive: she had opened her turquoise ski jacket, and her small breasts, gentle mounds under her red sweater, matched her boyish slimness in her royal blue stretch pants. Her face was pretty, small and delicate. But what I was taken with was that elusive, indefinable thing called "personality." I liked her.

Any reader—including my favorite one—who surmised two pages ago that Caroline will be my next "love interest" in this chronicle may be disappointed or relieved to be told that I was not in love with her. I really, actually, in fact liked her, without there being an overwhelming pull towards her, or a terrifying fear of losing her, or a yearning of my soul to adore her, or any of the other telltale signs of lovelorn lunacy. I liked her and I hadn't felt this way about anyone in a long time. That was all.

I said it was an uncomplicated feeling and on one level I remember it as such. But on another level the feeling was surprising and strange. It was as if something had cracked the iron door of my loneliness—that six-inch-steel barrier set in concrete—and I sensed through the crack that someone was outside, close by, and that maybe I didn't need to be alone.

When we got hungry, we skied back to the lodge and stood in line at the cafeteria. There Caroline's brother spotted her, and she introduced me to him (tall, dark, manly) and a friend of his (tall, blond, manly) and we all had lunch together. Brad, without being in the least subtle about it, checked out whether I met the standards he set for anyone escorting his sister. Apparently I passed muster (which suggests that his procedure was inadequate, or that I was a superb actor, or that on that charmed day my deeply buried but nevertheless existent decent self surfaced). At the end of lunch he shook my hand and advised me and his sister to have fun.

Which we did. We skied and talked, skied and laughed, skied

with style and verve. And somewhere, while standing on the brink of some steep slope high up, I thought: I'm happy. My God, is it so simple to be happy?

Characteristically, I didn't believe it was so simple and I tried to eternalize in my mind the feeling by connecting it to the images surrounding me, the blue sky, a few whips of clouds, the dazzling white of the mountain. Miraculously I succeeded. Even now, sitting in my cramped and drab cage—and so unhappy—I can will the image of the mountain to appear before my inner eye. And for an infinitesimal instant I know what it is like to be happy.

My golden day on the mountain and whatever promise it held had to be ruined, of course. A narrow gap, a glimpse, a breath of air—and the door of steel was once again slammed shut. Not, I quickly concede, that I hadn't worked long and hard to fashion the tool of my wretchedness.

When the lifts had shut down for the day and Caroline and I had parted after agreeing where we'd meet in the morning, I waited in the parking lot for the rest of the Avery clan to join me. The first arrival was Diana, unhealthily red-cheeked.

"Who's your little friend?" asked Diana.

"Who?" I asked. "Oh, Caroline?"

"Is that her name? The one you had lunch with?"

"Yes, that's her name," I said, annoyed at having been spied upon by my nosy cousin. "And her brother's name is Brad, and his friend's Ted, and Ted plays intramural ice hockey."

"I suppose she's an ace skier," Diana said, not about to be intimidated or diverted.

"She's all right; not sensational."

"But better than me, I suppose." She tried to sound sarcastic but managed only bitter.

This was starting to have the ring of a cross-examination and I didn't like it. "Isn't everybody?" I said.

"How about blow jobs? How's she at that? Or haven't you gotten her to that yet?"

My reaction to my foul cousin pouring filth on my golden day was the impulse to hurt her swiftly and devastatingly, but her guardian angels showed up disguised as Rex and Phaedra and I had to content myself with scenarios of slapping her silly. I don't know what internal recriminations, acrid and spiteful, she had to content herself with since she had no chance to further vent her spleen that evening.

In the morning she was snappy on the drive to the slopes. I tried to ignore her comments about how fantastic a skier I was, and everybody else was, and how she'd donate her body to science so they could isolate the bad skiing chromosome. We split at the parking lot and I fled to my rendezvous with Caroline.

But although I liked her as much as on the day before, and the day was as beautiful as the day before, my cousin had planted a barb that I couldn't dislodge, try as much as I did. I laughed, I joked, we skied, but I felt an undercurrent of dread and was unable to shake off the conviction that something good had been irrevocably tainted. I thought I hid my feelings well enough, but on one trip up the lift, Caroline said: "Is something wrong? You seem sad."

I felt a wave of gratitude and a surge of self-pity at her having noticed, and I told her that I had had a silly argument with my cousin and since she had a lot of psychological problems I was mad and at the same time worried about her.

Caroline said, "It's nice of you to worry about her," and I accepted her praise gladly and tried for the briefest moment to worry about Diana in order to be able to see myself as the thoughtful and considerate individual Caroline had made of me (and who's to say she was so very wrong? who's to say I might not have been thoughtful and considerate if I hadn't been seduced, betrayed and left to die by my true love?).

The day was the last day of Caroline's stay at Aspen, and it sped by. In the afternoon I fought depression and tried to forget that in a few hours I would lose my new friend (I finally had a name for what she was, a name I'd never before assigned to anyone).

But this was where I was wrong because at the end of the day Caroline said she was glad to have met me and that we had become friends, and she gave me her address and phone number and took down mine. Then she hugged me and I realized to my great amazement that I believed she was serious about keeping in touch with me and that I was prepared to do the same.

⊑⊑⊑ My friend was true to her word. A few days after I had returned to Chicago with D, P & R, the first letter from Dayton arrived: two pages in a small, precise hand, relating anecdotes from the trip home and reminiscing about Aspen. Caroline wrote in an engaging style and was often funny. I wrote back in the same vein.

About a week later, there was a call for me in the evening. Diana came upstairs to fetch me—all phony flippancy and exasperation at being forced to play the servant. It was Caroline. I talked to her in Rex's never-used study, ruing for the first time that I had not, like every other wealthy teenager in the country, insisted on having my own phone in my room. We talked about nothing in the least noteworthy but I enjoyed the conversation.

In the weeks that followed, letters and phone calls became a routine part of my days, and I kept catching glimpses of something that had been missing from my life and that I didn't identify for what it was until years later. It was a friendship based on mutual liking and concern (I soon found out that my friend had the bugbear of a possessive mother in her life and needed my concern); an honest, open relationship, without hidden agendas or manipulation of any kind.

I say I caught glimpses of this friendship because a glimpse now and then was all that was granted me by Diana, who observed my innocent correspondence and innocent phone calls with stealthy malice and made me defensive about anything having to do with Caroline. She never repeated the obscene charge she had flung at me at Aspen, nor did she outright accuse me of anything else having to do with my friend (and how could she have, given the innocence of that relationship?—unless devoting affection to someone, and not devoting it to her, can be counted as an offense). But I could feel her eyes on my back when I looked through the day's mail to see whether there was anything for me, and there was snappish resentment whenever I emerged from Rex's study after an hour-long phone call. She would have been easier to handle if she had been open about her jealousy. I could have responded to any overt charges with resentment and countered them by accusing her of not understanding me and trying to turn something perfectly innocent into something sordid. But since she said not a word about Caroline, all I could do was shoot her the occasional baleful glance when I felt she was spying on my affairs.

Meanwhile, under my baleful eyes and the nose beneath them something was happening of which I was oblivious until Phaedra pointed it out: Diana was losing weight—had, by the time Phaedra first mentioned it and I first consciously looked, lost about twenty pounds.

"You're so much slimmer," was how her mother put it, and Diana looked at her and me with an Oh-that?-I-almost-forgot look that ill disguised triumph and spite. She said that it was easy, she simply had decided to lose some weight and was eating less. Anybody could be skinny as a rail if she really wanted to, she said pointedly to me; there was nothing to it. Phaedra uttered congratulatory sounds. I said nothing because even I sensed that there was something objectionable about my not having noticed Diana's trimmer self. (I did, after all, still avail myself of her carnal services once a week—would it have been asking entirely too much of me to notice that the flesh I was pawing and pounding was less hefty?)

Of course "easy" was the last thing losing weight was for Diana.

Her genes (beefy Rex's, not lean Phaedra's) were against her. It is probably safe to say that in those weeks and months of dieting there was not one moment when she was not ravenous and using every available ounce of mental energy to keep herself from wolfing down a five-course meal. She was still the cook and kept serving up the same dishes, but at the table, surrounded by delectables of her own making, she took (as I now noticed) portions that she knew couldn't possibly keep her alive, and with resentful eyes munched her way through mountains of lettuce to stuff with wads of greenery the gaping hole that was her stomach. And still there must have been nights when she woke up doubled up by hunger pangs and bit into her hands and pounded her stomach to keep from running downstairs, tearing the door off the refrigerator and eating and eating and eating.

Her suffering must have been extraordinary. And for what? For the wildly improbable hope that one day, after once again mindlessly fucking her, I would suddenly look at her graceful naked form and the scales would fall from my eyes? I would gaze upon her and suddenly I would know that I loved her, only her, my slim love, the light of my eyes, the delight of my heart, the delectation of my spirit? To belabor the point: fat chance.

Fat chance also of my escorting her when she went shopping for new clothes since none of her old things fit. She asked me to, but I begged out, arguing that I was busy and that she had learned enough about style from me to be able to fend for herself. She had and did—the things she bought were fine, but if her plan was for me to become attracted to her, it failed, since the entire Dior spring collection plus all of Givenchy would not have had that effect on my jaded eye.

⊔⊔ Meanwhile life's rich pageantry was unfolding in other
areas. In March, Diana received in the span of a few
days letters of rejection from Harvard and Yale and fell into a pit of
gloom not noticeably brightened by Phaedra reminding her that she
had warned her that this might happen if she applied at only two—
and especially those two—places. Sometime later (which made me
wonder whether the powers that be had spent more time contemplating my application) I received Harvard's rejection. I suppose this
development cheered Diana in giving her hope that the torment she
was living in by virtue of her proximity to me was not going to be
discontinued by my departure for college. But for once the fates
were kind to her although she could not then have understood that
she ought to have fallen on her knees and given thanks: I was
accepted by Yale—not my first choice but adequate after I read up
on it in the self-congratulatory literature provided. Diana's gloom
deepened, needless to say, but I could hardly take the blame for her not
having done well enough in school to be judged worthy of becoming a
Yalie.

At Dayton, meanwhile, another family drama was unfolding:
Caroline's mother stepped up the clinginess characteristic of her
relationship to her daughter, and in call after call my friend talked to
me almost in tears about how more and more her mother dressed
like her (to show how easily they might be mistaken for sisters),
tried to be a pal to her friends, made her feel guilty about wanting to
lead her own life.

I did my best to furnish a shoulder for her to cry on and tried to
put things into perspective: Her mother was using guilt to manipulate her; she should ignore her as much as possible; in the fall she'd
be away at college (which was, I suggested, why her mother was
becoming more and more possessive—she had to be in a near panic
at the thought of her little girl cutting the umbilical cord). Sometimes, at the end of a long call, Caroline would say, "I'm so glad
you're my friend," and I'd be delighted at the thought that I was a
true friend in need.

95

Then high school ended forever for Caroline and me. I got a part-time job at a bookstore, joined an amateur theater group and made up my mind to go to Connecticut early to avoid another vacation with my kinfolk.

In June, Caroline's father came to Chicago for a meeting and she, in the idiom of the Midwest, "came with." We met in the lobby of the hotel where they were staying and spent an afternoon together. I was glad to see her again and happy to find that she enjoyed herself with me.

On the home front (read: Diana) this meeting and the continued phone calls and letters did not go over well. Diana, consumed by jealousy, was no doubt convinced that Caroline and I were lovers despite the distance separating us. Maybe her imagination had us rendezvous on alternate Thursdays at a halfway point between Dayton and Chicago and rut in the roadside shrubbery, or maybe we talked dirty to each other on the phone while masturbating now that I had a phone in my room (connected to the less-used and less easily listened-in-on of the house's two phone lines) and could lock my door on the world.

The irony was that whatever lustful scenarios Diana was torturing herself with missed not merely the target but the barn, since I had months earlier begun to court Theresa, my shy, voluptuous sophomore, and had by the summer progressed to nakedness and mutual masturbation albeit not yet to full-fledged coitus. I *was* furious at Diana's dragging my innocent relationship with Caroline through the slime of her filthy imagination. Still, I understood, even if I didn't forgive, her resentment: between my job, my amateur theatrics, my friendship with Caroline, and the sexual novelty of Theresa, there was barely enough time in my schedule to give Diana my business once a week; of course she felt neglected.

That all of this—my inattention and general lack of interest in Diana, her nerves being screwed to a high pitch by hunger, longing and jealousy—was rapidly approaching a climax of pathos and stupidity seems obvious in retrospect, but when that climax arrived I saw it as merely another example of Diana's ever-more-exasperating clinginess.

The stage for the final act was what appeared to be an empty house in mid-afternoon—no eagerly waiting or indifference-feigning Diana in living room, den or kitchen. I went upstairs, not particularly interested in where she'd gone off to. When I opened the door to my room I was treated to a sight: Diana on my bed, clad in black lace garter belt, black silk stockings and black lace brassiere. She wore nothing else. The odalisque pose she had adapted (legs closed, buttocks prominently displayed, head resting on palm so she could look at me over her shoulder) seemed forced and uncomfortable.

When I said nothing, she sat up, folding her legs under her in a rehearsed alluring move, and smiled a weak, frightened smile that looked absurd on her heavily made-up face. "Do you like it?" she asked, trying not to see the disapproval written all over me.

I said, "It's cute but I just came to change shirts and pick up a script." The glib lie was kinder than the truth, which was that I couldn't stand the sight of her in that outfit.

I will for a moment leave Diana suspended in mid alluring pose and frightened smile to answer an obvious question, namely, why I couldn't stand the sight of my cousin in provocative black lace after having used her sexually for close to three years. Given my lecherous record, it may seem incongruous that my pants weren't off two seconds after I'd laid eyes on her. Or has the psychologically sophisticated reader already taken into account my peculiarities, the most basic one being that when it came to Diana I insisted on having total control? Yes, if the idea of lascivious lingerie had been mine, Diana would long ago have been strutting about in split-crotch panties and nipples-exposing bras, and I would have panted over her and her scanties. But the idea being hers, I simply wasn't interested.

Another peculiarity, namely, my keen insight into the inner process-es of others, also worked against my cousin because I saw the frantic worry behind the dress-up—the desperate attempt to pull me back, hold on to me by the only part of my mind or anatomy she had ever had the slightest hold on. I saw it and I felt trapped. Finally, and I don't know if this qualifies as a peculiarity, I probably did at that precise point realize that I had turned a reasonably normal, unhap-py girl into a whore. The result was instant, visceral loathing.

I have left whorish Diana suspended in compromising get-up and weak smile. But the smile faded of course the moment I told her I wouldn't stay. She said with a quaver in her voice, "You don't like me wearing this," and without waiting for my reply burst into tears.

I opened my closet door, took out a shirt and began unbutton-ing the one I was wearing. Without warning, her crying changed into a high, keening sound and when I glanced at her, I was startled to see her rocking back and forth as if she were a small child con-sumed by grief over the loss of her favorite toy. She looked ridicu-lous in her tart's costume, and I found it hard to believe that I had ever been able to rouse sufficient interest in her to fuck her. I put on a fresh shirt and hastily buttoned it, eager to get away.

"Please don't go," she suddenly said in a little girl's voice. "I know you hate me but please don't."

"I have to," I lied. "Rehearsal."

"Just stay a little while," she said. "Please, help me just this once."

My rage was sudden and intense. "I don't have time for this; I'm already late," I said. "I don't have time for this shit."

"I feel terrible," she said. "Now you're angry at me. I've done everything wrong and now you really hate me."

"That's right," I said and went through my desk, looking for the script I had purportedly come to get, "I hate you. Whatever you say."

There was a pause, then she said, "No, you don't hate me." She was suddenly rid of her little girl's voice, and sounded quite calm. "You don't care enough to hate me. You're indifferent."

Her sudden pretension to sophistication made me even angrier. "Yes, you got it; indifferent is the word."

She paid no attention to me. "You've never cared about me at all, not for a single moment," she said calmly. "Never."

"That's right, not for a single moment," I said.

"And now you'll go and you don't care at all how I feel. It doesn't matter to you."

"You got it. That's me: good old uncaring Paul," I replied and left her sitting there in her ridiculous get-up and runny mascara. In the driveway I revved up my Impala Coupe and for the first time in my life laid down rubber in a squealing-tires getaway.

I don't know what I did the rest of the afternoon and evening and whether I stayed angry or lost interest as soon as I had put a few miles between me and my idiot cousin.

I didn't come home until late, to a house that was a hubbub: Phaedra, Rex and a sister and brother-in-law of Phaedra's jabbering away in the living room, all just back from the hospital where Diana was under observation after having tried to kill herself by slitting her wrists with one of her father's razor blades (in fact, two shallow cuts that barely nicked a few veins and tendons, as I found out a while later—not before having formulated the vivid mental image of Diana bottomless, marble white, adorned in black lace on my bed, which was soaked, blanket, sheet, mattress, with blood streaming from her wrists).

"Did she leave a note?" I asked, fearing—and who can blame me—incrimination. ("Dear Paul, You've turned me into a whore and now you won't even touch me. I can't stand it anymore....")

"No," said Phaedra.

"Did she say anything on the way to the hospital?" I asked, somewhat relieved.

"No," said Phaedra.

"Yes," said Rex. "She said she wished she'd done it right because then she'd be dead," and he abruptly burst into tears, which embarrassed everyone there, but most of all his wife.

That night, I sneaked into Diana's room and found at the bottom of a drawer the "naughties" she had tactfully taken off before getting dressed properly and looking for her father's razor blades. I threw them into a garbage bin the next day, discreetly wrapped in a brown paper bag.

Diana remained under observation in the psychiatric ward for a month. By the time she was released, I had left for college, and I had no further contact with her until a chance encounter some twenty years later. Which closes the book on the never-to-be-amended story of Diana's adolescence and mine.

I did have sporadic contact with Rex and Phaedra at the rate of about two items of correspondence per year until I came into my meager inheritance at twenty-one. After that I rarely heard from them or they from me.

In the fall of 1979, dynamic, Type A Rex died of a heart attack on the golf course. Since I had to present a paper at a conference in San Diego on the day of the funeral service I had an excuse for not attending. I did send the obligatory condolences to the survivors expressing the proper sentiments of what a loss, and a privilege to have known, and he would have wanted it to happen at the fifth hole. Phaedra, astonishingly, responded at length, and in the following year took to writing me long rambling letters full of complaints about ailments and doctors. The letters seemed written by someone thirty years older—as if she were living out some private fantasy of widowhood.

My replies were models of courteous terseness, mentioning superficial details—the conferences, the new office, the condominium I bought—and repeating in their closing phrases the refrain: very busy; still very busy; as usual, very busy.

Then, about a year after Rex's death, his widow put away her psychological black garb and became interested in men. She continued writing to me what were now unabashed letters of her romantic experiences. At first this struck me as bizarre, but then I realized that, as a practicing psychologist, I was now, according to that woman's limited grasp on reality, a professional Father Confessor who could be made privy to all transgressions of the flesh.

This largely one-sided correspondence continued for about five years, then stopped abruptly when the widow married the divorced owner of a Pittsburgh brewery and the two lived happily ever after—that is to say, at seventy she's still alive and still married.

I should add that in those years of contact there were occasional references to the startling doings of Diana—the mother writing with a never-ceasing sense of astonishment about her daughter, who seemed to be (was this at all possible?!) doing all right. From the fragments, I was able to deduce—amazed—that Diana, my pathetic, slavish Diana, was making a success of her life. I don't remember at what point I knew what, but summarized the developments were as follows: A year after I entered college, Diana got a late start at UCLA, majoring in geology. She went on to the Ph.D. at the University of Washington, en route marrying a fellow graduate student. The work they did for their respective dissertations impressed a few important people in their field and as a result they were offered a joint appointment at the University of Hawaii. In a span of ten years, they acquired an international reputation as vulcanologists, traveling as a team to Japan, Alaska, Sicily—wherever lame Hephaestus set up his smithy with anvil and twenty bellows.

I ran into the couple about six years ago at the San Francisco airport. I was on my way to a conference; they were changing planes on their way to somewhere. She and I recognized each other at the same time. I stopped, said, "I don't believe it!" laughed (an astounding reflex at times of horror), said, "Of all the crazy things."

She was overweight and frowsy, and she distractedly introduced me as "My cousin Paul" to "David," an unprepossessing beanpole with red hair and pale blue eyes, whose grip when he shook my hand was a little too firm, making me wonder whether he knew of my role in his wife's adolescent erotic life. I was vastly embarrassed, told Diana how well she looked five times in as many minutes, told him that he was lucky to have her two or three times, talked about my professional doings, listened to her telling me that Phaedra and Chuck (the new husband) were fine. During all of this, I formulated the single coherent thought that she looked at me as if I didn't actually exist; I had the disconcerting sensation of looking into a mirror and seeing no reflection of myself.

Then I escaped to my gate and silver bird without having given David the chance to strangle the man who at one time, without malice aforethought, had done his utmost to harm his wife.

Theoretical Interlude Two

🔳🔳🔳. The psychodynamic context and dreary causes of "disorders" like my cousin's have been explained in too many stop-dating-creeps-and-learn-to-esteem-yourself paperbacks to warrant a lengthy digression. "Dependency addiction" is the au courant buzzword (replacing the far more intriguing "obsession" of a previous age) and it will do until the fashion changes and some other paradigm cum jargon replaces the outmoded concept of addiction. I myself have no quarrel with the term in the case of Diana since whatever euphoria, affection, tenderness and admiration drew her to me at the beginning was clearly soon replaced by a need that kept her clinging to me like a heroin addict desperate for her fix. Her need existed entirely on an emotional level, and whatever conscious (or cognitive) introspection she may have used to try to convince herself to break away from me was as powerless against it as an addict's conscious resolution to stay away from heroin.

According to the currently popular theory (and no popular theory without a gram of truth), the psychological underpinnings of dependency addictions are to be found in the immediate family. In Diana's case, my neglect, coldness and abuse struck a chord in her as things inseparably connected with the way the people most important to her, namely, her parents, related to her. This was what she was used to; this was the world she had always lived in; this was what she deserved. She may have been colossally mistaken in identifying as love her inability to break away from me after she had consciously recognized me for the monster I was, but she was dead right in recognizing my treatment of her as familiar in all senses of the word and therefore as what she had had to make do with in lieu of love all of her life. As a reasonably intelligent and introspective individual, she knew that, in having certain feelings for me, she was pouring emotional resources into a cesspool; as a creature capable of being hurt, she loathed me for hurting her; but as that same creature, she experienced the sick emotional bond that joined her to me as unbreakable—or breakable only through her death.

As for the hidden causes of my deplorable behavior during those three years, I've provided the odd non-clinical interpretation here and there in my account. For anyone who thinks those speculations too skimpy (as I'm sure my frowning journalistic conscience does), I list below a random assortment of other stabs—some more hilarious than others—in the psychological dark.

- Hatred of women with pronounced secondary sex characteristics—to be traced back to a repressed memory of being sexually abused by a woman with large pendulous breasts.
- Hatred of beautiful, slim women (read: Phaedra via Jennifer) and the urge to hurt them by hurting what belongs to them.
- Hidden depression and the urge to fight it (and feel alive) through promiscuous sexual activity.
- Aversion to large-breasted and -bottomed women—attributable to latent homosexuality.
- The need to prove to myself that I could win and hold on to a woman, and the fury that the one I won and held on to was the wrong one.
- An affective disorder stemming from a dysfunctional family (my poor parents).
- Hatred at seeing my enthrallment for Jennifer mirrored in Diana's feelings toward me, and hatred of myself through hatred of her.
- Borderline simple schizophrenia, i.e., a chemical imbalance.
- Other possibilities too close to the "truth" for comfort, to which my own analytical faculty is ever denied access.

When my cousin and I are considered together, it becomes obvious that mutually compatible psychological disturbances were required before a situation so thoroughly bad could develop. Our problems dovetailed as smoothly as parts of our anatomies and, in a less obvious sense than in her case, I was as dependent on her as she was on me—that is, until my problems demanded a solution other than that of sexually victimizing her and I broke away from her.

Diana's behavior when we met at the airport suggests that she, too, broke away eventually and that in the process I became a figure of no importance whatsoever to her, something dimly remembered as distasteful but so far removed from her life that it didn't merit the effort of remembering. I suppose her beanpole husband was instrumental in exorcising me, but maybe she was also helped by therapy—amazing to picture myself appearing in a psychologist's office as one of the ogres tormenting a patient's childhood. ("He wanted me to...And I didn't want to...but he..." Tears, uncontrollable sobbing.)

I ask myself now what would have happened if during our encounter at the airport I had asked Diana to forgive me. I see travelers hurrying past us, hear arriving and departing flights announced in the metallic twang of intercoms, but I cannot picture her reaction. Would she have laughed? cried? told me to go slit my wrists to prove the honesty of my remorse? Or would she have made the greatest effort that is ever demanded of any of us, that of trying to understand another human being? And having understood, to forgive?

Maybe. But given the missed opportunity, there are other possible scenarios: Diana may learn about and read Fair Vanity's article (a feeble joke since my journalist friend is fair but not vain), or the unabridged version may accidentally fall into her hands. Especially in the latter case, she may relive some of the hurt of those years and be exceedingly short on charitable feelings toward me. And she may be gratified to find that in Part Three of these memoirs, their hero gets his comeuppance, and poetic justice triumphs.

Part Three

The denizens of my past did not altogether vanish from my life when I turned to a new chapter at hallowed Yale. There was still Caroline, for one, now on the other side of the continent at the University of Washington—a proper Husky (on the swim team) since in my imagination she still appeared against a backdrop of snow, exhaling white puffs of condensed moisture in the arid cold. I had told her about Diana's "nervous breakdown," omitting the role I (and indirectly she) had played in it, and she, good friend, had commiserated with my feeling bad about the episode. Once we were settled in at our respective campuses, we regularly wrote to each other about college life, which in her case was not untroubled because there were daily maternal phone calls from Dayton. I was self-consciously pleased at this sign that I was able to maintain a contact based on simple liking and concern. No monster, I.

But there, too, pride came before the fall: before the end of our freshman year, Caroline committed the unforgivable sin that began the slow death of our friendship. And there wasn't a thing I or she could have done to prevent it. The unforgivable sin? My friend fell in love. I forget the details: some fair-haired schemer who dumped her after a few months, not before having initiated her into sex.

Her calls revolving around the stupid affair had an odd effect on me. While I listened to her detailing her woe and waited through the long pauses of static crackling in the line when she couldn't talk because she was overcome by feelings, I sketched doodles—all sharp edges and daggers and darts—on a note pad. Vexation and annoyance informed these pointy, cutting shapes, and impatience made them darker and denser as I retraced and thickened them. For some reason, which I didn't then understand, I was incapable of concern or even interest in her romantic debacle. My blunt advice during one exasperating, one-sided conversation to "forget about the asshole and get on with your life" must have struck her as not the most empathetic thing in the world, but it was all I could muster.

When asshole A was followed in rapid succession by bozo B and creep C—each the same gregarious, athletic, glib, brainless, unfeeling type—I couldn't help suspect an element of complicity on her part in insisting on becoming emotionally attached to superficially attractive nonentities who were guaranteed to hurt her. My response was boredom and thinly veiled annoyance occasionally enlivened by an attack of acute vexation at her inability to see how utterly idiotic it was to spend more than half a second's thought on anybody who didn't care about her. (None of which recriminations and their underlying reasons require an advanced degree to be made psychological sense of.) On her part, she couldn't help but become aware of my lack of support, and she confided in me less and less.

She graduated with a degree in history and found work at a company in Milwaukee doing genealogy research. A few years later she got married to an all-American type—their wedding picture showed a cornfed fullback. Looking at his dull blue, smug eyes, I thought, Watch out, Caroline! By then our contact had become sporadic, one or two superficial communiqués a year. The last I heard from her was in a letter ("I ran into a box of your letters and started remembering…"). She sounded unhappy. A statement that Greg was "away on business a lot" made me read effortlessly between the lines the worry that business deals were not all that Greg was negotiating when he was away. She enclosed a photo of her holding the hands of her five-year-old and three-year-old—a bright smile for the camera by Mom, cute frowns by the kids.

I ought to have written to her or given her a call to find out whether she needed a friend, but I suppose I was already exasperated at the thought of being told about another one of her hopeless relationships. Plus, I was fighting my own battle with depression, about which more shortly, and had no desire to expose myself to what was sure to depress me. Finally, let us not forget the cold reality of the shrink as a young jerk: I was beginning to be paid good money to listen to people tell me about their hopeless relationships; to do in my spare time what I did professionally held no appeal.

Just to complete this wrap-up of the past and avoid the label "all-around heel": I had not abandoned Theresa, my voluptuous sophomore in Chicago: Her mother and father had gotten back together and the family had moved to Cincinnati shortly before I left for college (and before I got around to persuading her to "go all the way"). And Theresa had not, repeat, not, been heartbroken at having to part with me.

My major at Yale was psychology. Why I chose that rather than one of a dozen other possible majors I have no idea. I was tempted for the sake of plausibility to invent for this chronicle and its painstaking reader a sudden dawning of an interest in the workings of the mind, or a sophomoric dream of becoming the inventor of a brilliant new theory ("Avery's Paradigm of the Subversive Id"), but the truth is that I have entirely forgotten, or at least am unable to retrieve by conscious effort, the impulse that first planted my foot on the road to my future profession. The mind's a wondrous thing.

For my minor I chose English because I had always been a prodigious reader and found writing essays a cinch.

Socially I took no part in the life of the campus. Since I had a high draft number and was by nature apolitical, the anti-war rallies didn't interest me, and my sole concession to the climate on campus was the wearing of a black-and-white-enameled peace symbol pin.

My hair was shoulder-long, I occasionally wore a poncho, but otherwise I showed no sign of being affected by the major social and political movement of my college days. My not running with the crowd and having no friends meant also that I was that *rara avis* in that decade: the college student leading a drug-free life.

On the romance front, I practiced complete abstinence, possibly because I had been used to easy sex and lacked the patience for even the minimal courtship required in those days, or possibly because Diana's suicide stunt had been a cold shock to my libido from which it had not yet recovered.

In my senior year I found myself devoting more thought to my English than my psychology assignments—which by then had deteriorated to the unmitigated boredom of statistics: the statistics of sampling, the statistics of charting, the statistics of statistics, the mean, the median and the mode—all gathered and computed in the earnest aim to arrive at pseudo-scientific conclusions about a pseudo-world in which 2.3 people in 10 experienced 7 of 25 listed sexual fears between the ages of 12 and 15—unless they misunderstood the question, or misremembered the past, or lied. Writing essays on Shakespeare and Byron was more entertaining and made me feel in closer contact with the "real" world. By observation, I determined that the life of a professor of English offered—in addition to research that was not mind-numbing—a life of leisure, control over one's sphere of interest and a decent income, and I decided to continue for a fifth year, to graduate with a degree in English as well as psychology.

Graduate work in English took me to the University of California at Santa Barbara, an institution that unlike Yale was not consumed by the (again) pseudo-scientific claptrap of critical literary theory—the New Criticism being in those days still the final answer to all literary questions that had puzzled scholarly brains from the time of the first poetic utterance—but believed in traditional historical, psychological and genre-based scholarship. My aim, which solidified sometime in the course of my second year, was to write my dissertation on the representation of love in literature, an ambitious project, I realized, but one for which I was, I thought, uniquely suited since who could possibly have more interest and experience in the topic than I?

My qualifying exams out of the way, I began my research. I read or reread *Tristram and Isolde*, Ovid's *Amores* and *Ars amatoria*, *Of Human Bondage*, *The Sun Also Rises*, *The Portrait of a Lady*, *A Midsummer Night's Dream*, *Lolita*, *The Good Soldier*, *The Sorrows of Young Werther*, *Death in Venice*, etc. etc. etc., and I of course pored over that milestone of ill-conceived thought, *The Art of Courtly Love*. I collected notes on my finds on 4x6 index cards, which I kept in first one, then two, then three cardboard boxes. I bought a filing cabinet, and then another when I had stuffed the first one with folders containing more elaborate notes and copies of relevant passages. After not too many months, my studio apartment looked like a set for a parody of the academic life. My desk sagged under the weight of books, the spillover was in stacks on the floor, and I could truly say that between the stove in the alcove and the sofabed against the opposite wall love was everywhere.

And I was happy because I was in the privileged position of the expert to appreciate the artistic renditions I was collecting of turmoil, torment, pain, agony, and grief occurring when one crackbrained member of the species grossly overvalues another. I, remote from the visceral ache of love, could look and record, laugh scornfully, and shake my head in wonder at the fabulated but ever-so-true examples of folly displayed on the pages of books. At the same time I could learn, without having to pay the emotional price of actual experience, about this strange thing that had seized me so completely a decade earlier and had almost left me dead. As I saw it, the great free bonus of my scholarship was that in explaining to the world how artists saw and rendered love, I myself would understand this bizarre phenomenon and would lay the ghost of summer past.

Meanwhile there was one nagging problem—that of my adviser periodically requesting an outline, an abstract, an introductory chapter. I stalled, told him I wasn't ready, I'd give him something next week, next month, before the end of the year. For some reason, no matter how thrilled I was to make a new discovery for my encyclopedic work, no matter how eagerly I filed it under the appropriate category ("Love at First Sight," "Love Obstructed by Misunderstanding," "Love Unrequited," "Love for La Belle Dame sans Merci," "Love Leading to Suicide"…), I did not feel the impetus to write about my discoveries. My excuses were obvious: I didn't have enough material; no point in starting to write if there was a good chance things would have to be rewritten by the light of new insights; plus, no point starting now that the term/school year was almost over and there were the distractions of grading papers and exams; better wait until there would be more time next term/summer.

All of this may sound like the stuff of humdrum procrastination, but if I did anything impressive in those years it was elevating writer's block to an art. No mere sharpening of twenty pencils, no cleaning a spotless typewriter, and rearranging notes in alphabetical order by title or author or subtopic before sitting down to write a single word. On most days I was buried at the library, shoveling like a demented mole through the detritus of literature. I scanned texts whose pages hadn't been disturbed by a reader in fifty years: nineteenth-century novels by unknown writers in which mercantile-class heroes fell in love with barmaids or seamstresses and faced the wrath of their families, eighteenth-century plays in which doomed lovers jumped off cliffs or swallowed poison and expired in each other's arms, Tudor poems in which the poet was tied in "dark and obscure labyrinths of love."

Then one day, I woke up with the sure and certain knowledge that I would never write my dissertation on Love in the Literature of the Ages, and that, to compound the problem of my professional future, I was uninterested in any other literary topic. I quit graduate school at twenty-seven with nothing to show for my effort but a wide knowledge of who fondly gazed upon whom, and why—or fondly fondled whom, and how—in books.

A called-for P.S. is that not until much later did I see any connection between my monumental difficulty in doing something as
trivial as writing a dissertation (a few years later it took me a mere
eight months to produce one practically out of thin air in another
field) and my father's heroic writer's block. I don't know what deep
roots of doubt or fear kept Avery Père from writing, but I can take a
guess at the straitjacket that fettered me. Maybe I was, without
knowing it, dismayed at seeing the romantic impulse, unreasoning
and insidious, triumph in book after book, with no attempt made
to understand its sources or come to terms with its destructiveness—
as if the mere existence of a debilitating epidemic disease justified
filling volumes with lurid descriptions of it. Or maybe I felt on some
level that even though the information I was gathering on love was
in the public domain, my interest in love was private, and that in
writing about it I would bare to the eyes of all the world something
deeply personal, something that had hurt and harmed my most
secret self. (If so, I have changed, as is evidenced by my willingness
to be seen—scars and all—by the thoughtful eyes of at least one fellow being.)

Out of school, I spent a few months of near terminal boredom
as a textbook editor, then applied for admission to graduate school
in psychology at the University of Washington (it's a small world). I
did the course work and in record time wrote a Ph.D. dissertation
titled: "Interpersonal Bases of Abnormal Behavior," about which I
remember virtually nothing even though the title suggests that my
learned work may have been a rewrite of my misbegotten literary
thesis—never underestimate the mind's knack for following its own
obscure agenda. The paper I extracted from my dissertation was
published and received a patter of applause for its entirely spurious
but superficially arcane-seeming modeling of "primary, secondary,
and tertiary relationships" and their connection with psychological
aberrations.

I was thumbing my nose at my chosen profession because I had
by then developed a heartfelt contempt for the types of midget

brains endemic in the field who had but to memorize Freud or Adler or Skinner or Maslow to become unshakably convinced that the roots of all actions were now known, all psychopathology explainable, no mystery of the mind left unsolved. Or maybe my emerging cynicism was an early symptom of a condition that was to attack me and pursue me without let or hindrance shortly after I had finished my internship at a mental hospital, established my practice in San Francisco, and settled into the routine of the therapist guiding a mottled assortment of patients along the pitfall-strewn road of mental disorders.

Metaphorically speaking, my emerging illness was like a slow poison that was depriving me gradually, at an almost imperceptible rate, of avenues of pleasure, things that engaged me, activities that made me feel—without prompting me to analyze causes or inspect the "true" state of my emotional life—that being alive was worthwhile. More and more I was walking around with a sense of numbness that insulated me from my surroundings and made it difficult to give anything my full attention. And more and more my mental state made it difficult to believe that I had not always, at all times, been monstrously unhappy.

I was professionally familiar with the distorting lens of psychological states, and I tried to remember my past as more than a stream of unrelieved misery. But even taking into account the distorting effect of the condition, I traced its first symptoms to my childhood. Introspection placed its initial appearance around the time I was twelve (in other words—and I hated to let her off the hook of culpability—before Jennifer). My sense was that a constant busyness, changes in my life, new surroundings, new experiences, new interests and obligations had kept me from becoming aware of what the therapist I finally saw diagnosed (concurring with my own diagnosis) as an affective disorder, namely, endogenous unipolar depression.

I'll take time out here to note that my seeking the help of a therapist proves that even though I took a dim view of many of the field's practitioners, I did, when I became desperate, try to find help in the field—not, to be truthful, with a Ph.D. psychologist but an M.D. psychiatrist, but nevertheless I clearly hoped for relief through therapy. The point being that I was never a charlatan who set himself up to practice what he didn't believe in in order to soak poor, troubled wretches. Although I was not nearly as optimistic as the majority of my colleagues, I believed—or tried to believe—that by listening and by understanding the dark, painful places holding my patients' minds captive, I could devise a course of treatment that would crack a rusty shutter and let in a beam of light, even if it did not dramatically sunder an ironclad door. A curiously modest aim for someone not known for modesty, but my own affliction was having a humbling effect on me, and, at any rate, my more ambitious side was satisfied through flurries of activity in which after a minimum of research I tossed off surprisingly cogent and interesting papers for conferences and flew to Dallas or Vancouver or the Virgin Islands and derived sardonic amusement from observing the strutting and preening of the pretentious mediocrities in the field.

There is no point in dwelling at length on my disorder. It followed the standard script of depression: a general lack of vitality, times when I found it almost impossible to get out of bed in the morning or to draw breath into my lungs, the fight with tooth and claw against an awful sadness lurking at the edge of my awareness and ready to attack me at any time with minimal warning, the kind of warning—a sudden urgent speeding of water around the calves— that a child playing in the surf may receive at the approach of a monster wave. I fought my monster waves of despair with the antidepressant drugs prescribed by my therapist—none effective for long—and with the tools of cognitive therapy: trying to avoid "negative ideation" (in my specialty's jargon), trying to concentrate on my patients, taking an interest in furnishing my office, hiring a more competent receptionist when my first one kept losing messages, having sex with my competent—and married—receptionist on the non-therapeutic, modern-Danish couch in my office. (She was not my first partner in sex as an adult—I had had a brief fling with a secretary at the hospital where I interned.) Every one of these strategies temporarily separated me from my dismal state, but it was an embattled life I led, and in addition to being attacked by sadness, I fought the other horsemen of depression: irritation, anger, fits of rage at trivial annoyances blown up out of all proportion. When I lost the fight once too often, my competent, willing receptionist quit her job, calling me "a moody bastard" and, in an uncalled-for and unjust display of spite, "a lousy lay."

But the most cruel turn was that on one supremely dismal day I suddenly began to think of Jennifer again, and that thinking of Jennifer was like opening a secret door, overgrown with flowering branches and hidden from view, to a place and state that had remained inviolate and sacred. It was as if I had always known about this door and what waited for me behind it but had been kept distracted by things of no consequence. And now the hold of mundane concerns had been broken by wretchedness and I turned my attention toward what mattered. I've said that I can no longer see Jennifer's face in my mind's eye, and that is true. But on the day when despair made me push aside bloom and leaf and open that secret door, she returned to me, and for a spell I could see her face, and could see all of her, as clearly as if she had stood where all I needed to do was stretch out my hand and touch her. With her image came a sea smell and a sea swell, and sun and moon and stars.

In actuality, what happened was that once Jennifer returned to my consciousness I woke up many mornings with her before my inner eye and with the serene knowledge that I was with my heart's desire. I'd see her looking at me with a conspirator's smile or a pensive frown, or I'd see her glimmering palely in the moon's shadow. And with those images would come perfect happiness, a feeling so pure and clear and true that it seemed like a part of me that could never be dislodged, an infinite bliss that was mine forever. Then I'd wake up more fully and misery would claim me like a black tide.

Leafing back through last week's autobiographical outpourings, I notice that I've managed to compress seventeen years of my life into about as many double-spaced pages of typescript. The next six years ought to make for an even terser summary since the only noteworthy thing that happened to me between 1982 and 1988 was marriage—not as surprising a development as it may seem at first glance since perennially depressed and horribly yearning not to be, I was alert to the minutest fluttering in me that carried any hope of improvement. When I encountered in my third receptionist a pleasant face, an engaging vivaciousness and attentiveness to me (she'd notice when I was "in the dumps" and she'd express sympathy and concern), those qualities and small acts of kindness fused with my desperate wish not to be unhappy and I was finally able to deceive myself.

One evening, when I was through with my last patient of the day and almost paralyzed at the prospect of going home and fighting my depression alone, Shirley, standing in my office, said, "You feel down, don't you?" I looked at her and noticed the hollow of her throat in the soft light of my desk lamp. I felt the stirring of a wish I couldn't have put into words—although it was probably the simple wish not to be unhappy—and I said without thinking, "Will you have dinner with me?"

She said, "I thought you'd never ask," and suddenly a pall lifted off me and I felt I could breathe and move about in a world that was not entirely awful.

Over dinner Shirley told me that her predecessor had confided in her about sex with me and told me also that she didn't want our relationship to become sexual. I laughed, disarmed and pleased by her candor, and said I respected her wish but she'd have to allow me to fall in love with her.

Our relationship did, of course, become sexual not too many weeks later. I was in love, I was happy. Being happy and in love, I was charming and irresistible to Shirley, who admitted to having been attracted to me from the start. By my standards our encounters between my bachelor sheets were tame since my partner felt uncomfortable with sex that departed in the minutest way from strict orthodoxy, but I really didn't mind since I really thought I was in love with her.

We were married a few months later and divorced almost to the day three years after the wedding (one child, a son I haven't seen in seven years). That the marriage didn't work was neither her nor my fault. In love I was a different man, the man Shirley fell in love with—and she thought that, with her around for me to be in love with, I would stay that man. But, although nursed by me like a glimmering twig held in cupped hands, fed dry grass, blown on to keep it alive, my in-love feeling died and when it died, back came depression, anger, foul moods, thoughts of Jennifer—all of which I took out on—who else?—the woman who failed to make me happy.

I did make a few pathetic attempts to return to her the power to please me. (It is one of the great sad truths of human relationships that an unloved woman can exert any amount of effort to delight us—bathe in milk and honey, cling with rapt attention to our every word, offer herself for any erotic experience we may fancy—without awaking more than an indifferent sexual interest, whereas one we love can work a toothpick in her mouth with an ill-mannered scowl and there is a special charm in the act.) We went on a two-week vacation in idyllic southern France, strolled down country lanes arm in arm and enacted in a variety of other trite ways our second honeymoon. But my good mood was forced, and although Shirley was not, as I had discovered, the most sensitive woman ever married to a suffering man, even she recognized the enormity of the effort I was making to be pleasant, and grew irritable. (How had I discovered that Shirley was not the most sensitive woman ever married to etc.? When I had told her about Jennifer, hoping she'd understand, she had outright refused to believe that I could still be having feelings for someone I had known for less than a week almost a quarter of a century ago, and she had all but accused me of having an affair.)

An even more ill-starred romantic enterprise was my attempt to rekindle some feeling for her by getting us to engage in somewhat less orthodox sex. My argument was that a more imaginative eroticism would help me get to know her better or help me see her in a new light. After a single "go" at oral sex, she bluntly told me that she found the practice and all my other suggestions disgusting—not exactly the thing to convince me that she was willing to walk the extra mile to hold on to me or our marriage.

We were divorced in the spring of 1985. ("In the spring of the year, / I walked the road beside my dear.")

Interestingly, although the marriage had not worked almost from the beginning, the divorce strongly affected me, which perhaps explains what I did on the day it became final. I should preface my account with the statement that I had never, in all my years of ferocious depression, contemplated suicide. It was as if having once swum close to the black maw of oblivion, I could no longer turn in that direction. But during the divorce proceedings I did begin to have dispassionate thoughts about ending my life, and on the day the divorce became final, I drove to a gun shop on the peninsula, bought a .38 Special revolver with a four-inch barrel, and, after the required waiting period of a week, smuggled it and a box of ammunition back into the city (where gun control was unsuccessfully trying to keep the citizenry from murder and mayhem). As will be seen, this purchase was to have, to belabor the phrase, "far-reaching consequences."

My visit to that homicidal toy store, incidentally, was a moderately amusing adventure. The owner—beer belly suspended over a massive American Bald Eagle belt buckle—bad-mouthed the San Francisco ordinance ("The biggest buncha bullshit!"), but was despite his bluster unsure of what to make of his egghead customer. I gingerly inspected the revolvers he placed before me and asked which of them were the kinds used by policemen (reasoning astutely that anything "packed" by a cop was bound to be lethal). He lectured me on the increasing popularity—because they could be reloaded faster—of semiautomatics in law enforcement, and he produced a weapon straight out of a spy thriller and demonstrated how to change the magazine. Since reloading was not one of my concerns, I settled for the more straightforward revolver after having been assured that a hollow-point .38 Special bullet in the "breadbasket" would "do the job on any creep." I assumed that it would have the same effect applied to the cranium of a particular creep and was satisfied.

I stress that I had no intention of using the weapon and thought of it as the equivalent of a suicide pill to be taken only when torture was imminent. Nevertheless, I didn't tell my therapist about the loaded instrument of death concealed in my sock drawer, knowing that he, young and well-meaning, wouldn't trust my rational motives and would want to have me committed for observation. It stayed loaded and unused in my drawer, but sometimes, when I was in torment, I would think of it in loving terms as sweet peace waiting for its rendezvous with me. Whether in the end I would have found that peace and expired with my lips pursed about the barrel and my finger caressing the trigger—and a slug of lead lodged in the ceiling with bits of my brain—if I hadn't discovered another use for my lethal friend, is anybody's guess.

Another postscript is in order before I move on to the happiest time of my life and, shortly thereafter (*shortly* being the operative word—we are talking about *my* life), the most wretched. I have charitably said that my mental condition may have begun before Jennifer, but even if my depression was with me at the first breath I drew, and even if fighting it was my appointed destiny, Jennifer did something unpardonable. She showed me that I could be happy and then cast me into a pit of despair when she deprived me of the source of my happiness. It is one thing to recognize melancholia as your lot in life and another to be shown that there is no earthly reason why sorrow should gnaw at you all your days when all it takes is someone's presence for your pain to be soothed and gladness to be yours. I blame her, ashes though she is and beyond mortal reproach, for being the unfulfilled promise, the squelched hope without which I might have led my not very happy life not utterly unhappily.

After the spike of relief provided by my illusion of having found love, my state of mind returned to fluctuations about its baseline of misery: some days bearable on top of cold, dry hills, others vile torment in chasms filled with clammy fog. Nevertheless, the years after the divorce found me surviving, doing my daily little of good, planning therapeutic strategies, charting my patients' progress (or regress). Predictably, my chosen method was cognitive therapy, the approach custom-tailored for the therapist with an imperious personality, with its underlying aim to get others to stop thinking "maladaptive" thoughts and come to their senses through "positive ideation." As a therapist I was, of course, more subtle than when I, say, had told Caroline to stop falling in love with assholes. I was also more conscientious, aware that it was within my power to harm my patients, and concerned not to. I thought of cognitive therapy as relatively innocuous in its goal to change self-defeating and destructive patterns of thought.

For the benefit of anyone unfamiliar with the method, I give as an example "Patient Foe," one of my success stories, trite and unexciting but true. Foe had been afraid of girls and women ever since adolescence, paralyzingly shy in their presence, fearful of any social situation in which he might be approached by anyone female. This was, he claimed, simply the way he was, and he had no control over his response. I began treatment by asking him to examine what he thought immediately upon seeing a woman. He claimed he thought nothing; he felt awkward and tongue-tied, that was all. It took many sessions of gentle prodding before he reported that he did have definite thoughts he hadn't been aware of. The moment he was confronted by the possibility of having to talk to a woman, he would think: She'll think I'm a jerk; she'll hate me. Once he understood that these reflex or "automatic" thoughts were dictating his feelings, he was in a better position to actively counter them. When last heard from, Foe was going out twice a week with a pleasant, unassuming woman who had probably noticed that he was an agreeable enough fellow when he wasn't being hounded by feelings of inadequacy.

To anyone who scorns cognitive therapy on the grounds that it treats the symptoms, not the disease, I say that in the milder neuroses the symptoms may be the major part of a patient's problem and far more amenable to treatment than the causes. The cause of Foe's condition may well have been repressed anger at a dysfunctional mother, but his problem was that he could not talk to women. There is, at any rate, no clinical evidence backing the claim of detractors that if one symptom is eliminated another will presto appear elsewhere. (The Saturday-Morning-Cartoon school of criticism: Daffy Duck pushing one object out of sight only for another one to pop up elsewhere.) Still, I *was* concerned with the root causes of disorders as well and followed Jung in paying close attention to the symbolic content of my patients' minds and Freud in not ruling out childhood experiences and sexuality as powerful influences on the psyche.

On the physician-heal-thyself-front, I tried to use the common-sense nostrums of my trade on my depressed self and believed that they were doing me some good. It took the appearance of "Model Two" to show me what a naive fool I had been in believing that common sense was any kind of weapon to fight the fire-breathing monster Obsession: a tin sword brandished against the fierce blaze licking my face and searing my soul.

Until I was confronted by that compelling evidence, I indulged in the luxury of believing in the efficacy of cognitive therapy and was convinced that I was a decent (in both meanings of the word) therapist. In terms of documentable success, I had, by the middle of 1988, lost no one to suicide; I had not, as far as I knew, made anyone worse; I had not had sex with any of my patients despite some egregious and tempting overtures coming out of transference. It was a decent therapist who in early fall of 1988 ("In the fall of the year,/I walked the road beside my dear") accepted a new patient—Michelle Passatour, age 27, married, no children—and thereby sealed his own demented doom.

On the phone my new patient sounded businesslike, asking for an appointment without any of the usual signs of nervousness and unease emitted by people seeking help for mental problems rather than for a socially acceptable ailment like a pus-swollen appendix or gangrened toe. We agreed on a day and time and I wrote her name into my appointment book. That my hand didn't tremble when I formed the curlicued "...elle" ending her first name and rhyming, as the Beatles had discovered years earlier, with "belle," or my pen vomit a black splotch of ink on her married name, can in theory be construed as evidence that there is no such thing as clairvoyance. Surely even the feeblest mechanism of premonition should have sent back from the future a hint about the arrival in my life of someone who was to have as momentous an effect on me as Michelle Passatour, the true love of my adult life.

I did not fall in love with Michelle when I opened the door to my office and laid eyes on her in the waiting room, looking smart in blouse, jacket and skirt, her fair hair pulled back from a face wearing a minimum of makeup. I greeted her, returned a polite smile, shook a cool hand, led her into my office and indicated the two chairs she could choose from. She picked the one closer to my desk. "Something about a buffer zone, isn't it?" she asked. "You want the patient to feel comfortable with the distance."

I said yes, wondering whether I'd have to contend with the remembered lore of Psych 101. We both settled down, she with legs unstudiedly but elegantly crossed, I with a note pad on my lap. (I did not play the authority figure by interposing my desk between me and my patients; it faced the window and my chair was swiveled toward whatever chair the patient chose to sit in.) I asked her to tell me about herself.

"Do you want me to tell you why I'm here or about me in general?" she asked.

"Whatever you're more comfortable with."

She thought for a moment, then said that I'd never understand why she had come to see me unless she told me "the whole story." In the account that followed, she leapfrogged back and forth as bits of information from the nearer or more remote past were needed for me to make sense of what she was telling me. I listened, taking notes and occasionally asking a question. To myself, I observed that she was a beautiful woman and that six years earlier, the point at which her tale proper began, she had to have been as pretty as Marvelle's coy mistress "while the youthful hue sat on her skin like morning dew."

Her account during that first meeting was perforce a summary of highlights, and it took many additional sessions for the wealth of details to accumulate from which I could form a comprehensive picture. I'll present below material I gathered in the course of many weekly sessions rather than duplicating the slow accretion of information, much of it elicited by my questions, from which the story emerged. In everything I report, the limitations of my memory obviously compound the limitations of hers, multiplying the likelihood of inaccuracy. But since what I remember is more important here than what actually transpired in my patient's life, there is no meaningful loss.

She was the younger of two children. Her father was a civil engineer, her mother a librarian. She remembered her childhood as having been happy, its most traumatic event occurring when, at six, she saw her brother run through a plate-glass door and bleed from cuts requiring hundreds of stitches. She had gone to Stanford and had majored in drama, specializing in acting. At Stanford, she had had two physical relationships by the time of her senior year.

In her senior year she fell in love with a visiting professor from England, who directed her in *Mourning Becomes Electra*. Dennis was married but distantly so, since his wife was in England, and unhappily so, as he told Michelle at the same time he told her he loved her—moments before having sex with her. They had seen a lot of each other for several months until the unhappily married wife had paid her husband a surprise visit—whereupon Michelle had become persona non grata at his apartment.

They did continue their relationship via clandestine trysts in his office on campus while he was "sorting things out" with his wife, whom, he told Michelle, he intended to divorce. After several weeks of sex on the floor of his office, linoleum covered by a threadbare carpet, a wastepaper basket in her line of sight while they were "making love," she overheard two of the department secretaries discuss his and his wife's travel itinerary after the spring quarter ended: a week in Vancouver, then several weeks in New York on their way back to England.

Hurt and furious, she confronted him with the truth. He seemed bored by her revelation, said, yes, he and Bess had decided to give it another try and he had hoped she'd be grown-up about it. She was not grown-up about it, cried, accused him of lying to her, of having used her, of never having loved her at all. He said he wished she could bring one tenth of the emotional engagement she was exhibiting now to her acting. He also said she should look at what had happened between them as an experience to be drawn upon in the future and that he was glad to have helped her mature as an artist and person.

After that argument she went to the cafeteria and in a daze bought a cup of coffee and sat in the remotest booth crying large tears that bathed her face with a hot, salty wash—until someone stopped at her table and waited for her to look up: a bearded, bespectacled stranger holding a briefcase in one hand, a cup of coffee in the other.

"Can it possibly be that bad?" he asked.

A new flood of tears welled up and blurred his image. She began to sob uncontrollably. He sat down opposite her without asking her permission and said, "O.K., it *is* that bad." He opened his briefcase, extracted from it a packet of tissues, pulled out several and handed them to her. She took them and blew her nose and kept crying while he said nothing but sat patiently, every now and then taking a sip from his cup. Eventually her convulsions subsided, and he said, "Do you want to talk about it?"

She said, "I can't," but when he continued looking at her gravely and attentively, she began to talk, and out came the entire tale of love and betrayal.

"And now you can't imagine that you'll ever recover," he said when she had finished. "Your insides feel all raw and you don't believe that it'll ever hurt any less or that there'll ever be anybody other than him."

She was amazed at how this stranger could so accurately summarize her feelings. "I'll miss him so," she said. "I can't imagine being without him."

Before she could start crying again, the stranger pulled from his briefcase a pad and wrote something on a sheet. "I'm late for a meeting," he said. "But please, if you want to talk some more come to my office any time tomorrow." He handed her the sheet. On it was his name, Max Passatour, and the name of a building and an office number and campus extension. She took it, suddenly feeling shy about having opened herself so completely to a stranger. As if he were reading her thoughts, he said, "Don't worry. I know what you're going through and I'd like to talk to you some more." Then he walked away, trim, middle-aged, no doubt a professor in his sports coat and tie. She folded the sheet, wondering where on campus the building was, and she found herself thinking the surprising thought that she was attracted to him.

The next day, she looked up the building on a map and found that it was in the medical school. She made her way there in the afternoon, located his office, large, with a view of trees and a fountain, and more opulently furnished than anything to be found in the Humanities Quad. His door was open and he was sitting behind his desk, talking to a young woman in a white coat sitting opposite him. When he saw Michelle, he said to the woman, "We'll have to cut this short. I'll talk to you next week." She left, giving Michelle an unfriendly look.

"Students," Passatour said, after he had invited her to come in and sit down. "They'll drive you crazy. Present company of course excluded."

Michelle laughed. "I'm sure I've driven my professors crazy," she said. "Do you teach at the Med school?"

"Yes, when I'm not up to my elbows in somebody's chest."

They talked and Michelle was awed to find out that her compassionate stranger was a professor of medicine and one of the hospital's chief cardiac surgeons. But Passatour didn't dwell on his accomplishments. He asked her how she was feeling today. A little better, she said; not as totally awful. He asked her about previous experiences with men, and, amazed, she found that she could tell him things she had never told anyone, without feeling shy or embarrassed or apologetic. First she thought this had to do with his being a doctor and therefore someone she felt she could confide in, but she soon understood that the way he behaved toward her was what invited her to unburden herself. He listened, asked thoughtful questions, made remarks that were sad and funny at the same time. Then he told her about his recent divorce, his marriage of twenty years, his seventeen-year-old son. He had fallen in love with the thirty-year-old wife of one of his patients some five years earlier; she had requited the feeling; he had wanted to marry her but she had refused to leave her husband. They'd had an affair; her husband had found out and had called Passatour's wife, which had been the coup de grace to a marriage that hadn't worked in a long time.

"I loved her very deeply," he said, smiling wistfully. "And then this wonderful thing that happened to me turned so godawfully ugly and painful and bitter." It was like something out there couldn't stand the thought of his being happy, he continued. He hadn't been happy in a long time, and then he'd found her. But she hadn't been able to let go of her joke of a husband—he sold industrial vacuum cleaners—even though she loved Passatour. He hadn't talked to her or seen her in two years.

They talked until Passatour had to leave for a dinner engagement. "Will I see you again?" he asked her on their way out the building.

"I'd like to if you have the time," she answered.

"In my business you have no time unless you make it," he said. "How about lunch tomorrow? Meet me at my office at noon?"

She agreed.

In the weeks that followed, she and Max had lunch and talked, met in his office and talked, had dinner and talked—about her childhood, her thoughts about herself and life; about his childhood with a doting mother and remote, alcoholic father, his marriage, his son, his failed romance. Max was intelligent, funny, worldly, charming, and he continued to exhibit an intensity of interest in her that was enormously flattering. It was as if a dazzling searchlight containing all of his energy, vitality and brilliance were trained on her. She glowed in that light and discovered herself witty, charming, clever and delightful in its radiance.

They developed a routine whereby she'd meet him at his office, they'd have dinner at a restaurant, and after dinner he'd drop her at the apartment she was sharing with other students. Before she got out of the car, he'd lean over and kiss her on the cheek. She'd kiss his bearded cheek and they'd say good night.

Then came the night when he invited her to see his place and she accepted. It was a stupendous house in old-money Atherton, his parents' home before the death of his father, with quoins, alcoves, fireplaces and French doors giving on a backyard where the jasmine was fragrantly in bloom.

She thought that this would be the night they would make love. They had talked about sex in quite specific terms—what they liked, what they had and hadn't tried in bed—but without having referred to the possibility that they might get sexually involved. Michelle was of course deeply in love with him by that time, thought about him constantly, felt for his unhappiness, couldn't see why his wife hadn't been more understanding when he had fallen in love with that idiot (Barbara by name but always referred to as "Barb" by him, as if he meant to stress both attachment and irritation) who had stayed with her husband when Max had been in love with her and had wanted her to marry him. Michelle was in love with Max, and Michelle dared to hope that he had similar feelings for her since they did spend a great deal of time in one another's company and since he was attentive, charming, etc. toward her and made her feel wonderful.

Passatour showed her the house, including the master bedroom, where with a small smile he admitted feeling lost in his king-sized bed. Then he fixed drinks for them, and they sat in the living room and talked. When they had finished their drinks, he said he would drive her home.

"Don't you want me to stay?" she asked.

He took her hands in his, pulled her to her feet, embraced and kissed her, and said, "I'd like nothing better, but I have surgery in the morning. When next you come here, we'll make love all night long."

A few nights later, they made love, and even though it was not all night long, it was wonderful. Max undressed her, kissed her throat, breasts, abdomen, and was more patient and persistent at sex than any of her former lovers.

When they lay next to each other after sex, he said, "*Post coitum, omne animal triste est.* But not me tonight." He translated the Latin for her and she said, "Not me either; I'll never be sad again." He laughed, rose on his elbow to kiss her and said, "An unlikely but sweet thought."

A little later he told her he was in love with her, and she was finally able to confess to him that she had been deeply in love with him from the moment she had first seen him, and thought of nothing but him day and night. Awash in gladness, she told him how much he had meant to her all these weeks, how much she admired him; that from the start she had replayed in her head what he'd said and how he'd looked when he'd said it; that she was forever having imaginary conversations with him and planning what she'd say to him when next they would meet; that she always kept track of the number of hours it would be before she would see him again; that her first thought on waking up in the morning was how happy she'd be all day long because of him.

He pulled her close to him and said she made him happy and he was so glad to have found someone other than Barb who could do that.

They were married six months later. On the day of their wedding, which was attended by Passatour's many friends at the medical school and by her family, he was forty-seven and she twenty-two. The age difference did not bother her in the least, even though her father was two years younger than Passatour.

The first sign that she would not live happily ever after as the wife of Dr. Passatour, was subtle. About a month after the wedding, she paid her husband a surprise visit in his office. He was with the same white-coated student he had been talking to at her first visit. This time, he acknowledged Michelle with a frown, and asked her to come back in fifteen minutes: he was in the middle of something. She said she'd get a cup of coffee and withdrew. But rather than going to the cafeteria to kill time, she decided to wait in the corridor. Without any intention of eavesdropping, she overheard Passatour talk to the student about problems the student was having with her boyfriend. Passatour's comments showed thorough familiarity with the woman's difficulties, and professor and student related to each other like old friends.

When the woman left a little later, Michelle pretended she was just returning from somewhere. The student, dark and pretty, cast a triumphant smile at her and breezed by.

"Sorry about that," said Passatour and got up to kiss her. "I've been playing adviser all morning."

Even as the question left her lips, Michelle knew that she was biting into the fruit of knowledge and might find the seeds hard to swallow. "What's her problem?" she asked.

"Lucinda's? Oh, the usual. Falling behind in her course work, wanting to take an incomplete."

"How long have you been her adviser?" Michelle hated herself, but there was always the chance that what she would hear would miraculously show all worry to be unfounded.

"I don't know, maybe a year; seems like forever."

No more was said about Lucinda.

A subtle sign, but one that, as further evidence began to dribble in, was recorded by her as the first proof of two essential truths: 1) that in the life of Max Passatour, she was not at all times the most important thing, and 2) that Max Passatour was an accomplished liar.

I said that I did not fall in love with Michelle Passatour on the day of our introductory session. But when I apply a subtle probe to my remembered feelings on that first day, the needle does not sit stock-still at zero but trembles, an indication that even this early on my response to her was not unemotional. What I most clearly remember is the jubilant thought that I would be able to help her with a condition I diagnosed (from more evidence than I've so far provided) as what currently goes by the name of "narcissistic personality disorder" but has been hounding mankind since the first caveman developed a brain large enough to nurture the concept of feelings hurt by the indifference of others. That I was jubilant should have alarmed me but didn't, since I was able to attribute my exuberance to an unusually good mood and an unusual gladness to be by vocation a healer of the unhappy. Michelle was unhappy and I was in a position to help her. After I had told her about the pattern of sessions I proposed and she had left, I was in high spirits, organized my notes, read a chapter in Kohut's *The Analysis of the Self.*

During the next several days I found my mind drifting in the direction of my newest patient whenever it wasn't otherwise occupied. I looked forward to seeing her again, and on the day of our next scheduled session I came to work with more energy than usual, joked with my receptionist and felt that I was after all leading a fine life and practicing a fine profession.

Then my new patient did not show up on time—was five minutes late, was ten minutes late. I called her house and got an answering machine, a man's gravelly voice reciting the number I had reached and asking me to leave a message. Michelle walked in as I was hanging up annoyed. I told her, "I just refused your husband's request to leave a message."

She apologized for being late with a shy smile, and I forgave her in an instant.

That I was annoyed at her tardiness, as if she were late for a date with me, rather than considering it as a possible example of Freud's psychopathology of everyday life (the subconscious need to assert control over the threatening therapeutic situation, or the subconscious reluctance to reveal herself, or…) suggests that I had already lost my professional objectivity with respect to her—as does the fact that, again, I felt alive and glad throughout our session, and was moved when on several occasions she fought back tears when talking of Passatour—with whom she was still so much in love even though there were times when she felt he didn't love her at all and times when she saw him as the most self-centered, manipulative, false, self-indulgent individual she had known in her life.

One interesting thing was that psychotherapy had been Passatour's idea, not hers. She did not believe in any psychological theory and did not believe someone else could tell her things about herself that she didn't already know. And according to her view of mental states, whatever bothered her simply bothered her and talking about it to a stranger with a degree on the wall wouldn't make it go away. Passatour, however, had told her that he would no longer put up with her insecurities with respect to him and other women, and that she had better do something about her problem before she ruined their marriage. Hence, there she was, trying to explain to a stranger with a degree on the wall how her insecurities were turning the man she loved into a monster before her eyes, how afraid she was of losing him, and how she knew she'd have to learn to deal with the way he related to other women.

Regarding the latter, she had found out over the years that listened-to, advised, lied-about, triumphant Lucinda was a minor player in the battle for Passatour's affection. There were other female medical students, interns and residents who saw more of Passatour than

Lucinda did; for a year there was even a teenager majoring in biology who was doing a special studies project and fell in tearful love with the professor, who, since she was a long-legged, peach-skinned beauty, stooped to wipe away her tears. As far as Michelle knew, none of these attachments led to sex, but they were important to him—more important than she, she felt, once Passatour had determined that she was firmly under his spell and could be taken for granted. He lapped up their admiration and affection "like a dog let loose near a toilet bowl" in Michelle's scornful terms, and they had higher priority in his life than she did: "He wouldn't talk to me on the phone when he was with one of them; he'd just tell me he was busy. Or I'd want to have lunch with him and he'd claim he didn't have time because he had to get ready for surgery—except, a little later he'd forget the lie and let it slip that he spent an hour talking to some new intern about the abortion she had when she was sixteen, or some other personal thing."

When Michelle challenged him, not about lying to her but about spending time with these strangers (when he was forever too busy to come home in time for dinner), he became angry and said he felt good about being able to help people who had problems and he was disappointed that she didn't appreciate being married to someone who cared about others and felt empathy for them—hadn't they met precisely because he had been willing to talk to her when she'd had problems? What if on that day he'd been too busy for her? Since Passatour's normally forceful personality became overpowering when he was angry, Michelle apologized for her accusation and promised to be more understanding in the future—which, in practice, meant until their next argument about this topic.

I asked her whether as far as she knew all of Passatour's "groupies" (her expression) got along. No, she said. Max complained that he had to be forever careful not to appear to be favoring one over the other. If he wasn't careful, someone like Lucinda (whose personal problems he had told her about when admitting that he was something of a Father Confessor to his students) would suddenly play remote because she felt ignored, and he'd have to take her out to lunch to smooth the waters again. Without going into clinical details she wasn't ready for, I told her about what I called the "Palace Intrigue Syndrome": People with certain psychological problems could be enormously charming when they chose to be, and they used their charm to pull in admirers. But since they devoted most of their time and effort to whoever currently best satisfied their ego needs, jealousies were rampant among the courtiers.

Michelle's face lit up with the glow of a sudden insight: That explained why she always had the feeling that Max basked in his groupies' jealousies even when he complained about them. He was in fact saying: "Look how much they admire me and care about me and want me, and how important I am for them," wasn't he?

Precisely, I said.

As it turned out, the main problem of the marriage was not the waifs and orphans Passatour lured to his lair by promising them succor. In the third year of their marriage, Barb, his lost love, reappeared on the scene, still in love with him but asking for a purely platonic relationship—just to see him and talk to him as a friend. And he, although full of unabated fury at her rejection and forever complaining to Michelle about the basket case, and disaster area, and selfish and manipulative bitch she was, felt the need to see her and spend time with her—to get her out of his system once and for all by understanding the effect she had on him, as he told Michelle. He added that when the human heart got itself entangled in snares, no one was to blame, and that he didn't believe in lying about his feelings—which she translated to mean that he was still in love with Barb and (a) accepted no responsibility for his feelings or for any actions prompted by them and (b) needed someone to talk to about Barb, she being the most convenient someone, bizarre though it soon struck her to be cast in the role of the sympathetic soul listening to her husband incessantly holding forth about another woman.

When after a few weeks of Barb she got tired of being unfalteringly that sympathetic soul, Passatour resented the signs she showed of being hurt, upset and worried about his renewed contact with a woman with whom he had had an affair. They suggested to him, he told her, that she didn't trust him and didn't understand that he needed to come to terms with his feelings toward Barb. He was disappointed in her, he said, and he accused her of having no empathy for him, and contrasted her lack of understanding with his own compassion for her in the matter of Dennis the director.

The upshot was that Michelle, having been made to feel guilty about not being more understanding, agreed that it was all right for Passatour to meet Barb once a week to do whatever he needed to do to recover from her. She also continued being the recipient of Passatour's endless stories about Barb (her childhood, troubled adolescence, unhappy marriage, general unhappiness), of his Barb-induced highs when things went well between the two of them, his black moods and ranting when Barb acted like a bitch by not showing up when they were supposed to meet or contemplated another vanishing act from his life. But Max also exhibited thoughtfulness and concern: he told Michelle that he needed her (Michelle), that he knew he could always rely on her (which he never could with Barb), that she didn't lie to him (unlike Barb), that her actions showed she loved him (unlike Barb's despite all her vows of love). Michelle sought to draw comfort from these comparisons and kept to herself, except in overwrought moments, the thought that although Barb might be a bitch, she was a spectacularly talked-about and thought-about bitch (unlike Michelle).

From the point of view of therapy, it was soon obvious to me that there was more than a fragment of truth to Passatour's accusation of his wife's insecurity. Michelle did feel threatened by his contact with other women and was very ready to feel ignored and cheated out of what she considered hers. Although she made much of Passatour's involvement with students and others at the medical school, she also nursed a hidden resentment of his patients, especially the women who sat up straight, breasts thrust out, under the doctor's cold stethoscope, and who allowed his knowing hands inside the gaping red cave of their chests.

During one session she told me of a daydream she used to have, one far more revealing than she could have imagined: She had developed a heart condition requiring surgery—and there she was in the operating room anesthetized and unconscious, and bent over her was Max in his surgical gown and mask; Max delicately and with the highest concentration making incisions in her heart; Max using the professional skills acquired in a lifetime to try to save her—fighting back the terrible fear that he might lose her forever. (I had to hide a smile at the squeamish and self-important scene she conjured up for herself under his knife; my own imaginative, unsanitized version had Max up to his wrists in her blood between her spread ribs in what the uninitiated observer would construe to be an act of butchery—his mind certainly on the diseased organ before him but with no tearful emotional link to its owner.)

Self-serving daydreams of being the star surgeon's most important case aside, Michelle resented the time swallowed up by Passatour's career—the late hours, the emergency calls taking him to the hospital at two in the morning. But since she knew that complaints about his professional life were unacceptable, she rarely allowed her resentment to surface even in talking to me; her official feelings were respect and admiration for his devotion to his patients.

But her problems were of course not limited to Max exclusively: she also demanded attention and devotion from anyone else she was even minutely interested in and begrudged attention and devotion being given to others. As I gradually discovered, her pathological insecurity had some of its roots in a mother who had paid little attention to her because she had been wrapped up in her own impossible dream of writing a history of the Romanoffs with no training in historical scholarship, no access to the major documents and an "Ivan goes to the station to meet Tasha" command of Russian. I say "some of its roots" because I think it absurd and simpleminded to assign a single cause to any psychological disorder. If Michelle craved attention, dedication, constant concern, total involvement with her, it was not merely in a hopeless quest to be compensated for the blows she had been dealt as an ignored child but for less readily identifiable reasons as well, reasons that appeared in my picture-making mind as a succession of rooms from each of which she emerged subtly changed by things done to her. I imagined them to be dark rooms—all but the most recent one, the one that had done the most harm. That room had been a blaze of lights because for a few glorious months, Passatour had dazzled her by giving her all she craved, for reasons he himself no doubt didn't understand but that had to do with the need to perceive himself as someone who excelled in empathy and compassion, as well as with the aim to secure a rapt listener for all those times when he wanted to talk about himself—the one topic for which he had unlimited patience and enthusiasm. That the adoring slave he was grooming for the job was an extraordinarily beautiful girl could not have been a detriment in the world of someone for whom self-esteem was an elusive thing forever sought in the good opinion of others and weighted by their attractiveness, intelligence, social position, or other valued attribute.

I have leaped ahead in my account, and I ought to point out quickly that from the facts Michelle presented to me about Passatour, it was soon obvious to me that her own narcissism could not hold a candle to his. I recognized it as irony on a grand scale—and wished I could share the joke with Michelle—that Passatour, in worse shape than his wife, insisted on therapy for her. There he was, self-possessed, pathologically insecure, locked in his own cage of dependency on the admiration, respect, interest, love, devotion of others—ordering *her* to change or else…. I appreciated the humor, but I also had to bow to the logic of the situation: if Passatour saw no need for change on his part, and if Michelle could not fall out of love with him and wanted to stay with him without being hopelessly unhappy, what choice was there other than her getting rid of her insecurities, which (back to square one) was a formidable task since her own narcissism was by no means minor.

My insight into the peculiarities of that marriage prompted me after one session to draw a cartoon and title it, "When Narcissists Collide": A man and a woman are standing face to face, both talking at the same time. The bubbles emanating from both of their mouths read: "I, I, I, I." I submitted it to one of the pop psych magazines and was pleased to see it reproduced on glossy paper beneath an article on hypochondria.

Then there was the small matter of another love—that of me, poor unloved me, for Michelle. I don't know how long I was able to keep my feelings hidden from myself by attributing them to the concern of a dedicated, "caring" therapist for his patient. Not very long, I suspect, self-awareness and honesty with myself being two of my more conspicuous traits. I suspect that only one or two sessions were required before the truth began to seep into my conscious thinking, and I know that not many sessions later my heart recognized in that tormented, screwed-up woman sitting opposite me its sweetest desire and began softly, softly to call her "my love."

There she sat, my love, probing her inner self, subjecting herself to scrutiny in order to tell me the truth about her fears, anguishes, delights, complicated feelings about the man she loved. There she sat, young, easily hurt, more beautiful with each passing week, her hair loose and locked now—a new style, sweet and fetching—her eyes gently shaded by a soft gray, her lips the color of a blushing rose. There she sat, wincing at an insight coming out of something I had said, and hiding the wince with a grimace and a joke. And there sat I, inhaling her presence like a bracing, head-clearing aroma that expanded the chest and generated a sense of well-being and wiped the mental slate clean of all disagreeable thoughts, leaving nothing but gladness.

I was in love. Unfortunately my self-awareness and honesty with myself did not extend far enough to prompt me to inform Michelle at once that I could no longer be her therapist since my being in love with her compromised my professional objectivity. I did consider the problem fleetingly, but reasons for continuing as her therapist jumped into the breech with lightning speed. One was that if I told her how I felt about her and ended the therapy, she might blame herself for this development—she showed some leanings toward guilt. Another, more compelling, reason was my earnest conviction that I could help her out of a pit more dreadful than she imagined and that I could not abandon her. Even if I was bound to suffer anguish as a result of my feelings, to refuse to continue treating her would be selfish and unconscionable. My conclusion was that as long as I kept my feelings to myself and didn't allow them to interfere with the therapy, she couldn't be harmed by them.

Needless to say, what I knew about the deviousness of the mind when it wants to have things its own way should have told me at once that objectivity was out of the question when it came to "love," but such is the mind's cunning that it can selectively block off avenues leading to uncomfortable insights—even for people making a living from what they know about its workings. Whenever questions of possible biases flitted through my mind, they were promptly diverted by thoughts of how ideally suited I of all possible therapists was to treat Michelle for her emotional disorder.

And undeniably I was the most conscientious and concerned therapist Michelle could have found if she had searched throughout the U.S. and all of Austria and Switzerland. I pored over my notes—as if I needed them, every word of hers being scored in my brain the moment it left her lips—read up on affective disorders, made lists of questions I would ask her at our next meeting. The irony of being asked to help her to learn to live with her husband—I who would in an instant have taken her away from him to have her for myself—did not occur to me, possibly because, even though that was my task as she (and he) saw it, I—with every other therapist in the world—had my patient's well-being as my primary concern, and if that well-being should in her case turn out to be achievable only by her leaving her husband, then helping her leave him would have to be my aim.

As her therapist, one essential need I identified was for her to learn far more about Passatour than she knew. Since every one of our sessions was primarily devoted to talk about him, I found out a great deal about the good doctor, all of which confirmed my initial diagnosis of him as a textbook case of narcissistic disturbance (the currently fashionable term, as I've pointed out—an earlier age, viewing the condition from a moral perspective, excoriated it with the name *egotism* and felt no compunction to apologize for our instinctive aversion to it). One of my tasks, as I saw it, was gradually and gently to make Michelle understand that when she was hurt by some display of outstanding thoughtlessness on Passatour's part, she was not hurt by the willful action of a monster but by the uncontrollable symptom of a disease. That disease had one of its causes in Passatour's childhood with an alcoholic father, whose neglect had dealt him a wound from which he had not recovered and might never recover. His wound made him pathetically eager for affection and admiration, no amount of which was ever enough to satisfy an endless hunger for someone to validate his existence to him, or, in one of the celebrated metaphors of psychology, to "mirror" for him what he wanted to believe was his true being. This hunger kept him forever looking for new people in his life who might give him what he desperately needed, and his disorder made him prey to anyone whom he could, on a visceral level, believe when he or she told him he was admirable, remarkable, worthy of being loved. Fatal Barb was the one who was able to validate or mirror his "true" self to him—which was why he could not let go of her—Michelle was not.

In psychological terms, it was not a question of him caring about Barb and not caring about Michelle, but of him looking for a way to love himself and, for obscure psychological reasons, finding that way in Barb. The fact that Michelle could not do for him what Barb could was neither her fault nor something she could do anything about. To live with him without being made desperately unhappy, she would have to understand his pathology and to learn not to accept responsibility for it or be profoundly affected by it. Her emotional response, if she insisted on having an emotional response, ought to be pity for someone tormented by internal forces he neither understood nor had any control over.

Those were some of the things I would have to make Michelle understand about the man she was married to and in love with, the main insight to be derived from them being that she did not know Passatour at all. In the therapy, my difficulty was compounded by the fact that her condition was only a somewhat milder version of Passatour's. I had to be careful not to make her recognize that I saw in her the same defects she loathed in him. Fortunately people have an infinite capacity not to see their own most glaring deficiencies: although Michelle was surprisingly quick to agree with my assessment of her husband and, after I lent her a book on narcissism, came back excited and elated at how closely Max fit the description (which meant, she announced triumphantly, that she was not the only one to blame for their marital difficulties), she saw no resemblance to herself in the picture.

She was, I should add, far from an isolated case in her inability to recognize absurdly obvious parallels between her own personality and neurosis and those of someone else. While I was treating her, I had at least three other patients who had colossal blind spots of this kind, which prompted me to write a short paper drawing an analogy between behavior exhibited by patients in certain psychic states and that shown by people hypnotized to have negative hallucinations. I argued that the hypnotized subject's inability to see people or pieces of furniture in the room, while nevertheless safely navigating around them, bears a strong resemblance to a patient's repression of knowledge threatening, say, the grandiose self, coupled with an aggressive/defensive reaction indicating that the knowledge is being perceived on some level. What forces take the place of the hypnotist's compelling voice in the latter cases was "beyond the scope of my discussion."

Also beyond the scope of my discussion was my realization that it was a hilarious thing to watch someone refusing to see what any outside observer would see in an instant. To cite one particular case, I had to suppress laughter whenever patient M. exhibited conspicuous blindness to the obvious similarity between her and her monstrous husband. But seriously, folks, I didn't know whether to laugh or cry the time I mentioned Passatour's alcoholic father as one cause of his compulsive selfishness, and she blurted out, "My mother ignored me all her life, and I didn't turn into someone who thinks only about herself."

I did not answer, But of course you do; that's why you think about demented Max all the time, because he's the one who, if he graciously chooses to, has the power to make you feel wonderful about yourself—whereas I, who am a great deal more qualified to tell you that you are remarkable and terrific and worthy of being loved, don't have that power and don't exist for you except as someone to talk to about bloody Max.

🔲🔲 While the subject is selective thinking, I ought to mention at long last someone whose existence I knew nothing of until six months into Michelle's therapy. A distracted reference to something "George" had said about Max made me ask, "George who?" George, she told me, still distracted, was Max's oldest friend. When I asked her to elaborate, she explained that George and Max had known each other since college. George was an English professor at San Jose State University. He had since her marriage to Passatour become her friend as well—with a minor complication: he had fallen in love with her.

I managed to limit my reaction to a polite raising of eyebrows and noncommittal, "Oh?"

She elaborated that George had, some three or four years earlier, confessed his feelings to her. He had at that time also told her that he knew how deeply in love she was with Passatour and that he expected nothing from her and only wanted to remain her friend. He came over frequently even when Max was at the hospital or out of town, and she liked talking to him and confided in him about her difficulties with Max, her new therapeutic insights regarding Max, etc.

I said, "I see." Then I pointed out that George seemed to be of some importance in her life and asked her why she hadn't told me about him earlier. She frowned and said she guessed she simply hadn't thought of him.

Poor George, I mused. In love and simply not being thought of by the woman he was in love with. I asked Michelle whether she didn't think Max would mind her spending time with George if he ever found out that George had been in love with her all this time.

"Why should he mind? I'm not in love with George. Plus, I'm not supposed to mind when he's with Barb even though he's in love with her."

The impeccable logic of jealous hearts, I thought. But still, poor George.

George, I found out after a bit more prodding, was not only a frequent visitor but would occasionally spend the night at the Passatours' place—sometimes when Max was out of town. I thought of what it would be like to be in the same dark house with its fair-locked lady in the small hours of the night, knowing her in her connubial bed down the hall—asleep in the quiet, when a stealthy foot might approach her across soft carpets and a lover might gaze upon her dark form under silk sheets, and dream himself under those sheets, clasping her.

"What would you do if George tried to make love to you one of those nights?" I asked.

"He'd never do that, he's too decent," answered George's love.

"But isn't this a painful situation for him?" I prodded.

"I don't see why. He gets to spend time with me. Anyway, he knows I don't feel that way about him."

I secretly cringed at this summary dismissal of a fellow sufferer's pain and vowed never to tell the unconcerned creature before me of my own pain regarding her.

With respect to the two men "in Michelle's life," the perceptive reader may surmise that with my love literally madly in love with Passatour, my jealousy had swooped down on that obvious prey and was clinging to it with beak and talons and a raptor's singlemindedness. But although Passatour was my heart's prime detestation, I also found time to resent this new (to me) arrival on the field of romance. Michelle was not in love with good buddy George, nor did he occupy more than a fraction of her interest, but when he talked with her, it was not for a measly fifty minutes, my allotted weekly span, but for hours. I deeply envied George those hours and the intimacy they implied. This despite being painfully aware of how hopeless he had to feel at hearing the woman he loved go on and on about her sole true topic, Passatour—how much gnashing of teeth and clenching of fists he had to hide from the thoughtless bitch who was making him privy to the secrets of her disastrous marriage and who was not reluctant to call him and keep him on the phone half the afternoon when she was in turmoil over some Passatourish offense. How he must have bled at hearing his silly darling agonize over his worthless friend! How he must have been hurt at the thought that she, knowing how he felt about her, was oblivious to the pain she was inflicting on him by talking about another man and by showing him she cared only for that man. Only for Max, not at all for him.

Still, understanding and empathy did not keep me from resenting George when Michelle would mention some remark he had made about Passatour or about her in relation to Passatour. I found that I had to be careful not to give vent to my spleen by declaring George's psychological observations amateurish bunk the instant they had left her lips. When she told me that he agreed with my diagnosis of Max suffering from a narcissistic personality disorder I almost said, I'm indebted for the corroborating opinion, and, by the way, did he tell you that so are you, or does he stab only his oldest friend in the back?

I was generally subtle in discrediting George and tried to persuade her gently that she was not doing herself a favor in looking for solace and enlightenment in a man whose feelings for her clearly biased every one of his utterances. (My unvoiced theory concerning George's feelings, incidentally, was that George, sensible and stolid if left to his own devices, had been infected by the Passatours' perennial moanings about love.) I should have saved my breath to cool my porridge: Michelle was not interested in enlightenment from George, she simply wanted an adoring soul who was willing to listen to her talk about Passatour, which meant in psychological point of fact talk about herself.

Regarding the latter insight, I now wonder if George would have derived comfort from the knowledge that when Michelle was talking about Passatour she was really talking about herself seen through the complicated optics of "object/self reflection." Probably not, since I, who did clinically know, felt hot prickles of vexation when Passatour was the topic (and when was he ever not the topic?). Today's lesson: Not even "mental health professionals" are immune to irrational responses.

As far as George as a potential rival in love went, I was soon convinced that Michelle didn't give a damn about him other than as someone she could whine to about her problems. My lack of concern about George as competition probably also had to do with my spontaneously assigning to him the remembered face and figure of an English professor I had in college, an almost completely bald, fattish man with a pasty complexion, who lectured on the Romantics in an agitated manner—large gestures and a vocal range from a whisper to a bellow—that irritated me because of its blatant phoniness. Interestingly, the one specific thing I remember about him was raising my hand during his lecture on Blake's *Songs of Experience* and asking, "Why do poets write about things they know nothing about?" His affronted response had to do with experience depending upon the perception of the one doing the experiencing.

George or no George, in the matter of my emotional life, pain was of course the key word by then. In the first weeks of our sessions, I had been happy at having "found" Michelle, at thinking of Michelle, looking forward to seeing her, planning strategies for her therapy. But quickly that happiness had become isolated moments of bliss brought on by her presence in the same room and by sudden flashes of the improbable hope that somehow things would work out for us. These buoyant moments were separated by oceans of sadness, turmoil, hurt at seeing her attachment to Passatour, her suffering because of him, her lack of interest in anyone but him.

After eight months of sessions, I was in a nearly constant state of pain from which I found relief only when Michelle walked through my door and I knew that for the next fifty minutes she was mine, would listen to me, would treat me as someone who was important to her even if my importance was limited to what she was able to tell me—and I was able to tell her—about Passatour. When what she told me brought her to tears, I fought with the mask of a thoughtful frown (and my toes curled in my shoes, to make up for not being allowed to ball my fists) the impulse to tell her to forget the bastard, leave him, let him rot and come live with me.

Admittedly, some of my pain was self-inflicted. After months on end of talk about Passatour, I asked Michelle to show me a photo of him. She took out her wallet (the first stab to my heart, since I had hoped she would tell me she'd bring one for our next session) and took from it a picture. I don't know what I had expected, something formidable and impressive—haughty features made dark and com-pelling by mesmerizing eyes, perhaps. Instead I saw a nondescript roundish face, somewhat ravaged, somewhat sad despite a small smile, possibly, if I stretched my imagination, somewhat sardonic because of its trim, Don-Juanesque beard. I handed the picture back to her, saying that he looked tired and she, inspecting it before she put it away, said (the second stab to my heart), "Whenever I look at it I think he's been through some vast catastrophe and I want to put my arms around him and say that everything will be all right."

I was in nearly constant pain, but there were times—for instance, when at the end of a session she smiled at me and said she was glad she had me to talk to; she'd go nuts if she didn't—at which my hap-piness returned with a surge of pure delight that turned the rest of my day lighthearted and carefree and convinced me that everything would work out in the end. And lighthearted and carefree I'd marvel at how easy it was to be made happy: a smile, a few words, so very little.

I also had opportunities galore to marvel at how easy it was to be moved in other ways. Two examples out of hundreds that tugged on me and pricked me will suffice to make the point. One day, a fine summer day, Michelle showed up for her session wearing a pair of low-heeled, beige sandals with a minimum of straps. As usual, she sat opposite me with her legs crossed. Listening to her, I allowed my eyes to rest on her unstockinged, sandaled foot. And from nowhere came a feeling of intense, breath-catching pleasure at the sight of that high arch, the dry, taut skin over fine bones and sinews. I thought I saw a silky dusting of sand on her skin and a shiver of delight ran through me.

Example Two is possibly even quainter. On another day, I was greeted by my unsandaled love in the role of a prim scholar looking at me through horn-rimmed glasses.

"You look formidably erudite this morning," was my comment as I escorted her into my office. She told me she had scratched an eye with her contact lens. She was astigmatic, she added—had been since childhood.

She settled down and started talking about the week's events, but I kept being entranced by how different, earnest and studious yet vulnerable, she looked in spectacles. Then she took off her glasses and touched the corner of an eye with a finger. Suddenly I was flooded with pity for the weak eyes of my astigmatic dear. I wanted to kiss them and take away with my lips their saline dew of grief at their imperfection. I wanted to tell her that I loved her eyes no less behind spectacles. Even if the lenses should assume the thickness of coke-bottle bottoms, I'd find the twin stars in the depths of their glassy wells.

This moment of heightened emotion is given poignancy by the facts that I myself had been nearsighted for at least ten years and had never felt an inkling of grief at the condition and that the dozen or so other patients of mine who wore glasses had elicited no compassion on my part for their impaired sight. Choice feelings reserved for the select few. Others need not apply.

Which brings to mind the issue of Passatour's choice feelings for the select one (and Michelle need not apply). As I should have predicted—but didn't, since all the evidence notwithstanding, I couldn't ultimately imagine anyone to whom Michelle belonged interested in anyone else—Max's platonic relationship with Barb reverted to its unplatonic state one balmy evening in late summer. Since he believed in honesty in relationships (not a joke; he really believed he believed), he told Michelle at the first possible moment that he had had sex with Barb, asking her to understand that he had these feelings for Barb and that there were bound to be times when he'd succumb to them. This did not mean—he stressed—that he loved *her* any less. It simply meant he couldn't help himself when it came to Barb.

I had by then (by then being about a year into the therapy) a tolerable idea of Passatour's peculiar brand of honesty, which was in operation when he insisted on other people being honest with him and when he wanted to talk ad nauseam about something no matter how disagreeable that something was for the person he told it to, but became non-functional on any number of other occasions when the truth was inconvenient or self-incriminating. Nevertheless, I was bewildered by a man confessing his own infidelity to his wife and asking her to accept its continuance as unavoidable. My bewilderment grew when Michelle, almost in tears, said she was afraid to tell him that his having sex with Barb hurt her since he had several times mentioned that he might be driven to divorce by her lack of understanding and empathy for him: it was too painful not to be understood by the woman he lived with.

I couldn't help letting out a strangled guffaw at this blatant browbeating, but I quickly checked myself. "Do you think he's at all worried that *you* might contemplate divorcing *him?*" I asked gingerly.

"No, he knows I'd never do that. I couldn't live without him."

"So you're going to let him continue having an affair with Barb as long as he wants to?"

She bit her lower lip, an unattractive habit she had recently acquired, and said Max knew she couldn't really get on her high horse with respect to sex with someone else.

It was my turn to exhibit a mental state with body language. I raised my eyebrows dramatically and discovered what Herr Doktor Freud had discovered long since: that patients do not always choose to tell the truth, the whole truth, to their naive therapist. Out came, with more lip biting and some nervous laughter and petulant head tossing, that the woman I loved had had a six-month-long affair with an architect who was also an amateur actor. The episode had occurred about four years into her marriage; she had told Max she was in love with Ron, and Passatour had been understanding.

Not wanting to put her on the defensive (as well as being close to stupefied) I did not ask why she hadn't given me this not entirely negligible information earlier. "*Were* you in love with him?" I asked instead.

"Maybe a little. He's very good-looking and charming and it was nice to be with someone for whom I was the most important thing in the world—I and not Barb or somebody else. Ron wanted me to leave Max and marry him—he really was very much in love with me."

"And did you consider leaving Max?"

"No. Not for a moment. I think half my reason for starting a relationship with Ron was my hope that Max would become more interested in me again if he saw that this handsome, successful architect wanted me."

"*Did* he become more interested?"

"I don't think so. I think all it meant to him was that now he could spend more time with whoever he wanted to spend time with, and if I complained he could always point to Ron."

Our time was up, but before she left she turned at the door and said with an unattractive mixture of brashness and feminine coyness (head tilted sideways, eye contact from the corner of her eye, a flirtatious yet rueful expression on her face), "Do you think I'm pretty horrible, now that I've told you about my 'adultery'?"

She caught me off-guard, and I mumbled something about of course having no such thought; we all had needs and desires that made us do odd things; life was complicated.

Life was complicated, but, as I realized after this unveiling of another suitor in the wings, my wishes were simple. I simply wished to make Michelle see Passatour as a hopeless case, someone guaranteed to make her unhappy the rest of her life unless she broke her emotional attachment to him and left him. I also wished for her to fall in love with me, to want me more than she wanted Passatour or Ron or George or anyone or anything else in the world, to marry me and be mine until the stars turned cold. Simple.

To accomplish my first wish, I had to make her understand on an emotional level Passatour the neurotic—the man she thought she loved and in fact didn't know at all (and, in additional fact, didn't love at all, in the sense of caring about his well-being or feeling empathy for him). I had to do this without revealing my own feelings about him. Which were? An unethical, unprofessional, heartfelt loathing. I loathed Max Passatour. Invisible, constructed almost entirely from words coming out of the mouth of the woman I loved, he was nevertheless as palpable and real in my imagination as anything had ever been. My dim recollection of his photo was fleshed out by repulsive attributes that gave his eyes a calculating gleam, his mouth a lascivious leer, his expression a phony pathos. From Michelle, I knew that he was fighting a midriff bulge with a machine that simulated cross-country skiing, and the thought of his blood-engorged penis protruding under a hump of fat, and that fat butting against my love's lean belly when he penetrated her made

155

me sick to my stomach. Not to hate him would have been a supreme spiritual achievement making me eligible for sainthood.

I did on occasion try to see him clinically, and did then recognize him as suffering from an affective disorder and being tormented by an abject craving for a figment, a rank delusion—since he no more saw Barb as who she "really" was than Michelle saw him, or, in the endless round of blind dancers, George saw Michelle. But it was always a relief to return to my honest, reflexive, visceral responses of hatred and revulsion. My excuse for indulging in hating hateful Max was that even if I had been able to forgive his odious personality, I would never have been able to forgive a man who hurt the woman I loved and who without the slightest effort held her in thrall.

To work some of the spite out of my system, I once compiled a list of Passatour's qualities. For a few days I toyed with the idea of leaving it prominently on my desk and, when Michelle was next in my office, pleading the need to run a quick errand. Might she not come to her senses if she read a professional—albeit rendered for the non-professional—grab bag of her husband's defects? To wit: small-minded, ungenerous, opportunistic, defensive, manipulative, lying, exploding with rage at any suggestion that he might be to blame for someone's hurt; a user of people, incapable of recognizing the existence—let alone the needs—of others, adroit at making others feel guilty when he feels guilty, convinced of his monumental importance, his role as the healer, his great compassion and empathy for others, incapable of loving anyone, self-deceiving, self-indulgent, self-pitying, vain, empty, poisonous.

I did not allow Michelle to run across my list, but I addressed the question of how to reveal to her Passatour's loathsome nature by now and then giving concrete meaning to topics discussed in the too-charitable book about narcissism I had loaned her. I explained, for instance, Passatour's grand illusion of caring about others as a reality he had created for himself to deal with his total lack of empathy, which on some level he recognized and was deeply disturbed by. His chosen profession as healer was his most obvious mechanism of denial, but his insistence that he felt concern for troubled interns and others came in a close second. That he prided himself on exactly what he was most deficient at—human relationships—was ironic but not uncommon in narcissistic personalities and explained why he flew into a rage whenever Michelle accused him of not caring about her: her charge threatened the sense of a generous, sensitive, compassionate self he had laboriously built and knew deep down to be wrong.

I also suggested, gently, gently, that her husband did not know her and had little sense of who she was or what things concerned her because he was so wrapped up in himself that he was unable to make the effort to get to know her. She agreed wholeheartedly with the latter insight, and I could tell that I had tapped into a rich vein of self-pity. Nevertheless, her response to my watered-down version of Passatour's lack of empathy and understanding was the usual, "Yes, but…" vacillation. I forget around what arguments.

I did not tell her (and maybe I should have, in order to shock her at least once out of her plaintive acceptance of the situation) that in one of my imaginative scenarios I walked up to Passatour, looked him in the eye and said: "Why don't you stop pretending you're interested in anybody or give a shit about anybody? Why don't you think back to that moment when you looked a little too closely at yourself and recoiled in horror at the freak you saw: blind, deaf, insensate, equipped with a midget heart and a huge mouth that recites tirelessly the litany, Listen to me, pay attention to me, be interested in me, think of me, feel for me, understand me, want me, love me!"

To accomplish my second wish (my beloved falling in love with me), I first had to make her see that Passatour was not the only man in the world—there were by a conservative estimate several thousand other possibilities. But I had to be gentle there too because the slightest hint that she might ever leave Passatour triggered a formidable battery of defenses in her. She reacted as if I were threatening her life—and from her warped perception of things, I was, since he held the key to her being happy with herself even if it was a key he rarely used. At any hint of there possibly coming a time in the distant future when she might be better off without him, she fell into a near panic, became defensive, accused me of not understanding what there was between her and Max. Then she would double back, apologize and say that she didn't blame me for not understanding because she hadn't done a good job of explaining what Max really meant to her—how he was the only man who could make her laugh, how complete she felt when Max paid attention to her, how she had never felt so happy with anyone.

And I'd double back and say, of course she got a great deal out of the relationship and it would be a mistake to give up on it just because Max occasionally drove her crazy. But those times when he drove her crazy and she was in pain and felt she was trapped in a hopeless situation, it might help her to think that there were other men and that she didn't need to be trapped.

"But there are no other men," she said. "That's what you don't understand."

"There is George, who worships you, and is there when you need him, and would never do anything to hurt you."

"George," she said, looking perfectly baffled, as if the subject I had recklessly introduced had been sea cows or lawn furniture. "George is nice," she then collected herself, "but I could never be attracted to him."

I did not ask her the eminently pertinent question whether I, too, was lawn furniture in the discriminating chambers of her heart.

Not in order to answer the question of my role in my love's life but a related one, I did something out of the ordinary a few weeks after she had told me of her affair. Michelle was a member of the Stanford Savoyards, an amateur theatrical company devoted to Gilbert and Sullivan, but until the mention of her fellow Savoyard architect/actor lover, I had paid little attention to her theatrical activities, since her acting was a pastime rather than vocation and unconnected with her condition (except as an example of the predilection of narcissistic personalities to be in the spotlight). Now, knowing that love had budded on a stage, I wanted to know more about that aspect of her life, and I clandestinely attended a performance of *Pirates of Penzance* in which she appeared, according to the program, as one of "a bevy of beauties." The question I set out to answer was that of my victorious (if physical intimacy can be said to be victory in the battle of romance) theatrical rival. Here was a man who had held, caressed, sexually possessed the naked form of the woman I loved. Maybe I would, by observing him, get a clue to what attracted her to another male. I was also (and who can blame me) curious to see how the two ex-lovers related to each other on stage.

On the evening I had chosen, I waited for the theater to be almost full before sliding into a seat in the back row, just in case one particular actress was inspecting the house through a peephole in the curtain. I didn't know what role Ron played in the production but a glance at the program showed only one actor with the first name Ronald, and the personality sketches of the cast informed me that he was an architect when he was not appearing as Major General Stanley.

It came as no surprise that Michelle would be attracted to someone playing a leading part. She herself might be merely one of several "blushing buds of ever-blooming beauty" (she was the fairest of the buds, all pink and lavender and golden hair), but it took "The very model of a Modern Major General,/With information vegetable, animal and mineral" to interest her; no humble pirate or bungling policeman need bother wooing.

I don't know what I had hoped to find in Ron, probably someone hilariously distorted by the lens of love and in reality quite ignorable. But he proved to be an arresting presence on stage, bearded, attired in scarlet and white, and black jackboots. He was short and somewhat stocky, supercilious, pompous, pathetic in pleading for his life, and yet there was something behind the strutting and trembling that kept my eyes on him even when other actors were in the foreground. He had a fine voice that rang true under the quaver he gave it for comical effect, but what kept me interested in him was that indefinable something of focus and energy that stars are reputed to have. I could see why a weak, silly goose like my love would be drawn to him.

I did pay attention to the play, and was moderately amused by its contrived dilemma of the apprentice pirate's split allegiance. Then came Mabel's and Frederick's lyrical ballad and I was suddenly in tears at hearing the sad girl singing in a voice sweet and clear

> Ah, leave me not to pine
> Alone and desolate;
> No fate seemed fair as mine.
> No happiness so great!
> And nature, day by day,
> Has sung in accents clear,
> This joyous roundelay,
> "He loves thee—he is here."

And Frederick's poignant answer

> Ah, must I leave thee here
> In endless night to dream,
> Where life is dark and dread,
> And sorrow all supreme!
> Where nature, day by day,
> Will sing, in altered tone,
> This weary roundelay,
> "He loves thee—he is gone."

Music hath charms, etc. Or was it the knowledge of being so close to my dear and yet so very far that drove me to tears? Or would any melodious lament of love have had that effect?

Regarding Michelle's performance: She was a member of the chorus and her voice blended with those of the others. But I can say without love-induced exaggeration that she was more artfully coquettish, more coy, more frightened yet flattered by her pirate would-be husband, than any of the others.

In the matter of her ex-lover, since she was one of the Major General's six or seven daughters there was little contact between them until the final scene. Then the pirates and their brides, she one of them, danced garlands around him, whereafter he danced with each daughter: a comical polka twirling the couple around and around in a swirl of color and gaiety. And did my eyes deceive me or did the Major General twirl his prettiest daughter with more vigor? Did his eye have a brighter gleam and his foot a livelier step? I wished myself up on that stage, dancing with my love, and forgot that I would have felt quite ridiculous in the Modern Major General's get-up and before an audience.

There was a reception after the show. I waited until a crowd had formed backstage and then stayed in the corridor and peered through the door. Under no circumstances did I want Michelle to see me and think her therapist was spying on her, but my heart pulled me toward the promise of just a glimpse of her, pink and golden and lovely in her lavender frock. I couldn't see her but the Modern Major General, still in uniform but sans hat and with steel-frame aviator glasses, was talking to a group of people. The beard, I saw, was real, and I wondered whether it was possible that Michelle had "a thing" about beards and would fall madly in love with me if I grew one. Then someone moved and Michelle talking to another beauty flashed into view. I quickly withdrew, too afraid a random glance would locate me in the crowd to linger and please my desirous eye.

By the time I saw her on that stage, I no longer had any illusions about my motives regarding my patient. The blunt truth I faced was that my aim was not the pious and creditable one of steering Michelle into whatever direction would help her—and if that direction meant she would learn to deal with Max and would stay married to him then so be it—but the do-or-die one to pry her from his clutches and have her for myself. Once that truth was out, my native cunning, which had so far been held in check by scruples, took over and I pondered my strategy. There had been no transference other than the minor one—standard for narcissists—of Michelle idealizing me as an eminent psychologist concerned for her. Passatour had too overpowering a personality for her to project him onto me, and I could therefore not use a therapeutic emotional engagement with me to my advantage (as an alarming number of my disreputable colleagues have done if surveys are to be believed). My approach had to be subtle. My clue was that at least once before Michelle had dallied with another male in order to rekindle Passatour's interest in her. Her actor/architect lover was attractive and charming, but then so was I when I put my mind to it.

The progress of my "courtship" on the road to my love's heart could have been measured in inches. It took place in the course of months and consisted of a softly-spoken phrase here, a gentle double entendre there, a piece of biographical information about my own romantic debacles, an expression of empathy for the hell she was living in courtesy of Passatour—all tailored to turn me in her eyes from the therapist into a person, a friend, a male of the species. (I decided against growing a beard because I was afraid that my intention would be obvious—clearly a faulty projection of my own hypersensitivity regarding her: I doubt she would at that time have recognized any change less conspicuous than a second nose or third eye. But I was forever afraid that I was accidentally broadcasting my feelings for her in blazing letters.) Her interest, similarly, awakened very gradually—it took many months before I was reasonably sure that if I had mentioned myself as an example of at least one man other than Passatour existing in this world she would not have stared at me in wide-eyed bafflement.

The message I strove to impart to her throughout these months was that she would be better able to deal with Passatour if she could learn not to focus her entire emotional life on him alone. She would in fact do not only herself but her marriage and him a favor if she could break out of her obsessive preoccupation with him. She would see him more objectively as a human being subject to the snares and pitfalls created by his own psychological problems, and this would make her less susceptible to being hurt by him. But she needed to look around with open eyes at other people. This did not mean, I gently advised her one afternoon in late summer, that she ought to jump into bed with the next pleasing face she met. The sort of contact I had in mind might well be non-sexual as long as it engaged her on some emotional level; I was imagining someone she liked and was at ease with and found interesting.

"Someone like George?" she asked.

"No," I said. "You don't find George interesting. Someone like me."

It was the first time I had directly brought myself into the picture. I hid my wildly beating heart behind a smile.

"Are you interesting?" she asked, returning my banter. "Maybe I'll have to start paying attention to you."

My heart leaped up. My love is a tease, I thought.

I was not in the habit of tape-recording sessions with my patients since scanning fifty minutes of talk for a few pertinent morsels was less efficient than glancing at the notes I took. But in the case of Michelle, I did secretly record several of our meetings—not, I admit with an abashed smile, for professional reasons but because I wanted to be able to listen to her voice in her absence. (A melodious voice, clear as a mountain stream.) I reproduce below parts of one of those meetings, one that took place shortly after she had teased me about being interesting, to give my gentle reader some idea of what it was like to be with the woman to whom I had confessed with a smile that she was "my favorite patient." I give stage directions wherever they serve to enliven the scene, and I indicate with asterisks omissions of discourse that struck as boring even love-drenched Paul.

P. (*After greeting M.—the reference is to road construction on the block*) Did you make it through the obstacle course in one piece?
M. Just barely. I snuck through after the guy had turned the sign to Stop and he gave me a dirty look.
P. To which you responded with a bright smile, which mollified him.
M. No, I tried to look crestfallen. I should have told him I can't be late for my shrink appointment or I'll go mad; he'd have let me through in a hurry.
P. Would you have gone mad?
M. (*Wide open eyes, mock solemnity*) Absolutely.

*** Chitchat about neither madness nor insanity being clinical terms while patient and therapist settle down.

P. Any particular reason you would have gone mad if you hadn't been able to see me?
M. Just the usual. Remember what you said last time about Max being a brilliant four-year-old? I thought about it and I think you're wrong—he's a brilliant three-year-old.
P. (*Laughs*) A bit early for arrested development but I'm willing to entertain the possibility. What's he done now?
M. The usual. You know Max. Inconsiderate, insensitive, there's no-

body but him in the universe. (*Snorts deprecatingly*) You know how he likes to talk about surgery at dinner even though he knows it makes me lose my appetite. Last night he told me about a bypass operation he'd done—quadruple or quintuple or whatever. He said the patient reminded him of Barb's husband—the same complications. Before I could remind him that he's told me the story of Barb's husband, and poor Barb at the hospital, about fifty times, there he went again. You know the story: how worried Barb was; how she didn't want to leave the hospital when he told her that it would be a while before he'd be able to tell her anything. How she was so pale and clutching a neck chain like a rope, and he wondered what it would be like to have someone so worried about *him*, a lovely woman so worried instead of not giving a damn about him like Marge (Passatour's first wife).

P. Did he actually use the word "lovely"?

M. Not this time, but he used it the first time he told me the story. Anyway, I was in a bad mood and I didn't want to hear about Barb. So I said, "Did you ask yourself the same thing with all the other wives who were afraid that their husbands might die? Did you wonder what it would be like to have them worry about you?" He gave one of his scowls and said, "I don't know. Sometimes." I knew he was lying and I said, "Isn't it strange that she was so worried about Bill when it turned out that she didn't love him? Or that you thought she was so worried about him when she really didn't give a damn and slept with you when he was still in the hospital?" (*She leans back and studies P. for the effect she's made*)

P. Interesting questions but hardly what he wanted to hear. What did he say?

M. He said Barb is difficult to figure out. She probably felt guilty about not loving Bill and worried that that had something to do with Bill's condition. I said, "So what made her worry wasn't that she loved him but that if he died it might be her fault. And if she'd been worried about you with a bad heart it might have been for the same reason." (*Another triumphant look at P.*)

P. (*Laughs*) Ten points for baiting the bear in his cave. I am amazed you're in one piece.

M. Just barely. He got huffy and said if Barb were worried about *him* it would be because she loved him. *That* he knew for damn sure. I almost said, Why don't you have a heart attack; then we'll see who'll be at the hospital worrying herself sick, her or me; if I know dear Barb she'll be too busy vacationing in the Bahamas to send a get-well card unless it fits in her busy schedule.

P. Why do you think you didn't?

M. Tell him that I'd be there and she wouldn't? Because it's pointless arguing with him about her. He has his rose-colored glasses on and can't see what a fraud that woman is.

P. What *did* you say?

M. I said it must be nice to know for certain that somebody one is in love with would worry if one were ill. He said, "Is that a crack about me not being concerned for you under similar circumstances?" I said, "No, I believe you'd be concerned for me."

P. Do you think he would?

M. Not if something happening to me would mean he could get Barb. That's an awful thing to say about the man you're married to, isn't it? But I really think that if some genie showed up and said to him, "You can have either Barb or Michelle, but the one you don't want will die," he'd choose her and let me die. (*Sudden tears streaming from lustrous eyes. P. hands her a box of tissues and imagines himself plunging a knife into Passatour's black heart.*)

P. Whoever said, "Being in love is the most selfish impulse" was certainly right. But I'm not sure that's the choice Max would make.

M. (*Sobbing into a tissue*) Yes, it is. She's more important to him. He'd divorce me in a minute if Barb left Bill.

P. Don't you think you're being unfair in creating that kind of all-or-nothing, life-or-death scenario? Suppose your genie asked you to choose between Max and George. Wouldn't you choose Max even though George is in love with you and a far better friend—

someone concerned about you, someone who doesn't constantly hurt you by his inconsiderateness?

M. Yes, but I'm married to Max and you're supposed to choose the one you're married to.

P. (*Punts, unable to attack the logic of tradition*) Was he satisfied when you said you believed he'd worry about you?

M. (*Blows her nose*) I don't know. George called and wanted to know if we wanted to go to an arts-and-crafts fair on Saturday, and afterwards Max had to read up on a case.

***Talk about the arts found at arts-and-crafts fairs until calm has returned.

P. Are you keeping in mind my suggestion to emotionally distance yourself from Max when he goes off on one of his Barb tangents? To remind yourself that he's someone who has severe emotional problems?

M. I try to, but it's difficult when he gets emotional. It's like he infects me with his feelings and it becomes hard for me to think straight.

P. Do you think it's similar to being married to someone who physically abuses you? In other words, you may know that he is ill but the beating hurts just as much and it's impossible to distance oneself from it?

M. No, I don't think so. I've told you that I'd leave Max if he beat me.

P. How sure are you of that? Are you sure psychological abuse is that much easier to handle?

M. I don't know. Maybe you're right. Maybe I wouldn't leave Max even if he beat me—if I believed that he's doing it because he's ill.

P. I never claimed you wouldn't leave him if he were physically abusive. The only point I was making was that there is an analogy between physical and psychological abuse. In each case, the abuser is unconcerned with the well-being of the one he abuses.

M. But what if you know that he loves you even though he does awful things to you?

P. "Know" or "want to believe"? And what if you do know? Does that make the awful things less harmful?

M. I don't know. Maybe. Maybe if you know, they are less harmful.

P. A fractured skull is a fractured skull is a busted head.

M. All right, maybe they would be less awful.

P. A fractured skull is awful.

M. (*Shakes her head furiously*) You don't understand. Everything you say makes sense and I agree with it but you don't understand and I can't explain.

P. (*Looks at her with a loving smile*) You're in love with him. He can please you in more ways than you think you can list in an hour. He hurts you, but then he looks at you in a certain way and you're lifted up by a wave of delight. You hate him for hurting you, but he takes you into his arms and you're elated beyond words. You spend 99% of your time suffering, victimized by the inconsiderate bastard, and yet you want no one else in the world.

M. (*In tears*) Yes. I know it's crazy, but that's how I feel.

*** Sermon by Paul (nth time told) on strategies designed to help deal with emotional dependencies. Patient nods, agrees, claims she'll try. Therapist hides his skepticism. End of session.

A few months after I made this recording came Christmas, on the first day of which—thinking of my true love—I typed on an index card the lines

Heartache is my middle name.
My first name is pain.
Is it a wonder my mailbox says I-N-S-A-N-E?

The verse had been given to me on embossed stationery by one of my patients, an elderly woman suffering from depression. I liked it, and kept it in my top drawer, possibly because the initials of my first and middle name are P.H. and it seemed custom-tailored for my state of mind.

Heartache was my middle name and one I strove to live up to at all times at all costs. But I made a special effort during the holiday season. I had hated Christmas ever since my years with R. P. & D. (Before then I had been largely indifferent to it since my parents had largely ignored it.) But Michelle told me she loved Christmas: there was a special feeling about it—anticipation or hope or she didn't know what. Her dreamy way of talking about the blessed season was enough for a special dread to accompany its arrival that year. It was our second Christmas as therapist and patient, but she and Passatour had spent the first one in Hawaii, which had helped me ignore it. This time I became acutely aware that Christmas was important to her and would exclude me, and I was in agony over being excluded from something she cherished.

I was also unable to fend off the thought of how I would have loved it if it had been our yuletide, hers and mine. I would have spent days shopping for her, looking at this elegant trinket, that pricey bauble, running my fingers over silk and leather and antique silver, wondering how she would look wearing or carrying, anticipating the moment when she would eagerly tear the red-and-gold paper and open the box, and give a gasp of delight.

Instead, she was too busy the week of Christmas, and specifically too occupied with preparations for the arrival of Max's present (about which more soon), to attend her session, and I spent a perfectly wretched Christmas Eve and Day at home watching TV to keep from going out of my mind with imagined scenes of domestic Christmassy bliss with Max.

Then, at our first post-Christmas session, I could not stop myself from worrying the scab; I had to ask her: "Was Santa nice to you?" And got the story of Christmas at the Passatours. Max had given her a gold bracelet—a dull, reddish glint encircling her slim wrist. George—naturally present during the opening of gifts—had given her three New-Age CDs (my poor fool didn't have the disciplined mind necessary to enjoy Bach or Mozart). George's present by the Passatours were a Giants baseball cap (he was a fan) and a sweater, both purchased, of course, by Michelle. Jealousy pricked me as I pictured George covering his bald head and encasing his fleshy bulk with the things Michelle had selected for him, had held in her hands, had paid money for. Max's present from George was a pair of leather house slippers. Being told about this frenzy of gift giving, I felt like Scrooge looking in on a merriment excluding him—inside, a blaze in the hearth, hot grog, gingerbread men, laughter; outside, cold, darkness, loneliness gnawing at the gaunt stranger.

But I had not had enough punishment. "How did Max like your present?" I asked, furiously biting the wound.

And got the answer I deserved: "He was amazed. We'd managed to keep him out of the study, so it was really a surprise. He took one look at it and I could tell he loved it."

As she had told me with great excitement before Christmas, Max's present was—hold on to your socks—a grand piano! A Steinway, no less, for a man whose most impressive achievement as a pianist had been playing afternoons in a hotel lobby when he was in college. (One can imagine the selection: *If Ever I Should Leave You, Some Enchanted Evening, What Kind of Fool Am I?* and for a humorous digression: *The Sadder but Wiser Girl for Me*—all transcribed for the insufferable mellowness of lounge music.)

But the loving wife wasn't done enthusing about the effect of her formidable present. "You should have seen him when we dragged him into the study and there it was. You may not believe this, but he had tears in his eyes, he was so touched."

I said I could imagine him being touched and amazed. It was after all quite a costly present in addition to being thoughtful. Whereupon she rummaged in her bag and pulled from it a small box, wrapped in green-and-silver paper. "This probably isn't legal," she said. "But I liked them and I thought you might too. Merry Christmas." It was my turn to be touched—except I had to hide my tears in the bustle of opening my present. In the box was a pair of silver-and-onyx cuff links, tasteful and elegant. I thanked her and muttered that I hadn't gotten her anything because she was right: strictly speaking, giving gifts to patients or therapists was against the professional code. But, I added, that didn't mean I wasn't delighted.

And I was. At least until in the cold light of day that settled over my office when she had left, I contemplated the difference between a grand piano—or, for that matter, a sweater or baseball cap—and a pair of cuff links. The latter was surely an impersonal gift, one notch better than cologne, for the man one didn't know what to give to and whose gift didn't merit an inordinate amount of time and effort. In other words, although I appreciated that she had given me anything, and put the cuff links on my night stand so they were the first thing I'd see in the morning, the fact that the gift wasn't more personal smarted once I pried open the gift horse's mouth.

The next memorable scene in the drama of my stealthy romance occurred in the spring, many months after my love's teasing, "Are you interesting? Maybe I'll have to start paying attention to you." Which attests to the fact that I really had the most extraordinary patience in the pursuit of my goal.

Not that patience wasn't forced upon me by the impossible situation I was in. My contact with Michelle was limited to a scant and precious fifty minutes per week, and I could use none of the standard ruses and ploys by which would-be lovers can speed up the progress of acquaintance and courtship. I could not "on the spur of the moment" call Michelle and invite her to a movie classic I had just spotted, or call her to inquire about gloves I had or had not left in her car the evening before, or call her to ask her whether she was mad about something I had said to her. I could not take her out to dinner and talk about one of ten thousand innocuous topics (fender benders, insurance rates, vacation spots, favorite movies, paranormal experiences, etc. etc. etc.), until over the third glass of Chablis the conversation becomes more personal and eyes are allowed to linger on eyes and flirtatious remarks to glide through wine-loosened lips. I could not explain to her, with a demonstration, how Germans drank from their glasses with intertwined arms to seal friendship. I could not compliment her on her open-neck, bottle-green blouse and the way the color turned her eyes into something between a mystery and a dream. I could not ask her for a picture for my wallet, and tease her about my carrying her likeness near my heart or (lovingly) on my left buttock.

All I had were my paltry, antiseptic fifty minutes during which I had to act within a narrow range of prescribed behavior, and there were miserable times when I didn't even have those, for instance when the Passatours acted like a traditional couple and took a trip to Greece, leaving me to contemplate the eternity of two weeks— fourteen days!—with no hope of contact with Michelle. (I had at the beginning of the therapy told her to call me any time, day or night, when she felt the need to talk to me, and while she was within a radius of thirty miles from me I always nursed a small hope that any moment my phone might ring with that call: "I feel so terrible.

Can I see you?" That call had never come, but the knowledge that it might come helped me through the week. But with her tramping about the Parthenon, there was no hope for a surprise call; there was only a vast distance and an interminable number of days before I would see her again and be at peace for the space of a smile.)

As I said, my patience as a suitor was remarkable, and even when my strategy of romance began to show signs of success, as in the episode of the teasing remark, I remained cautious. Many more months had to elapse before I had more conclusive evidence of interest in me than a pair of cheap cuff links.

The particular scene that furnished that evidence took place at the end of a session. We said goodbye, and Michelle was on her way out the door when she paused, turned and said, "You keep insisting that there are other men, but you're wrong. There is only one other man."

I must have gaped, unable to make sense of what I was hearing as the list of her former attachments ran through my head. The English director? the Modern Major General? good buddy George? "Who is he?" I asked.

She pouted and shrugged. "As if you didn't know," she said, walked out and closed the door.

My reaction was similar to what it would have been if she had exploded a grenade on her way out and left me deafened by the roar and choking in smoke. As soon as I had reoriented myself, my impulse was to leap up, fight my way through the fiery wall, find her in the parking lot, grab her by the shoulders and twirl her around, and shout into her face, "What did you mean by that? What exactly?"

I did not run after her, and I fought down with all my mental resources the urge to call her at home as soon as there was a reasonable chance that she had arrived and say, "You mentioned something very interesting on your way out of my office, and as your therapist I need to know what you meant—what exactly!—when you claimed I knew what you were talking about."

In the week that followed, I rehearsed a dozen ways to broach the question during our next session. When the session arrived after time sickly crawled through the appointed number of hours and days, I got to the point (I forget in which of my dozen rehearsed ways) as soon as Michelle was settled in her chair. I waited for the answer, concentrating on keeping my breathing regular, and was treated to a wide-eyed look, a frown, a bitten lower lip, and the claim that she had forgotten what she had said and couldn't imagine what she had meant.

I gnashed my teeth, tapped my pencil on my pad, described the scene in detail (in the session we had talked about…and she was standing in the door when she said…and I asked…and she answered…). This seemed, I added, somewhat important in view of the sort of things we were grappling with in therapy.

I got the same response, with a petulant shrug thrown in: She didn't remember; she couldn't imagine.

I dropped the subject and behaved remote during the session, offering few questions or comments about one of her typical Passatour stories (ever the soul of honesty about his feelings, he had told her he was depressed because Barb was on vacation with her husband). I took hardly any notes and did what I never did during sessions: checked my watch rather than discreetly glance at the large overhead clock. When she got ready to leave, I gave her a brisk see you next time, goodbye, and turned to a file on my desk before she had left the room.

I ministered to my next patient, a man suffering from borderline paranoid schizophrenia who was, I told myself sardonically, in closer contact with reality than either of those two basket cases, Dr. and Mrs. Passatour.

When I was through with him, my receptionist told me that there had been a call from Michelle. The message was for me to call her when I got a chance. I did immediately and she said, "You're sore at me, aren't you?"

It was my turn to be wide-eyed and puzzled. "No, of course not; why should I be?" I asked wide-eyed and puzzled.

"Because I didn't tell you what I meant when I said there was another man and you knew it."

"You don't remember."

"But I do remember. I was just afraid to tell you."

"Can you tell me now?"

"I don't think so. It's too idiotic. If I tell you you really will be mad at me."

By this time, my heart was beating against my rib cage like a crazed thing wanting out. "You're being silly," I said. "How can I help you if you don't tell me what's going on in your life?"

"I'll tell you next time," she said.

"That's a week from now," I wailed.

There was a small pause, then she said, "Max just got home. I'll talk to you next week. Bye." She hung up.

I don't know how I resisted the savage urge to call her back and say, "Max didn't come home; stop hedging and tell me that I'm the man you have in mind."

A week of agony and sweet dreams later, she sat opposite me and told me with the disarming frankness she affected whenever she wished to hide her motives from anyone, including herself, that I was the man she had had in mind, but she had been afraid to tell me that she had certain feelings for me because I might refuse to continue as her therapist.

I smiled gently, hoping to hide my wild elation, and said that of course I wouldn't dream of sending her away at this stage in the therapy, that I was glad she was frank, and that despite the obvious difficulty introduced by her being attracted to me, and—to be equally frank—my being attracted to her, we should be able to continue our sessions, provided we were honest about our feelings and accepted this complication as something to be worked through.

She gnawed her lower lip. "How attracted are you to me?" she asked.

"A not totally insubstantial amount," I joked. But I did not like that gnawed lip and I was right to see it as a manifestation of an unattractive (I won't say disgusting) trait of her personality, which I eventually labeled the "pull-me/push-me game"—push me (away from her) when I approached; pull me (to her) when I showed signs of retreating.

She promptly began to ponder audibly whether my having "feelings" for her didn't mean we should end the sessions and she should find another therapist.

I spent a frantic half hour trying to convince her that her worries were unfounded: I was perfectly capable of maintaining professional objectivity and distance; this complication could only help her crack the door of her obsessive cage; in no way could harm come from it. She kept rephrasing the same fear that there was something wrong with her being my patient if I had feelings for her. She seemed ready to walk out of my office and life forever, when, beyond panic and firing blindly, I said, "OK, maybe you're right. Maybe somebody else would be better at helping you with Max. As a matter of fact, now that I think of it it occurs to me that I may get in deep water with the profession if I continue as your therapist. People are fond of misinterpreting this sort of thing."

Whereupon the fickle creature paused, pondered and said that she needed me. She didn't believe anyone else would understand her and her problems with Max the way I did.

We parted, therapist and patient—the therapist ecstatic at having held on to his love and energetically keeping at bay his prescient fear of future hurt, the patient thinking who-knows-what confused and self-gratifying thoughts.

Long before Michelle, it had been my habit to compose lists of attributes describing my patients' characteristics, in order to get some grip on that elusive thing, their personality. (Anyone thirsting for a rigorous discussion is invited to peruse my article, "An Attributive Approach to Diagnosis," in *The American Psychologist*, August 1987.)

In the case of Michelle, the list evolved in the course of the two years I knew her, with some items being crossed out as the result of new insights and others added for the same reason. A few days ago I composed a final updated list based on my final updated understanding of her. I did the exercise for no reason other than to amuse myself since I no longer have the slightest interest in the psychological condition of my ex-patient, and I append my "findings" here for the possible amusement of others (including Busy Becky, currently a hyperactive beaver chewing on more pressing assignments than my sad tale). According to my list, my love was self-absorbed, self-serving, irresponsible, flighty, fickle, insensitive, thoughtless, callous, manipulative, opportunistic, mendacious, false, cowardly, greedy; a flirt, a charmer, a born survivor, a fucking bitch.

The pitiful thing being that I wanted that flighty, fickle, false, fucking bitch more than life with grace, peace, and health, more than the lifetime earnings of a lucrative profession, more than my immortal soul. I wanted her and loved her, and tried, with sweat beading on my brow and veins knotting in my temples, to believe in another, less incriminating, collection of attributes—which defined her as insecure, vulnerable, guilt-ridden, unable to esteem herself, confused about her own needs and wants, ready to use charm and beauty as tools because she had had to learn to use them or have no defense against the indifference of others, profoundly lonely, profoundly unhappy, suffering.

With that sad compendium as my breviary, I was able to summon up compassion for her and to cast myself in the role of the man who would take her hand in the fog enshrouding her mind and would guide her to a place of light and air, where she would stand upright and breathe freely—her own person at last, self-aware, happy with herself, in need of no one to assure her of the rightness of being who she was, desired (by me) for being herself, loved (by me) for being no one else.

🔳🔳 Which brings us to the question of how many weeks of pussyfooting there were after our confessions of "feelings" for one another—how many weeks of me wanting us to talk about us rather than about her disaster of a husband, and wanting her to talk about me, and wanting her to be in love with me—before that amazing moment when she stood in the middle of my office and said, "All right, let's do it. Let's have sex."

Some nine or ten is my guess since it must have taken at least six weeks after the I'm-attracted-to-you episode for me to buy and have delivered to my office a new couch, and since the couch was at least three weeks old before I put it to its intended use with Michelle, *ma nue belle.*

Why a new couch? Because the wood-and-fabric one I relaxed on between sessions, studying files or reading, was showing signs of wear, as I told my receptionist. She, economy-minded, suggested reupholstering, but I said it had never been that comfortable and I wanted something different, more classy, leather. Then I visited every quality furniture store in San Francisco looking for what my luxurious imagination had presented me with: a low, wide, soft couch (related to French *coucher,* to sleep) covered with supple leather the color of dark chocolate. In my vision of it, Michelle was lying on its sumptuous expanse, bare, white-limbed, pink-nippled, fair hair spread about her face and curling in golden locks below her abdomen. So powerful was this image that I drove legions of salespeople crazy when neither black, nor gray, nor tan, nor marzipan would do and when even the choices of browns (beige through burnt umber) they presented me with got nothing but shakes of my head and the excuse that I had a very particular effect in mind.

When I finally found the rich dark chocolate of my imagination, it was on a couch that was adequate for the act itself but too narrow for post-coital nestling. But I had finally encountered a salesman who understood the nature of obsession and knew that it was meaningless to try to talk me into another color with greater width or the narrow width with the right color; he got on the phone, and when he got off he had put in an order for couch model such-and-such with leather from dye lot number so-and-so. About a month later I accepted delivery.

The day the couch arrived and was divested of its protective plastic, I spent the night in my office and slept on it. Before slipping off to forgetfulness, I willed myself to dream of Michelle—Michelle on my couch, under me, feeling its suppleness on her back and buttocks while I possessed her. I dreamt instead a horrible dream about a horse that had been skinned alive and ran mad with agony across a prairie.

Michelle, at her next session, approved of the new acquisition, commented on its delicious color and laughed when I said I might yet turn into an old-fashioned psychoanalyst—couch, regression, Oedipal complexes, and so forth.

Two or three weeks later the amazing moment arrived: Michelle standing in the middle of my office before we settled down for her session, Michelle saying, "All right, let's do it. Let's have sex."

There she stood, brash, intense, clearly furious about something Max had done or had failed to do, so sweet, so vulnerable, so beautiful I wanted to weep.

After a speechless moment of elation and terror, I said, "You can't be serious. I could never do that. Think of the ethics."

"Screw the ethics," she said. "Besides, you yourself keep saying I need to relate to other people. Well, I'm relating to you and it's impolite for you to just stand there. Kiss me, will you?"

I took her into my arms and kissed her, finally, finally close to my deepest longing, holding it in my arms, drinking from a clear fountain after spending a lifetime parched in the desert.

I could have held on to her forever, but she shrugged away from me and began unbuttoning her blouse. I said, "Let me," but she was already done and out of the smooth cotton. Her brassiere closed in front and she undid its clasp and shrugged out of it. I folded a hand around each breast, leaned forward and tenderly kissed her again.

This time she lingered a bit longer, her nipples growing stiff in my palm, but again she pulled back sooner than I wanted her to and reached to the side of her skirt. "Aren't you going to get undressed?" she asked.

I mumbled that of course I would, but there was plenty of time. We had all the time in the world from now on. Without replying, she lowered her skirt and stepped out of it. I quickly unbuttoned my shirt and took off it and my T-shirt. She, in panty hose and panties, her shoes kicked aside, ran her hands up and down my chest, combing through its thicket of hair with her fingers and curling strands of it.

"Do you like that?" I asked, pulling her close and kissing her again.

"Yes," she said.

I had by that time a substantial erection and had trouble unzipping my pants. She worked her panty hose down to her thighs and sat on my chocolate couch to take it off. I watched her, my mind a jumble of thoughts and feelings. She stood up again and ran her hand over my testicles, still ensconced in my briefs. "That's nice," I whispered into her ear, and she took hold of the waistband and pulled my briefs down over my buttocks. I did the same to her panties. Suddenly she kissed me again, thrusting her tongue deeply into my mouth. I pulled her down onto the couch and after a bit of adjustment (my wide couch was not quite wide enough for total comfort) I fondled her and she fondled me, and I penetrated her and we made quiet, passionate love.

Afterwards I lay on my side connected to my love along my entire length, from my glowing forehead, awkward nose and tender mouth to my happily curling toes caressing the arch of her foot. "I love you. I do. I do," I said between kisses. "Do you love me?"

"Yes," she replied and kissed me. "So we're not doing anything unethical, are we?"

I wasn't sure whether or not she was joking, but in any event, the answer was, "No, we're not."

"Good," she said and sat up. "We've made a mess of your new couch," she added matter-of-factly.

I eased myself off my perch. "Don't worry about that," I told her. "I'll get a new one for every time we make love. What would you like for next time? strawberry red? licorice black?"

She laughed. "Dark honey, to go with your moody eyes."

We cleaned ourselves in my private bathroom and got dressed, all the while stealing a touch here, a kiss there.

"How about dinner this evening?" Michelle asked.

The thought of seeing her for the first time in a social setting thrilled me. "I'd like that very much," I said.

"And then we can go to your place and I'll spend the night," she said. "Max is in Chicago," she added.

So that there was of course a dram of sadness right there in my beaker brimming with happiness. She would spend the night with me because...

Still, hope is a powerful drug against sadness. I had gone from being her therapist to being her lover, from being obligatorily confided in to being made an intimate part of her life. What was to prevent things from continuing along a steady line of progress leading to our permanent attachment to one another? I had, I told myself, no illusions about this turning into a relationship never darkened by clouds—she had too many unresolved psychological problems for there to be perennial bliss, but knowing that we belonged to each other would help us surmount every difficulty we would encounter. If only I'd come home to her in the evening and wake up to her in the morning, all would be well.

After she had left, I entertained myself with pleasing notions of our future while wiping our bodily fluids off my chocolate couch and using the leather conditioner that had come with it to eliminate most traces of our activity. I do not, by the way, recommend leather for non-platonic trysts: in the weeks that followed, my couch began to show signs that would have left little to guess for the initiated.

If all this is starting to sound a tad sordid, I can only say that to me it wasn't in any way. Yes, we had sex during Michelle's sessions (for which I had to keep billing her since Passatour would have wondered why his wife was all of a sudden being given free therapy). Yes, we met in the evening now and then, and on some mornings when I was free, and, yes, very occasionally she spent the night at my townhouse. But I loved her and she loved me, and I would have married her at the drop of a hat if she had divorced her husband, and there was all the tenderness and loveliness and sense of closeness that make sexual intimacy between two people the private, untarnished thing it will never be in the eyes of others or when it is described on the pages of a book or other document.

Tender, lovely, private, untarnished our love was to me. Pleasing beyond words since everything about her, from the most overt to the most secret, pleased me—the way she greedily gulped coffee and whiskey sours, her long, awkward hands, the subtle scent of her perfume, the golden locks of pubic hair reaching far back between her buttocks, soft as the wool of a young sheep. Everything.

But was our love tender, lovely, private, untarnished to her? Without fear of doing her an injustice, I can answer, No, not to her. She loved me in word and deed, but while I was in a state of sustained, deep happiness, seeing promise for a glorious future everywhere (we had come this far, etc.), she was muddling along in a growing state of confusion. My own elation made it difficult for me to see what was happening, but even I, my powers of observation blunted by happiness, eventually couldn't help but notice her confusion and ask myself about its source.

Its source, I can now state confidently, was Michelle's growing awareness that she was not getting what she wanted out of this affair with me. Consciously or semiconsciously, she had thought she wanted my adoration, devotion, undivided attention, love. If I, her therapist, a clever, sophisticated, successful, handsome man, made her the most important thing in his life, that would offset the humiliation she was daily being dealt by her husband, in addition to satisfying her craving for being adored. Again consciously or semiconsciously, she had realized from her beleaguered position that if she could transfer to me the feelings she had for Passatour, then she would have paradise on earth since I would treat her the way she longed with every atom of her being to be treated by him. A corollary to this projected bliss was that, happy in my arms, she would be able to tell Max to go to hell.

Glorious notions, followed by a devastating blow when after a few weeks she realized that even though I gave her exactly what she most craved, the fact that it was I who gave it to her made what I gave her meaningless. Yes, I adored her, but it wasn't *my* adoration she wanted, it was *his*. Once she understood that essential truth, I failed in every other significant point of comparison, from the pettiest to the profoundest. To randomly name a few: I was successful in my profession, but helping people fight private demons could not compare with the scarlet pageantry of saving lives in an operating theater. I was handsome—certainly more handsome than Max—but it was his looks she viscerally responded to. I was financially well off, but I didn't own a palace. I told her she was remarkable, witty, charming, beautiful, but those words didn't mean anything coming from me. I would have given my life for her, but who gave a damn about *my* life? To summarize, although I met all the requirements, I was the wrong candidate, superbly qualified and disastrously wrong —because I was not Max Passatour.

I did not speedily arrive at this insight. How could I have, when every moment I spent with her was dear to me; when I felt so close to her, and so much at peace with her, and at the same time so full of exuberance and energy just because of her? Those first weeks of "our love" were the happiest of my life. I confided in her about Jennifer, and I told her more honestly than I had told anyone before about sex with my cousin. I told her a hundred other things about me, how unhappy I had been, how awful I felt about some of the things I had done, how afraid and lost and alone I had been; that she made me so glad, that she took away my sadness and made me feel I was alive and deserving to be alive because she loved me.

I opened myself to her, but I did not monopolize our conversations. I listened raptly when she told me things she had kept from me when I had been only her therapist. (I say "only" because I still occasionally thought of her as my patient, and still occasionally said or did things because I thought of her in those terms, even though she clearly no longer saw me in that role.) To me as her therapist she had confessed that she hated her brother and that when he had run through the plate-glass door, she had hoped he'd die so her mother would pay attention to her rather than him. To me as her lover she told silly things like that she loved squirrels and filed her nails because she hated cutting them, and that she was convinced four was an unlucky number for her. She also confessed to me her sexual fantasies—just as she had confessed them to her husband and Ron— which put me in the unenviable position of having to try to fulfill them as effectively as my rivals had. (I will not satisfy the appetite of the possibly prurient reader by providing details on my love's erotic delectations, which were at any rate more strenuous than depraved.)

And yet, at the same time this getting closer to her, and getting to know her, and so loving it all, was going on, she must already have suspected that she had made a mistake. I was not who she'd hoped I would be because I did not possess that unknowable something that Passatour possessed. A something that made her tremble and shiver and laugh out loud in aliveness and gladness—and that was what? his voice? his walk? the texture of his skin? his smell? or even less definable characteristics having nothing whatsoever to do with things worthy of respect, admiration or love.

⊑⊑⊑ I've said nothing about my subconscious life throughout these hopeless months, and I'll take out time and
invite the reader to set foot on the *via regia* to it and marvel at how
wonderfully opaque the analytical faculty can be when part of the
mind wishes to remain ignorant. To wit, none of the three dreams
I'll describe below struck me initially as relating to my own life and I
looked for their origins in two cases I was treating (one, a borderline
schizophrenic lost in the labyrinth of an unhappy love affair, the
other suffering from anxiety neurosis). Since it took me a while to
recognize the connections between these dreams and my own life, I
urge amateur psychologists as well as any interested ex-colleagues
who may encounter this document to sharpen their pencils and
interpret these fabulations of my subconscious in the light of the
events. Guesses may be sent to me, care of the authorities, for comparison with my own. The best match will be rewarded with a letter
suitable for framing in my own homicidal hand.

Dream One:

I'm in a desert at night. Overhead are two moons, one half, the
other full. The desert is flat and featureless but at its center
stands a giant monolith, tall, with smooth, polished sides. On
top is a woman. I think that she must be dying of thirst up there
and I see a pile of stackable chairs (the same ones I keep in a
closet for those rare times when I need extra chairs for a session). I see that by pushing against their legs, I can lock them in
a new configuration that allows me to put one on top of the
other. I begin to build a tower one chair at a time. Dragging a
chair, I climb up to whatever height I've reached and install it for
the next tier, then climb back down to get the next chair. As the
tower of chairs grows, it becomes unsteadier and I'm more and
more afraid of falling. I reach the height of the monolith, but the
woman is gone. The rock begins to sway. I hold on to the highest
chair and watch terrified as each swing brings the massive col-
umn closer to me. It bumps into my tower and I awake.

Dream Two:

I'm walking through a forest at night. From its depth I hear a voice calling: "Help me! Please help me!" I start running towards it. It seems to recede. I run faster. I can hardly hear the voice. I break out of the trees and stand in a clearing. At its center is a large house with columns. All its windows are lighted by red lamps. A tube-shaped structure is mounted on the roof; I know it to be a loudspeaker. From it issues the voice calling for help. I know that the loudspeaker is connected to a tape recorder inside and that the voice is on an endless tape. I feel stark terror. I awake.

Dream Three:

I'm watching a movie. In it, a woman wielding two large needles is knitting a net from the hair between her legs. More hair keeps appearing as she needs it, as if there were an inexhaustible supply of it inside her pubis. Two men come in; the woman is gone but she has left the net. One of the men picks it up and throws it over the other and begins to stab him with a butcher's knife. I suddenly remember that I can get inside the movie if I push a button. I do, but when I step through the frame I'm too late. The stabbed man lies on the floor, dead and covered with blood. The murderer sees me and says, "I made a mistake," and he heads for me. But I remember something else. "I'm invisible," I tell him, and he looks surprised and says: "You're right, but that won't save you." He begins to stab the air and moves closer. I dodge him, thinking I have nothing to worry about as long as I don't step on the dead man and get the soles of my shoes bloody and leave tracks. The woman is back. She's wearing a black brassiere, nothing else. "There he is," she says and points at me. The murderer can suddenly see me and he drives the knife into my belly. I think, This is like a Greek tragedy—Agamemnon in his bath, or Medea carrying on—and I begin to laugh. I wake up.

I add as a coda one dream told to me by my lady love when she was my lady love (again, I welcome interpretations). She was in a department store looking for something, but she didn't know what. Everything she tried was wrong because she thought that crystal bowls were shoes or watches were belts and couldn't make anything fit. It occurred to her that what she wanted was something called "Impossible Happiness," but she didn't know whether it was a perfume or candy or the name of a game. Then she saw a counter that had a sign saying in large red letters: IMPOSSIBLE HAPPINESS. She walked up to it, but all she saw under the glass were rows upon rows of gray clams. She felt cheated and angry because it was unfair that they made everybody else happy but not her. She awoke.

Then came Black Tuesday. A call at four in the afternoon, Michelle on the phone, furious, in tears. An argument with Max about to leave for a conference. He'd raised his voice, slammed his fist on the table, told her he refused to waste time on another one of her attacks of insecurity. He'd grabbed his bags and stormed out of the house—not giving a damn about how awful she felt.

"I've had it," she said, a tremble in her voice. "I'm not going to put up with any more of his abuse. When he comes back I'll be gone. I'll get a divorce and we'll get married. He can find himself another idiot to wipe his shoes on."

My reaction to what I was hearing was so intense I could hardly think, but I tried to hold on to myself. "You're angry," I said. "Are you sure you won't change your mind tomorrow?"

She wasn't listening. "He has this hilarious idea he's the only man in the world. He thinks he'll walk in here Friday and I'll be here all apologetic and contrite and admit that it was all my fault. Well, he's in for a surprise."

"But are you sure you won't change your mind when you're less angry?" I was afraid that my playing the voice of reason would make her reconsider, but I also wanted to drive home to her that she was making a serious decision and not following a spur-of-the-moment impulse. I wanted her to commit herself and know that that was what she was doing.

"Yes. I'm packing my bags."

She sounded grim and determined, and I was flooded with a jubilant glee. "How long do you think it'll take you? I can be at home in an hour and a half."

"No, I've already thought about that. I'll give him no chance to drag any of this to court. I'll stay at the Hilton."

I had already pictured her getting up tomorrow morning in my bedroom, having breakfast in my kitchen, making herself at home in my living room and backyard—soon to be *our* bedroom, kitchen, living room, backyard. But she was right about being cautious, and there was no reason why we shouldn't spend the night together in her hotel room and have breakfast sent up, and see each other every day from now on.

"I'll wait for you in the lobby," I said. "I'll be there by 5:30. We'll have dinner together and talk."

"I'm so glad I have you," she said.

"Not half as glad as I am to have you."

I was at the hotel at 5:15 and found an easy chair in the lobby with a clear view of the entrance and front desk. I gave her a generous hour and a half to pack and another half hour for the drive. I hoped she'd arrive improbably early, driven by impatience to be with me, but I didn't begin to expect her in earnest until 6 o'clock. Then I doubled my alertness, kept my eyes on the main entrance and the desk, in case she used another entrance.

People arrived, checked in. Groups of people sat down next to me, had conversations about restaurants and shows, a breed of dog

I'd never heard of, a cousin in the hospital for a gallbladder operation, a roommate in college who had qualified for the Olympic swim team. I waited. Seven o'clock arrived, 7:30. A man rose and embraced a woman who had come in. They seemed glad to see each other, joked about something having to do with his shoes, went to the desk. A woman came out of an elevator, scanned the lobby and left the hotel. I went to the one phone that allowed an unobstructed view of the desk, called Michelle's number, got the answering machine. At eight o'clock I tried again; still no answer. I called my office, listened to two messages having nothing to do with Michelle, called my home, listened to a message from a canvassing real estate broker.

When I sat down again, I lost from one instant to the next all ability to think up rational excuses for her lateness, having to do with packing taking longer than I expected, or George calling and her having to brief him on the developments, or a traffic jam. I was suddenly weak with fear. She'd been in an accident; she'd been killed. While I was sitting here, her body was at the morgue and officials were trying to reach her home. Maybe they'd gained access, maybe they'd found my number and were trying to call me. Were people informed over the phone about fatal accidents? Or would a uniformed officer be waiting for me at the door? "I'm sorry, there's been an accident. Would you come with me and identify your patient?"

At nine o'clock I drove home half out of my mind with worry and cursing for the first time the lack of a car phone. On the way, I plowed into the rear of another car, crippling it, and had to wait, seething with impatience, for the paperwork to be done and my car extricated from the mess.

I got home at 10:30 and raced to the phone and called Michelle's number. After four rings there was a groggy "Hello."

After an instant of relief so intense I felt faint, I thought, Oh God, she has taken something. She's trying to kill herself. "It's me," I said. "Are you all right?"

"Yes."

"Did you take something? You sound drowsy."

"No."

"Then why do you sound that way?"

"I was asleep."

I couldn't believe what I was hearing. "You were what?"

"Asleep."

"How could you be asleep? You were supposed to meet me at the hotel."

"I tried to call but you'd left."

"Call about what?"

"To tell you I changed my mind."

I still couldn't believe what I was hearing. "You changed your mind? When did you change your mind?"

"I don't know. I thought about it and I just couldn't go through with it."

"I waited for you. All this time. I just got home."

"I told you, I tried to call."

"Why didn't you leave a message?"

"I didn't feel like talking to a machine."

"So you let me wait all this time, knowing that I was waiting and worrying about you? I thought you'd been in an accident. I was afraid you'd been killed. I kept trying to call you and you weren't there. Where were you?"

"I went to a movie. I felt so rotten I had to do something. I'm sorry I didn't get killed. I guess that would have made you feel better."

"Of course not. It's just that I waited and waited, and I was sure something had happened to you or you would have called. You could have had me paged at the hotel. You knew I was there, waiting for you."

There was a pause, then she said, "You don't understand."

"Understand what? That you promised you'd be at the hotel and then you didn't show up?"

There was another pause, then, "You don't trust me."

I contemplated laughing hysterically at this non sequitur, but she said, "I'm tired. I need to get some sleep."

I tried to keep her on the phone. "We need to talk."

"I told you I'm tired."

"Just five minutes, so I can get my bearing back."

"I'm too tired. I'm exhausted. Maybe tomorrow," she said and hung up.

I spent the night in a black pit of fury, anguish and despair, railing at the thoughtless, selfish bitch, who had been to a movie while I had pictured her on a slab at the morgue, who had gone to sleep without bothering to inform me about her change of mind, who was asleep in her bed while I was being flayed alive by thoughts of her.

Michelle's lack of love for me might predictably have led to a rapid fizzing of our flash-in-the-pan romance if she had been honest with herself and me. Someone honest would have recognized the mistake and would have said to me: "I hoped, I tried, but this isn't working; I thought I loved you but I don't; I thought you would make me happy but you don't; let's call it quits before you get hurt even more." It would certainly have been the charitable thing to do: I would have been devastated and heartbroken and in pain, but I would have survived the honest admission of a mistake.

But if my dearie had her faults, a compulsion to tell the truth was not one of them. The unvarnished fact was that if she wanted something, she went after it; if the truth threatened to become an obstacle, she lied. I had witnessed enough slips in her accounts—disagreements in versions of events or thoughts referred to in different sessions, the accidental revelation usually showing her in a worse light than the rehearsed one of a week or month earlier—to know that whatever came out of her mouth at a given time had to meet the criteria of convenience and effect, not those of truth. But my clinical insight did not lessen my personal desire to believe her when, for instance, she told me a few days after Black Tuesday that she loved me—she truly did—but couldn't yet leave Passatour, needed time, was earnestly working on breaking her attachment to him—when she promised again emphatically that she *would* leave him and *would* marry me! Instead of confronting her with the truth—namely, that she spoke of leaving her husband only on those times when either he excelled at hurting her or when I, sick to death of the sordid affair we were conducting, said we should stop seeing each other and having anything to do with each other—I believed her once again and once again admonished myself to be more understanding. Only to be stood up again two weeks later for some trite reason that made no allowance at all for my having looked forward to seeing her for days and being cast into a pit of dejection when she didn't appear.

The "pull-me/push-me game," "Model Two," and "The Great Manipulator" were concepts that came out of my by then not too happy relationship with Michelle. Why did she keep pulling? Why complicate her life with me after she had determined that there was no profit? Because there was of course some profit. I was her slave, and it surely is flattering to have for a slave a successful man. I stroked her ego; she was flattered by my attention and devotion; her vanity had a field day. No, I could not satisfy her abysmal craving for self-worth, only my rival could do that when he felt inclined to do so, but I could sate a superficial appetite here and there, now and then—so why let go of me?

And I, most of the time in a white-hot rage at her callous disregard for my feelings and my own inability to stop being her puppet, could not walk away from her and commit her to whatever private hell made her the monster she was. Why? Because although when I was away from her all was darkness and pain, and I thrashed about in a blind fury ready to harm anyone who came within my reach, and a fist inside me threatened to strangle me, that darkness and pain and stranglehold left me when I was with her. I could breathe, look about me, be at peace. For the sake of those moments, rarer and rarer though they got with the passing months, I held on, tried to cope with the blatant manipulation, the falseness, the lies, by attributing them to her mental disorder, tried to fool myself into thinking that all was not lost, and that if I were patient enough and employed the right subtle strategies, she might change.

Meanwhile I still got a bellyful of Passatour stories from her, all told on implicit If-you-love-me-you'll-understand-my-still-being-hurt-by-him grounds, and I derived some sardonic amusement from considering the irony of her complaining to me about her husband complaining to her about Barb. In one of my daydreams I called the latter, introduced myself to her and explained how I was really getting the worst part of the deal and that she ought to fall madly in love with me so I could complain to her, before or after sex with her, how rotten Michelle was treating me. Michelle, of course, would continue to have the best deal in town since she was able to moan not only to me but also to good buddy George about her deplorable husband.

I say I derived sardonic amusement from the situation, but I cannot sufficiently stress that most of the time it hurt—it fucking hurt!—and that there were times aplenty when its central figure made humor too much of a luxury, and pain was the only thing I could afford in the coin of my emotional realm. Like the time the godforsaken bitch showed to me, her lover, a clipping from an article on *Faust*—two stanzas from *Gretchen at the Spinning Wheel* (Part I, Scene XV)—and told me in tears that when she had read them she had felt they were talking about Max; what Max meant to her; how she felt about him physically.

I read the lines fighting nausea:

> His noble form,
> His bearing high,
> His lips' sweet smile,
> The power of his eye;

And the magic sound
Of that voice of his,
His hands' soft pressure,
And, ah! his kiss!

And, ah! my aching, breaking heart!

I could write a mid-sized volume on similar occurrences that demonstrated how little my clinical understanding of my own Gretchen's condition served me in my fight against pain. It is easy to see that what was happening to me was happening in a realm that literally did not understand the voice of reason, but one might nevertheless think that knowing what symptoms to expect would have protected me from responding to them with the emotional intensity of someone ignorant—but it didn't. Take for instance the question of promises. Long before Black Tuesday, I knew that the idea of a pledge to do or not to do something was a meaningless concept to sufferers of a narcissistic disorder. They were quick at making promises, but since they had only a nebulous sense of the existence of others, the fact that these others felt hurt or betrayed when a promise was forgotten registered only as an annoying misinterpretation of the events. This, interestingly, despite the fact that they were keenly sensitive to promises made to them and deeply insulted and hurt when as minor a promise as a phone call was forgotten. Michelle, to return to my star example, kept breaking promises large and small (to call me, to meet me, to marry me) with a cavalierness that would have deserved my admiration if it hadn't enraged me and hurt me to the quick. When I'd accuse her of breaking any particular promise, she'd either not remember having made it, or something had made it impossible to keep it—in either event, a wide-eyed, hurt look accompanied the explanation, and "You don't trust me" was the standard pained retort. When I would patiently point out that it was by definition difficult to trust someone who broke promises, her reply would be that impossible-to-answer charge, "You don't understand."

I had, I should add, parted with my own therapist at about the time I fell in love with Michelle, hence had no one who might have reminded me over and over that I was dealing with a pathology and ought not to be unduly affected by the behavior I was witnessing.

A topical aside is in order here. Knowing what I know about personality, it should have been obvious to me when I was approached by Ms. Vanity Fair that the understanding we reached about our collaboration was absolutely binding—that is, until the moment the party of the first part decided that it wasn't. Which is what in fact happened when the excuses are discounted—a breathless note followed by a hurried phone call: very sorry about being forced to drop the project...out of the blue...part of the editorial brass's new policy of redirecting focus...blah, blah. I commiserated with her long-distance for her uncooperative superiors and didn't laugh until I had hung up about her lack of backbone and her ease in reneging on our agreement. After further thought, I did send her a somewhat facetious card stating that I didn't see her behavior symptomatic of anything that might not be profitably tackled by intensive psychotherapy. End of journalistic mini-drama.

Happily this development has made me realize that I have in effect all along in this project been conducting that most stimulating and rewarding type of conversation, the monologue. "Know thyself," is the oracle's motto, and I've followed it by explaining myself to myself on page after page, as if I believed that to know all is to forgive all—which I probably do not. But having come this far on my journey through the dark forest Self-Discovery, I'll press on until I'll reach the magic lake in the clearing and see reflected in it the villain or victim.

My "life" with Michelle could, as far as I was concerned, have lasted for all eternity since, no matter how
much pain I was in, and no matter how often I wished I could stop
caring for her—be shed of this endless ache—there were always
moments when a glance or word from my love made turmoil and
anguish and hurt rain from me like crusts of dead tissue, and I stood
glowing and beaming in my new happy skin.

But the situation was of course volatile and my love its most
volatile element. She continued to suffer greatly because of Passatour's lack of love for her, and she was too young to have arrived at
the insight that living in hell is something one can indeed do all of
one's life—quietly and without making a fuss. And so the day of
reckoning between husband and wife came. One Barb story too
many, or too emotionally told, or told at the wrong time, proved the
straw that broke my young camel's back. Out came the spiteful, triumphant announcement that she was in love with me and sleeping
with me, and that it was doing her a world of good: she really didn't
give a damn about him and Barb anymore; at any rate, he was the
one who ought to see a therapist since he was, according to the professional opinion of her therapist, a textbook case of narcissism.

Since, unlike in the case of her Modern Major General lover, this
scene was not one of repentant her asking understanding him for
forgiveness, Passatour's reaction was markedly different. He point-
blank ordered her to stop seeing me. It was unconscionable and
unethical for me to have used the therapeutic setting to manipulate
her into sex, he claimed.

"He was furious," Michelle reported to dumbstruck me, barely
able to hide her triumph at having provoked so emotional a reaction
from Max. "I've never seen him so angry. He said, he can't stand the
thought of me being used in this way; he threatened to report you,
and he said he'll wring your neck if he ever runs into you. But,"
added the conscionable whore, "I said it was my fault, too."

I regained the power of speech and said, "You're not going to obey
him, are you? Who's he to order you about? Suppose you ordered him

to stop seeing Barb, what sort of an effect do you think that would have?"

But she was too thrilled by her forceful husband's interest in her. (Max was angry! Max was jealous! Max cared!!) Flushed and excited, she dismissed my questions with a shrug. "I have to go," she said. "He didn't want me to see you at all, but I didn't want to do this over the phone."

"That was thoughtful of you. Just one question: what did he say about the narcissism comment?"

She didn't like the question, but she answered it with a flippant shrug, "Nothing."

I smiled an evil smile and finally gave her the unabridged version of my professional opinion about her husband: an ego bloated to the point of bursting, pumped up with the hot, noxious fumes of itself, engorged with the poison of self-love, wallowing in his own muck. A stunted, disfigured, warped, sick mannequin of a man infecting everyone around him with his disease. I stopped in midtirade when I noticed a blank, slack-jawed look on her face. "Do you understand any of this?" I asked.

She returned from whatever far-away place she had vacationed in and said (and I swear that this is true), "You're not mad, are you?"

I gaped, laughed, stopped laughing, laughed again, said, "Why, because you promised me that you'd divorce him and marry me? Because all it takes is an order from a man who is sleeping with another woman for you to break that promise?"

Her flushed face became even redder. She looked ugly, and for a moment I was able to believe that I didn't love her. How could I love a woman so ugly?

She turned to leave, then turned back and said, "He's right. You just used me like you used your cousin. I told Max about that, how you made her do all those filthy things she didn't want to do; he thinks you're slime."

"Tell him it takes one to know one. No, tell him I'm indebted to him for his diagnosis—it explains how I was able to swallow the shit you've fed me all these months."

She turned and left without another word.

I stayed, sat down, thumbed through a file that held no interest whatsoever. A while later, I told my receptionist that I didn't feel well and asked her to cancel my afternoon appointments.

I went home. From there, I called Michelle's number. She answered the phone. I said, "I'm sorry about what I said. I didn't mean to hurt you."

She said, "I can't talk to you," and hung up.

I called back but after four rings I got the answering machine: Passatour's gravelly voice telling me I had reached the number I had reached and asking me to leave a message.

I waited an hour, pacing back and forth in the living room, four round-trips per minute, to make the time go by faster. Then I called. Again, Michelle answered the phone. "Please don't hang up," I said. She hung up.

I called back, let the phone ring four times and hung up before the machine kicked in. I repeated this process twenty times keeping a tally on a sheet of paper, begging Michelle under my breath to please pick up the phone. Please, talk to me just for a minute, thirty seconds, just a few words so I won't feel so awful.

After a total of eighty unanswered rings I stopped. I waited exactly an hour and a half, then dialed the number again.

This time the phone was answered after the first ring, by Passatour. "Hello," he said.

"Hi, could I talk to Michelle?" I said.

"Who's calling?"

"Tom Parsons," I improvised, using the name of a patient.

There was a small pause, then he said, "Listen, Avery, if you don't stop harassing my wife this instant, I'll file charges against you. Do you hear me?"

I quickly hung up and sat trembling, my hands shaking violently in my lap.

Passatour's threat notwithstanding, I spent the next several weeks committed to the singleminded aim of contacting his wife. I soon gave up trying to call, realizing after two or three attempts that the answering machine—now kicking in after two rings—was being used to screen all calls. Michelle was in rehearsals for *Princess Ida*, and my next attempt was to call the theater and ask for her. Twice she did come to the phone, only to hang up the moment she recognized my voice. Then she was never able to come to the phone. "Could you give her a message?" I asked after the fourth or fifth try. I recognized the voice of the man who had answered the phone. He hesitated then said, "All right," which told me all I needed to know about my love the blabbermouth.

"Tell her to call Dr. Faust when she gets a chance. It's important."

"All right," he said.

I felt like adding, "Did you enjoy screwing her as much as I did?" but the Modern Major General had hung up.

I drove to Stanford twice, but the cosmos didn't love me: Michelle did not attend rehearsals on either day. I even looked up her address on a map and drove to the palatial Passatour residence and sat in my car for hours feeling like a madman, waiting for the wrought-iron gate to slide open and her car and her to appear.

And every day was torment, loneliness, hunger, hurt, a want that ate black, ragged holes into my soul and gave me not a moment's rest. Until all I could think of was that a few minutes in Michelle's presence would save my life, and that I would die in darkness and despair if I didn't get those minutes.

Then, after an eternity in hell, came the day when I was sitting in my office, having just said goodbye to one of my patients after having spent fifty minutes with a negligible fraction of my mind on his problems. My receptionist buzzed me and asked whether I had time to see Michelle. I had, and there she stood, framed by my door, my dear, my darling, lovely as ever, loved as ever, as I was lifted off my chair by a surge of relief. I embraced her, kissed her. She was crying, kissed me, cried harder. "I'm sorry," she said. "I'm sorry."

"No, don't be. I'm so glad you're here. I've missed you so."

"I shouldn't have come."

"Yes, you should have." I held her. She began to sob violently. Her shoulders heaved and her body shook while I ran my hands up and down her back. "It's all right," I kept saying. "It's all right."

After a while her crying became quieter, a forlorn keening, then wet breathing and an occasional sob. I let go of her and got a box of tissues from my desk. She blew her nose, dried her face and dabbed her eyes. "I must look like a complete mess," she said.

"You look wonderful. I'm so glad you came. I was going crazy."

She said, "I feel completely awful. I couldn't think of anyone but you to talk to to make me feel better. Do you think that's incredibly selfish of me?"

I was too happy at her presence to pay close attention to what she was saying. "No, of course not. You know you can talk to me any time, day or night."

"Even about Max?" she asked.

I felt a twinge under my sternum but my happiness was tenacious. "About anything," I said.

She sat down and began to cry again, softly.

"What is it?" I asked. "What happened?"

She settled back in the chair, and told me, her eyes lustrous with tears, about the night before. Max had come home after seeing Barb and had told her of Barb's resolution to stop seeing him. He had been so depressed he had hardly been able to talk. He had cried.

Michelle stopped her account and looked at me helpless. "I've never seen him cry. I couldn't stand seeing him so hurt and unhappy. At the same time I was furious and I hated him. How can he do that to me? How can he tell *me* how afraid he is of losing her and how much she's hurting him? As if I didn't mean anything and she's the only thing that matters. Like my feelings don't count at all; I don't count at all; I don't exist except as someone he can tell how unhappy she makes him."

I listened to this outpour with a mounting sense of disbelief. I found myself doubting the possibility that someone with as little self-awareness as this babbling idiot sitting opposite me could exist. Surely any creature this warped would have been strangled for gross insensitivity the moment she acquired the faculty of speech. There she was doing to me virtually to the letter what her monster of a husband had done to her the night before, and not a glimmer of recognition penetrated the self-serving fog enveloping her brain. I thought of what *I* had done the night before, during those same hours in which Passatour had cried over his lost love and his wife had participated in his grief and had thought of nothing in the universe but poor, suffering Max and poor, suffering her: *I* had cried myself to sleep thinking of *her*.

Michelle began to cry harder again. "But I really also felt sorry for him. It's not his fault that he's in love with that bitch. I know what it's like when someone you love doesn't care about you. But why can't he understand and feel sorry for me and love me just a little?"

A sharp pain was lodged at the center of my chest. I handed her the box of tissues. She took a few and held them to her nose and mouth while crying uncontrollably.

"Please stop," I said. "I can't stand to see you hurt. It hurts me too much."

Between spasmodic gasps, she managed to get out, "I know! Why isn't that true for Max? He can stand seeing me hurt forever and ever."

She kept on sobbing and telling me about her hurt. And apparently this crying-her-eyes-out cry helped her. She seemed almost her old self when, a little later, she told me that she wouldn't be able to see me again. It had been a mistake for her to come, but she had felt so awful.

I've lost all recollection of the rest of the scene. Somehow it must have ended. Somehow Michelle must have left my office (after washing her face? putting on makeup in my bathroom?), and somehow I must have told my receptionist to cancel the rest of my appointments and must have driven home.

My story ought to end here to make its point that the most amazing agony and grief and despair can be achieved by nothing more dramatic or dynamic than human brains doing what human brains do. As far as I can tell, that is the point all this has led up to, and it is unfortunate that the dramatic, dynamic action I performed in the late afternoon of the same day may end up muddling the issue. My excuse for turning a purely imaginary disaster into a real one is that the mixture of pain, compassion and hate seething in my brain became too virulent to be dealt with purely in the mental realm. The pain needs no explanation, the compassion was probably a figment of my imagination but seemed real enough, the hatred was not new but was colder and more deliberate than it had ever been.

From what I remember about my thoughts the rest of the day, they all revolved around the fact that Passatour had absolute, unchallengeable possession over the mind and body of the only thing I loved. He, as unworthy an object as there was, held in sway the woman I wanted and needed and was lost without. I had tried to make her see the ugly truth, but she, seeing it, kept clinging to this diseased, sickening creature, whom she didn't know at all. She kept being made unhappy by him, kept submitting to the worst kind of psychological abuse, manipulation, brainwashing, being made to feel guilty for normal human reactions to his abominable behavior toward her, being coerced into pitying him for the very thing that hurt her to the quick. I had hated Passatour for his compulsive self-indulgence, which allowed him to do anything he wanted without regard for how his actions affected others. I had hated him because he could make the woman I loved jump through hoops, and hurt her, and made her oblivious to anyone but him. Still, he had not been able to kill my hope to snatch her away from him. But now victory was his. I conceded that Michelle would not come to me. She would follow his order to avoid me. She would continue to prefer abuse from his hands to caresses from mine. I had lost utterly. Unfortunately, as many a winner has found out, accepting defeat is not the same as being a good loser.

Still, I entertained no homicidal thoughts when after Michelle's visit I drove home and, first thing through the door, dug under my socks to extract my loaded revolver and check to see whether it was indeed loaded. Nor do I remember any suicidal thoughts. Taking out the gun simply seemed the right thing to do, and once I had playfully spun the cylinder and clicked it back in place, just like in the movies, there seemed an equal likelihood that I'd return it to its place of hiding or that I'd tuck it in the waistband of my pants. But I must be mistaken. There must have been a higher likelihood of the latter than the former because I did the latter and left the house with the revolver.

Half an hour later, I sat in my car, the windows rolled down, waiting. The sun streamed in through the windshield, but wearing a mask of dark glasses I felt safe from its probing rays. I had sat at the same place a week earlier, feeling like a madman. Now I cast myself as anonymous death plotting destruction—remaining anonymous until the last instant. Only then would I show my true, vengeful features. I waited, knowing, as only a lover or lunatic can know, that my moment would come. All I needed to do was wait patiently.

When the sun sank behind pines flanking the road and I was in their long shadow, I replaced my dusky shades with my regular glasses: death needed keen sight to transfix his trembling victim. Waiting, I began whispering the last two lines of Gretchen's cruel stanzas: "His hands' soft pressure, / And, ah! his kiss!" The incantation would, I knew, draw out my enemy and lead him to his doom.

But when smoothly, silently, the iron gate rolled open, it was Michelle's car that glided out. She had the top of her golden chariot down, and by the light of the setting sun (no shadow dared touch my love) her hair gleamed and she seemed to smile. She turned the car in the direction away from me, and I wasn't forced to duck behind the dashboard and hide like a thief or assassin.

When she had rounded the corner, I got out of the car, the revolver tucked into the waistband of my pants, where its heavy bulk was ill concealed by my jacket. The iron gate had smoothly and silently slid shut, but I knew (this was the day for precognition) that the side door would be open. It swung soundlessly on its hinges and I walked up the blacktop driveway toward the two-story rosy stucco palazzo where my love laid down her head at night and dreamt of an impossible happiness. From the house no challenge rang out checking the progress of the unannounced visitor. Birds sang in trees and a large gray cat appeared from behind a flower box and vanished at the sight of the invader, who, unstoppable, purposeful like a mechanical man, walked up the stairs leading to the oak double door. The door was flanked by pots bearing crimson azaleas, which glowed as if they were radiating into the fragrant evening the sunlight they had absorbed.

The door was unlocked. I stepped into a cool, spacious foyer tiled with Mexican terra-cotta mosaic. To my left was the airy living room, minimally but expensively furnished. I stood on a huge Persian carpet, all glowing reds and blues and cunning intricacy, wondering what to do next. Ought I to call out, "Is anybody home?" or to summon the master of the house somewhat more theatrically to his moment of reckoning? ("You've done enough damage, sir; it's time to pay up!") Or should I make my way upstairs on tiptoes and surprise Passatour sweating on his cross-country-skiing contraption or voiding his bowels while reading *The Washington Post*? Not quite in his rage or in the pleasure of his bed but sufficiently unrepentant to slip into at least one version of hell. Careful homicidal maniac that I was, I had the gun in my hand by now, its hammer cocked.

Before I could conclude my internal monologue ("Soft you, now; who comes?"), Passatour entered stage center, saw me and stopped. In shirt sleeves and slippers, my foe looked more domesticated and less formidable than I had imagined him, less interesting than I remembered him from his photo, his beard not as Don Juanesquely trim, his mien not as sardonic. It took a moment's mental adjustment for me to see the seductive villain hidden under a facade of mediocrity.

Passatour saw me, stopped, saw the gun in my hand, opened his mouth to speak. Which, I realized with alarm, I couldn't let him. I also realized that I was terrified by his slippers. An instinctive sense of decorum told me that a man could be killed in a vast assortment of footwear, and even in his bare feet, but not in house slippers. If this middle-aged, slippers-shod specimen were to talk to me, to ask me what the devil I was doing here, I would never be able to harm him. Terrified of the sounds beginning to issue from his mouth, which I misheard as the question, "What are you?" I raised the gun and pulled the trigger.

It was my day for lucky breaks. I had never in my life fired a gun. He was at least twenty-five feet from me. Why should I not have hit an arm or shoulder, or missed him altogether and decapitated the surpassingly ugly autoerotic sculpture (*Nude Woman in Love with her Paps?*) to his left? Instead of pointing the gun exactly at the spot on his pale blue shirt that was connected by an invisible ray to his heart?

He did nothing I might have expected him to do from the depiction of death in countless movies and plays. His hands didn't clutch his chest, he didn't let out a frothy gasp, he didn't stumble or stagger. It was as if someone had kicked him in the back of the knees. They simply gave, and he folded at several other places on his way to the floor, and lay on his back, perfectly still, the *tableau vivant* disturbed only by a red spot spreading on the corpse's shirt. In my ears, wind whistled through a canyon.

Then there was a sound behind me, a laugh, I thought, but when I turned, it was Michelle staring wide-eyed at the dead man, bursting into tears, covering her face with her hands and sobbing, "Don't hurt me. Please don't hurt me."

I said, "Did you forget something?"

She kept sobbing and carrying on—pleading with me not to hurt her, please, please. All of which I found distasteful.

"I'd never hurt you," I told her stiffly. "I did this for you."

I left her there, sobbing out of control and hysterically afraid I might turn my wrath against her.

I drove from my love's sunny house to the darkling cold of the city, arriving when the sky had turned a somber purple. My townhouse had the typical minuscule backyard and this was where I repaired to, with a book in hand, thinking I'd do some reading while waiting for I wasn't sure what. I did not, however, turn on the porch light and sat instead in the deepening gloom, the book in my lap, thinking that it was remarkable—and I ought to write a paper on it—that one could actually be thinking about nothing at all.

I became dimly aware of the doorbell and a pounding on the front door and voices, and suddenly a head, darker than the surrounding night, and arms joined at the hands, where there was a metallic glint, loomed over the fence and a voice said, "Don't move."

Then there were footsteps behind me and more voices telling me what to do and what not to. I did and did not accordingly and in short order was bundled into a police car, under arrest for murder. Not, interestingly enough, the murder of Max Passatour.

I don't remember exactly when I found out that my day of precognition had also been my day of supreme irony, since the man I had shot dead was George O'Rourke, Professor of English, friend of the family, confidant and hopeless swain of the lady of the house. George had planned to spend the night at the house, a thing he frequently did when Passatour was away—as was the case that evening since the doctor had been called away on an emergency.

I do remember laughing sometime later, when I was alone in my cell, a conversion reaction to what I assume was authentic chagrin at having caused the death of the only decent individual of the lot—present company included—domesticated, slippers-wearing, unremarkable George, disguised behind a poor imitation of Passatour's beard only because of the improbable hope that facial hair might kindle Michelle's interest in him. Poor George, not the bald, fat figure of my imagination, but still the least likely candidate to die for love.—Or maybe not. Maybe George, too, longed for the romantic moment, the ecstasy of giving all for the beloved, the transcendence of the ultimate sacrifice. Maybe he would even have done himself harm eventually if his cruel love had kept disdaining him and using him—and if I hadn't removed that option.

Incidentally—and I mention this for the sake of anyone impatient with protagonists blind to the most obvious pikestaffs rising from the corpse-strewn field of their misfortune—it does not escape me that my killing George was a failed symbolic suicide since my intended victim was that thing endlessly useful in modern psychological theory, the double. I had meant to kill my evil doppelgänger—read, my evil self—and had instead punched a deadly hole through good George, who was (and here the plot thickens) bad Max's double. (Or, possibly a more interesting thought, did I punch a hole through my own good double? Irony in spades?)

Another thing worth considering is that I felt no compassion for Michelle at the thought that the mistake I had made meant Passatour was alive and would continue to be her torment. Which argues that any idea I might have had of committing this great bloody act to deliver her from a life of endless unhappiness had been bogus from the start. The more likely motive remains pure, uncompromised hatred of the man who had what I desired and would never call my own. But here, as elsewhere, beware of the easy answer!

There is little else to say. I am serving year two of a thirty-year sentence; Passatour—will wonders never cease?—has fallen out of love with Barb and is in love with an ex-patient of his; Michelle remains married to him and is probably, as I wrap up this meditation on desire and love, looking with eyes that are pools of limpid tears at her current therapist, telling him of selfishness and cruelty and hurt, and eliciting from him the empathy we feel for suffering beyond all hope.